INTERVENTION
THE
KING PIN

INTERVENTION
THE
KING PIN

JAMES HANFORD

Copyright © 2018 James Hanford

The moral right of the author has been asserted.

Apart from any fair dealing for the purposes of research or private study,
or criticism or review, as permitted under the Copyright, Designs and Patents
Act 1988, this publication may only be reproduced, stored or transmitted, in
any form or by any means, with the prior permission in writing of the
publishers, or in the case of reprographic reproduction in accordance with
the terms of licences issued by the Copyright Licensing Agency. Enquiries
concerning reproduction outside those terms should be sent to the publishers.

This book is a work of fiction. Names, characters, businesses, organisations, places, and
events are either the product of the author's imagination or are used fictitiously. Any
resemblance to actual persons, living or dead, events, or locales is unintended and entirely
coincidental.

Matador
9 Priory Business Park,
Wistow Road, Kibworth Beauchamp,
Leicestershire. LE8 0RX
Tel: 0116 279 2299
Email: books@troubador.co.uk
Web: www.troubador.co.uk/matador
Twitter: @matadorbooks

ISBN 978 1788032 902

British Library Cataloguing in Publication Data.
A catalogue record for this book is available from the British Library.

Printed and bound in Great Britain by 4edge Limited
Typeset in 11pt Adobe Garamond Pro by Troubador Publishing Ltd, Leicester, UK

Matador is an imprint of Troubador Publishing Ltd

*In loving memory of my father,
John Hanford (1932–2013),
and with immense gratitude to my
family for their encouragement whilst
I was writing Intervention: The King Pin.*

1

Rob Krane emerged from the ensuite shower room at the guesthouse where he was staying and pulled his long-sleeved T-shirt on before opening the curtains with a flourish. The room was spartan, furnished only with the bare essentials, but it was perfectly adequate for his purposes.

"Damn, that's bright," he muttered, crinkling his eyes into a squint.

The blackout curtains had certainly done their job. Add the room's poor lighting and the morning sun appeared very bright as it broke through the clouds. Instinctively, Rob suddenly stepped to one side of the battered, loose-fitting window. He brushed some blistered paint off his shirt while continuing to look down on the street below.

What is it with this place? he thought as yet another twenty-something man wandered along the street. The man was as equally out of place as himself in the small town, but there was a distinct difference; Rob was a legitimate tourist, and these guys did not give that appearance.

Despite himself, Rob tensed as the adrenalin rush of butterflies hit his stomach. It was the same feeling he had before meeting a senior executive at work. Well, that had been until a few weeks ago, when he had lost his job. He also had the same feeling prior to a championship fight as he anticipated an unknown combatant's moves. Shaking these thoughts away, he recalled how uncomfortable he had felt the previous evening, and during his morning's run, when he saw these characters wandering the streets of Postojna.

Everyone he had spoken to and all he had read indicated that travelling around Slovenia was safe. However, the number of times he had seen these out-of-place, twenty-something, lone men was distinctly disconcerting. The similarities were evident. Their dress-sense, swagger, and expressionless faces all resembled those of the guy who was currently disappearing from Rob's sight. They were certainly not locals, so who were they? And why were they here in such numbers?

Okay, there had been similarly dressed men elsewhere when he travelled to Postojna the day before. But this was different. Something was up. He knew it. Regardless, why should he be bothered? Rob was having a great time on a holiday paid for from his redundancy and prize money. Two weeks ago he had won the gold medal at the European Combined Martial Arts and Unarmed Combat Championships at Wembley Conference Centre in London.

A sufficiently loud gurgle from his belly reminded him that he was hungry. *Breakfast!* He picked up his iPhone from the bedside table, scanning the screen to read the time. "Damn it!" The low-battery indicator was flashing.

Rob pulled a small day sack from a far larger backpack, smiling as he rubbed a thumb over the flexible solar panels on the face of the bag. It was a new toy—one that he had been unable to resist because he was planning a few days camping. After looking out of the window again at the weather, Rob decided he would go out for breakfast. It was warm enough and certainly bright enough for him to test his new purchase. He could also check his e-mail instead of having an ingratiatingly painful conversation with his hosts.

Jogging down the stairs, Rob waved to the unconvincingly jovial owners of the guesthouse. "No breakfast today, thank you. I ate too much last night."

While that was partially true, the pleasant weather gave him the opportunity to avoid the unnecessarily large and unhealthy breakfast Madam Kos insisted upon rustling up. And, of course, he would avoid having to converse with the elderly couple.

Closing the door gently behind him, Rob turned and headed towards the Kras Hotel. He had noted the previous night that breakfast was served outside in the square, and, since it was the only four-star hotel in town, he hoped for reasonable fare. Breaking with habit, he didn't bother looking around at the buildings and the general environment; he had seen enough during his run. The area where he was staying was really rather bland, the house frontages having very limited architectural appeal.

Few of the exterior tables were occupied, and those that were clearly contained tourists. Schools had restarted after the summer holidays, so the number of tourists was dwindling, which was by far Rob's preference. There was little movement inside the hotel foyer, all he could see was an attractive woman with a fidgety young girl sitting down, looking out into the square. The woman was a few years older than himself, had pleasant but not striking features, shoulder-length, straight blond hair, and the tired looks of a concerned, caring mother. Rob recognised the signs from his sister-in-law. He settled himself at a non-shady table not far from the hotel door, set up his solar-panelled backpack, and plugged in his iPhone, iPad, and other gadgets to recharge.

The pretty waitress gave Rob more attention than he really wanted, distracting him from his e-mails and reading the day's news. Not that he really minded. The girl was a few years younger than him, and engaging her with some idle banter and reciprocating her playful flirtations was fun. Rob felt good as he noted her name, Irina Vidmar, and ensured he used it as they chatted. He made a mental note to come here more frequently, particularly after he returned from his planned hike in the hills and mountains to the south and east of Postojna.

Half an hour later, Rob broke off from reading the news and drinking his coffee when an apparently distinguished, well-built man in a dark tailored suit and open-neck shirt walked into the hotel foyer. Only the tanned face and purposeful, almost-cold demeanour suggested something entirely different. Ignoring the man, Rob continued to read the ridiculous intrigue and implications of the latest sex scandal involving a government minister. Rob shook his head slightly, *Why do they always dice with the illicit? Eventually the press always finds out.*

A few minutes later, the same man left the hotel, holding the young girl's hand, with the mother walking along beside them. The girl was smiling, half-skipping, and happily chatting away to the man, whose demeanour had softened markedly. Rob watched their progress across the paved, pedestrianised square, their direction suggesting they were headed for either the Karst Museum or transportation towards the Postojna Caves. Rob presumed the latter; a museum of predominantly archaeological collections would be of little interest to the young girl. She did not have the grumpy air of a child going somewhere that, in her mind, would be dull and boring. Instead, she exuded excitement and joy. As they approached halfway, one of the young men Rob had seen earlier appeared at the far corner, talking on a mobile phone. Moments later, a black saloon and a red four-door Nissan pickup with white cover over the rear charged into the square, tyres squealing.

The man froze, his free hand inching into his jacket. Glancing at the woman and young girl, he dropped his hand to his side and became a spectator to the impending horror in which he would play a central role.

The black saloon raced over towards him while the Nissan screeched to a halt adjacent to the hotel. Young hooded men jumped from all doors of both cars, each wearing dark jeans and shirts. *It's like a uniform!* Rob thought, remembering the many dubious characters from the past few days. Each also carried a machine pistol. Those from the saloon approached the man, woman, and girl while the others turned their attention towards Rob and the others having breakfast.

Without hesitation, Rob grabbed his belongings and flipped his and a neighbouring table over to provide a semblance of cover. As the other hotel guests looked on with bemused, uncomprehending expressions, the square was filled with bursts of gunfire and bullets slammed into walls and pinged off the metal tables.

As bullets started piercing nearby tables Rob realised that his cover was decidedly limited. Quickly assessing his position, Rob glanced over his shoulder towards the hotel lobby and the relative safety that being behind its walls would bring. Screams from the other guests punctuated the racket hammering in his ears, making thinking hard.

As more bullets whined overhead, ripping through the windows and glazed doors, Rob rolled over to the table behind him, drawing closer to the hotel entrance and hoped-for shelter. With a whooshing, chinking sound, the glass doors collapsed in a myriad of glistening beads and gleaming shards, spraying across Rob's back.

With his heart thumping, he shuffled on hands and knees behind the next table, scrunching painfully over the pieces of glass. Groans from injured hotel guests gave a constant, disconcerting background sound, reminding him that each and every move could determine his fate. Looking round the edge of a table to check the route for his next dash, Rob recoiled as he came eye to eye with Irina, whose lifeless body was surrounded by pieces of broken crockery and food from her tray. Summoning all of his willpower, Rob shook his head to remove this nightmarish vision to focus on his next move. With a final roll and dive, Rob made it through the door into the hotel lobby, and behind a wall, followed by a volley of bullets.

Mesmerised, Rob watched in horror as the apparent terrorists went about their business, spraying bullets in all directions. The smell of cordite floated into the lobby on the gentle breeze, making him shudder.

One of those from the Nissan flung the tailgate open, hauled out a couple of large sacks, and ran over to where his accomplices had surrounded the man, woman, and girl. While the man was punched to the ground, gagged and a handgun removed from his jacket, the girl was shoved into one sack, kicking and screaming, before also being gagged and the sack firmly tied. The dazed mother was grabbed roughly by one man and shoved in front of another, who, after the briefest of looks, shot her twice in the chest. Her body collapsed onto the stone slabs, a pool of blood forming, even as her partner reached out a hand from where he was lying to briefly caress her face. He was then bundled, struggling, into another sack, and both writhing sacks were dragged slowly back across the square towards the Nissan truck.

The other terrorists, meanwhile, fanned out across the square, firing in all directions, at passing cars and the windows of the surrounding buildings. Two headed towards the hotel as they fired. Calmly walking between the carnage of the upturned tables and chairs, they shot in the head all those lying on the ground, whether apparently dead or not.

These guys don't want witnesses! Rob realised with horror, as he once again slid across the hotel's floor. Everyone else was momentarily frozen in disbelief. Milliseconds later, however, they were screaming and running in all directions as the two men walked into the lobby, calmly spraying bullets all over and cutting people down. Rob had no choice but to jump up and dive through a broken window to head back outside. Rolling over, Rob came to a halt behind a table and some chairs, his back sack cradled in his arms.

Once outside, Rob wormed his way through the morass of up-turned furniture, seeking an escape; he had no doubt the area would be thoroughly checked for survivors. Looking about, it became obvious there was no opportunity to make a run for it down the street. Instead, the Nissan with its open tailgate was nearby and it was directly between him and the men dragging the sacks. Risking becoming trapped, Rob sprinted to the rear of the vehicle and leapt in. Relief flooded through him on seeing the cluttered interior. It didn't take long to slide a large toolbox out from the rear and duck behind it, covering himself with other sacks and rugs that were lying around.

Every sinew was tensed, virtually to the point of snapping, as Rob tried to control his breathing and listened to the approaching footsteps. For the first time, he heard voices.

"Well?"

"All taken care of in there." Rob surmised the speaker was referring to the hotel.

"No survivors, then?" demanded the first voice brusquely.

A third voice replied, "We think not. We thought one jumped through the window but didn't see anyone when we got to look."

"Idiots!" the first voice yelled. "Boss will deal with you later if that turns out to be correct and details reported. Orders were no witnesses!" After a momentary pause, he continued, "Get those two into the truck, and let's get moving before the police arrive! Stephane! You're in the back to watch over the packages!"

They had all spoken in rough English but with varying accents, suggesting differing nationalities.

There were grunts of exertion, followed by two soft thuds, as the sacks were heaved into the rear, the truck jiggling slightly in the process. Rob heard the sound of sackcloth being pushed over the bare metal of the truck floor before he was squeezed by the large toolbox as the man and girl were shoved as far in as possible. Rob barely suppressed a groan. A third jiggle signalled that Stephane had climbed in before the tailgate slammed shut with an eerie finality.

Doors slammed, engines roared, and they moved off quickly, the sound of the tyres thrumming on the road surface. Hard braking compressed the heavy toolbox against Rob, alerting him to either a road junction or corner. He braced himself against the car's sides to avoid slipping and potentially giving himself away.

When the hard cornering ceased a short while later, Rob guessed they had joined one of the nearby main roads. It was also telling that, judging by the steady thrumming of the tyres, they were not travelling at breakneck speed anymore. He could only presume the kidnappers were hoping that no one had survived to describe the vehicles to the local police, or *policija*, and therefore did not want to draw attention to themselves by travelling too fast.

There was no way of knowing in which direction they were travelling. However, with the periodic slowing down and subsequent gentle acceleration, Rob was sure they were going through other small towns or villages. That meant he wasn't on the A10 highway between Italy and the capital, Ljubljana. Instead, he decided, they were either travelling north, further into the heart of Slovenia, or south towards Croatia.

Occasionally, Stephane shifted his weight and growled, "You still alive in there?" as he thumped the larger of the two sacks. On hearing a grunt or moan, Stephane chuckled. Occasionally there was a gentle whimper from the young girl.

Rob's limbs soon started to ache from his cramped position, but he dared not stretch, let alone move to try to alleviate his discomfort. This was a trifle compared to whatever would befall him were he to be found.

2

The emergency services arrived rapidly, and the medical workers ran from victim to victim, searching in vain for any sign of life. The local policija initially stood around in undisguised disbelief and horror. A radioed message from one of them brought their chief racing to the square, by which time the officers had started to corral the remaining hotel guests around the corner into the neighbouring park. Having quickly cast his eyes over the devastation, the chief knew he had to radio for expert support from Ljubljana.

Chief Horvat then set about ordering and directing his men, building-by-building enquiries were needed to determine if there were any other casualties, or if there were any witnesses prepared to come forward and describe what on earth had happened.

"Don't forget," he yelled into the radio, "make sure that everyone understands they're not to touch or move anything." Then, after a short pause, he followed up with, "However small! It must not be touched! Locate all bullets! Seal off the entire square, including the roads. I don't care how inconvenient. Just do it! Report everything back to me and write it down. I'll be in my car!" With that, he stomped away to where he had parked on the opposite side of the square.

◆◆◆

An unexpected jerk indicated they had turned off whichever main road they were on. Stephane cursed loudly as he slid about, not having expected the sudden change of direction. They had been travelling for barely fifteen minutes, but it seemed like an eternity for Rob cooped up where he was. The cornering became more frequent and more pronounced as time ticked past and Stephane's curses came thicker and faster in a language that Rob did not recognise.

The girl started whimpering far more frequently as she slid around the floor, crunching into the metal sides. Barely a sound came from the man, except for when he was punched by Stephane, who alternated using his fists with the gun that he carefully kept below the level of the tailgate. The road soon inclined steeply, so the toolbox would slide away from Rob slightly. This was short lived as Stephane rammed the toolbox back, hard against Rob. The journey went on for an indeterminate amount of time, and the oily rags and rugs coupled with the violent motion started to make Rob feel queasy. He swallowed hard a few times as bile rose in his throat, almost gagging in the process.

Oh man, how much longer? Okay, I'm better off than those slaughtered in the square and the two poor souls in those sacks, but even so. Argh! That hurt, he thought as his head thudded into the side of the truck once more. Keeping braced against the truck's sides to reduce the impacts of each corner had become a real challenge as his strength dwindled.

This section of the journey was easily the longest. *I really hope they don't turn off onto a dirt track—that will be horrendous!* Rob thought to himself as he braced against yet another sharp corner.

The truck eventually slowed to a halt, without any dirt tracks. Doors opened and then clunked closed. There had been no bumps, no scrunching of gravel or other surface that could be expected from a lay-by or from pulling off to the side of the road. Rob held his breath, every muscle taut and every sense straining to work out what was about to occur.

"Quick about it!" Rob recognised the first voice from the town square in Postojna. "Unwrap the packages away from the road and remove the gags so they can breathe for the walk."

Moments later the tailgate squeaked open, and the two sacks were manhandled out of the rear of the truck. To Rob's relief, the tailgate was slammed shut again.

"Ali, Gustov!" the apparent leader barked. "You buffoons will guard the base of the path just back from the road. You'll hear what the boss says about your idiocy later. You two," the leader continued, pointing to the two drivers, "dispose of the vehicles while the rest of us take KP and the girl to the base. Make sure you're not followed."

The engines started, and the two vehicles turned around. *Damn, should I bail here or later?* An image of the girl's terrified face flashed into Rob's consciousness, so, as the truck reversed once more, backing into the bushes at the side of the road, Rob gathered his belongings, plus the rug he had been lying under, and leap-frogged from the tailgate, landing in the midst of some tall grass and bushes. *Phew! No reaction from anyone. I must have got away with it!*

The two vehicles raced off and disappeared around a bend fifty metres away. For the first time, Rob noticed just how steep the landscape was, bushes having prevented him from rolling further and creating a greater commotion. He crept as close to the edge of the road as he dared to watch and listen.

"Ali, Gustov! Beware you don't stray, and set off any of the alarms we set. Stephane will bring down some food later. It would be bullets if I had my way! But you're lucky! There are no reports of cars following us, and the policija appear to be in disarray, so if someone escaped, you appear to have gotten away with it—so far.

"Right, you idiots! Why are you standing around gawping? Get them out of the bags! Now!" The leader was almost screaming at the remaining three men, clearly confident of their isolation and that no one else would hear.

That also means that there's no chance for me to find help easily, Rob realised dejectedly. *I'd better get moving, I can't afford to lose these guys, particularly if they're setting alarms*!

Rob wormed his way deeper into the forest before scampering downhill to the bend in the narrow road. After a quick check, he sprinted across the road and made his way back uphill towards the terrorists, or thugs, or whoever they were. When Rob approached, the thugs were standing around, while the man and girl, both well bound with their hands behind their backs, were slumped on the ground among the damp leaves and earth.

For the first time, Rob considered his surroundings. The fresh, damp, earthy smell of the forest filled his lungs, which was immensely gratifying after the oily rags in the truck. He was also filthy and underdressed. *Okay, I've got my waterproofs, this smelly rug, and some semi-decent footwear, but that's it!*

While he knew he should save himself and seek help, when he saw the girl, who couldn't have been more than ten or eleven, he could not leave. She was snuggling up as close to the man as she could, her eyes wide with terror, her thin dress a mess and her hair all awry. The man, while outwardly composed, was clearly weighing up the situation. He gently leaned his head against the top of hers and whispered something to her, trying to give some level of comfort through his proximity and words. *There is clearly a relationship there. Very possibly, he's the girl's father,* Rob decided. The man's suit was a complete mess and as equally unsuitable for this environment as the girl's dress.

There's nothing I can do here. It's too dangerous, but I have to find out where they're going. Then I can go for help. Must be careful of twigs, he warned himself as he moved to a new vantage point. *This is for the girl. The dad looks as dodgy as you can get, so tough on him.*

Glancing at his watch, Rob saw it was already 11:40. They had been travelling for over two and a half hours.

Chief Horvat was soon trudging disconsolately back across the square from his car. He had just taken a call from Franc Kovač, a revered inspector at the Slovenian Intelligence and Security Agency in Ljubljana, and had come out at the end feeling rather dim witted.

"What are you doing just sitting in your car? Go commandeer some conference rooms in the hotel. I will need a base to conduct operations, won't I? And make sure there's a side entrance available for use so the crime scene is not disturbed."

That was two hours ago. Now Kovač had arrived with a small team by helicopter, landing in the nearby park. More were to arrive by road. Mercifully for Chief Horvat, Kovač and his team had immediately swung into action and taken charge. Chief Horvat, although grateful to be still involved, was out of his depth—he was more used to petty theft, speeding, the occasional burglary, and alcohol-related fights.

They were in one of the hotel's conference rooms, a number of tables rearranged throughout the space. In one corner, to provide a little isolation, Kovač had set up a position for himself, together with a couple of flip charts and an outlying desk for his assistant to act as gatekeeper. Chief Horvat, Janez Potočnik, the hotel's manager, who was looking haggard and shell-shocked, and a couple of others were gathered together with Kovač, peering through a scribbled list of names.

One of the local policija approached and nervously cleared his throat. "We've been through all receipts and tables-in-service records, as Chief Horvat requested. All paperwork can be accounted for and associated with either a body or a guest." He hesitated briefly and then, taking on a serious expression, continued with, "Except one, that is—a single male who is not resident at the hotel. We know this because the kitchen staff told us how Irina Vidmar, the waitress covering the outside area, kept talking about a non-guest diner who she fancied. All the kitchen staff were encouraging her on because she, well, was feeling…"

"Enough!" barked Kovač. "That's great work and very helpful, but we don't need the unfortunate girl's life story, at least not yet. Please go back and find out if there's any description of this man. Did the waitress say anything, whether descriptive or anecdotal, like nationality or where he's staying and for how long? Did any of the kitchen staff take a look at the man? Put a message out across town for anyone who had breakfast here to come forward and check the hospital. I don't suppose there's CCTV there?"

"No, sir. No CCTV. I will go and start those enquiries, sir." And with that, he turned on his heels and headed off, relieved to be doing so.

"Now that *was* interesting and helpful intel," Kovač commented, emphasising the word *was*. "So we have fifteen people dead; seven who were eating breakfast outside, two ladies and one man on reception, four who had been sitting in reception, and crucially, a mother whose daughter has disappeared, presumed kidnapped. I understand, Chief Horvat, you have initiated a search just in case the girl escaped. But at this stage, looking at the location of the mother's body and the tyre tracks, I consider that unlikely. Remarkably, no one else was injured, just a lot of irate motorists with bullet holes in their cars, presumably designed to dissuade them from paying attention to what was going on. This was clearly a well-planned and efficiently executed operation, so we are dealing with an organised group. We now also have a missing man who had been eating breakfast outside the hotel."

"The mother and daughter were staying by themselves," the hotel manager commented. "They arrived last night in time for dinner and were not due to leave for another two days."

Kovač nodded. "Killing the mother and kidnapping the girl, leaving no one against whom she can be used as leverage, is not rational. The missing and unidentified man may be pivotal to this, or simply be a mystery man in the wrong place at the wrong time. He may have been a spotter for this gang, or he may have been taken as well. I want to know who he is and why he was here. At this stage, the girl appears to be central and the reason for this carnage, and I want to know why!

"Have I missed anything, or does anyone have something more to add? If not, get working!"

"Guv," said a member of Kovač's team who had been reviewing a paper on the desk, "The mother, her name is down here as Evelyne Dubois. She was a French national. The daughter's name was registered as Anja. Shall I contact our counterparts at the DSGE?"

Kovač thought about his opposite number at the DSGE, The Direction Générale de la Sécurité Extérieure, the French intelligence service. "Glad someone's alert. No, I will call Henri Simmonet, myself," he looked meaningfully at his assistant.

With that and after a momentary silence, everyone started to drift off, leaving Kovač poring over the various papers. After a few minutes, his mobile phone buzzed on the table beside him. Kovač snatched it up, recognising the name flashing on the display.

"Henri, *bonjour. Comment va-tu?* Many thanks for calling me back."

"You are always welcome, *mon ami*. I am well, and how are both you and your good wife?"

"We're both well, thank you, Henri."

"Good, good. I'm pleased. Now tell me, how can I help? A call in work hours is a sign of activity, *n'est pas*?"

"Exactly, and sadly, in this case you're right. A French woman, Evelyne Dubois, has been shot dead in Postojna, where I am now leading the investigation."

Despite a pause, Henri did not interject, and Kovač continued. "Her daughter, Anja, aged nine, is presumed taken. Fourteen other people are also dead. One person, a white male, remains unaccounted for. Tyre tracks suggest two vehicles, and from the clusters of cartridges, up to eight hostile participants, so a large group for just one young girl." Following another pause for breath, Kovač finished with, "Motive unknown."

"*Mon ami*," Simmonet whistled, "you have certainly been an unwilling host to a most horrific and strange situation. I assume you wish checks on this Dubois woman?"

"Absolutely, together with anything on the girl's father if he is known."

"I shall do so with pleasure. Presumably you can send copies of the documents lodged upon her arrival."

"Yes, they are ready and will be e-mailed very soon. Thank you for agreeing to help and speak soon."

"*Au revoir*." And with that, Kovač hung up and put his phone back down on the table.

Rob kept his distance from the group and watched cautiously from behind a clump of bushes. *Muppet!* Rob cursed himself suddenly. He shrugged out of his back sack, opened it, and pulled out his iPhone. *Bother! No signal.*

He was about to drop it back into his bag when a thought struck him. Holding the gadget between the branches and leaves of a bush, Rob zoomed into the man's and then the girl's faces, taking a photo of each separately and then together. Flipping through the menus, Rob opened another app. The words "Media Face Recognition" flashed across the screen, followed by a command to upload the desired photo. Rob found the man's photo, and pressed "OK" and set the app running. *Yes! Now you're thinking. E-mail—let's do an e-mail. Who to?* he asked himself.

Just then the group of terrorists or gangsters—Rob had still not made up his mind as to which—broke up as the apparent leader handed a radio to Ali and Gustov. They moved away, inserting an earpiece as they did, each in his own direction to find a suitable place to stand guard.

Rob stuffed his iPhone back into his daysack without composing any e-mail while trying to note where the two went, but he lost sight of both. *I'm going to have to move carefully,* he thought as he eased deeper into the forest while still keeping an eye on the remaining four, who were pulling the hostages to their feet. Rob cursed as they headed off directly away from him. He was going to have to catch up while avoiding the two guards, wherever they may be. Keeping as low as possible and scanning the ground for noisy materials, Rob followed as rapidly as he could. The thick foliage proved a huge hindrance as he zigzagged around trees, stumps, bushes, and other clumps of plants. At least the dampness supressed any scrunching from the thick mat of leaves upon which he was forced to scamper, often on all fours.

The group soon found their intended path and increased their pace. *Damn! If I'm not careful, I will lose them and get horribly lost!*

Periodically, Rob lost sight of his quarry behind a mass of trees or bushes, but he plunged on regardless, trying to parallel track whatever path the group was taking. The going became harder as the ground started to slope upward more steeply. It wasn't long before he spotted, quite a long way ahead of him, that two of the group had stopped and were bending over their back sacks. The other two were still guiding the bound hostages forward. The girl was in front, with her guide holding a gun close to her head, the display obviously for the man's benefit.

Damn, they are setting alarms, Rob muttered. *At least I've seen this set.* When the two men finished their work, one on either side of the path, they promptly jogged up the path after their colleagues, leaving Rob far behind.

After another hundred metres or so, Rob paused. Trying to ignore his hunger—it was well passed lunch—Rob sat down to assess his situation. *I'm going to have to keep creeping up to the path to check for changes of direction or turn-offs,* he concluded.

Grateful that he had donned his waterproofs sometime earlier—it had started getting cooler the higher he climbed—Rob pressed on for nearly five hours. The path had kept changing direction as it weaved up a narrow valley. As a result, the path was often not where he expected. Consequently, he had to re-trace his steps to recover his intended direction. To do so, he crept up to the path, terrified of being seen, to search for the tell-tale scuff marks on the ground left by the group's footwear. The ground became increasingly rocky, slippery and treacherous.

Easing back from the path once again, Rob identified a small area suitable for a breather. Taking his iPhone from his bag once more, he checked for a signal. *Bother!* No signal again. *Oh well, e-mail time.* He tapped in his password and was welcomed by a flashing icon indicating that his face recognition app had returned a result. At some point during his ascent, he must have picked up a signal. Forgetting his intention of composing an e-mail, he opened the app and found himself looking at the man's mug shot. The photo was associated with a report in the *Independent* newspaper entitled "Legitimate Face of Corruption?"

Burak Demir walked free from a Parisian court yesterday after the spectacular collapse of the trial into his alleged involvement with criminal activities. The secretive, fifty-one-year-old Turkish billionaire was the alleged indirect owner of and, more importantly, the 'instructing director of operations' for three businesses in France. Each business, under express direction and knowledge of Mr Demir, was alleged to have laundered millions of Euros over at least five years, avoiding tax on the associated activities and being fronts for an array of other criminal activities.

The trial was expected to run for a further five weeks when it collapsed suddenly today. For the fourth consecutive day, the prosecution failed to introduce any evidence or substantiate any of the allegations. Papers and other apparently incriminating evidence were mysteriously lost from police files. Witnesses for the prosecution have variously recanted their testimonies, failed to turn up at court, or outright contradicted the prosecution's allegations, and in one unsettling instance, one witness was found dead two nights ago following an apparent suicide.

Prosecution lawyers were unavailable to comment on how a case three years in the making, involving the police and intelligence services of many countries, could collapse quite so spectacularly.

Burak Demir left the court building rapidly, refusing to answer questions, and disappeared in a waiting car. Frustratingly for the UK authorities, the current whereabouts of Burak Demir are not known. They had hoped to interview him about a raft of similar matters across Britain during the course of his confinement here in Paris—a fact Burak Demir was apparently aware of.

A voice alerted Rob that someone was heading his way. "Okay, guys, I'm on my way with some food and clothes. Boss is still not happy, so you're parked down there for the long haul." Stephane then appeared from around a corner on the path, his attention focused on a two-way radio in his right hand. Rob slipped further behind a tree for greater cover, once again stuffing his technology back into his bag, index finger fumbling for the off switch so no sounds could give him away.

"Bad news is that the police are talking about an unaccounted for person, so you did miss someone. Good news is that they don't appear to have anything to go on." Stephane continued on his way and disappeared down the path.

Rob settled back against the tree to think and give his heart time to stop racing and the thumping in his ears quieten down. *That was too close for comfort!* he thought as he took a series of deep breaths.

Kovač was sitting at his desk with a dry sandwich, a half-eaten bar of chocolate and a large, freshly brewed cup of coffee. He had become increasingly frustrated as the day slipped past. Government ministers were on his back for updates, as was a multitude of reporters. It had been necessary to issue a statement that a large number of foreign nationals had been killed—Australian, Belgian, British, and French. The fact that a nine-year-old French girl may also have been abducted had sent the reporters wild with excitement and speculation, at times bordering on the ludicrous. He was impatient to hear from Henri Simmonet, he wanted to know about this Dubois woman as quickly as possible.

The only piece of good news had followed the 5:00 p.m. radio broadcast requesting information on the still unaccounted for man. Kovač's assistant had just announced the arrival of Madam Kos, who ran a local guesthouse. She had telephoned about her only current guest and was promptly invited for an interview. Kovač stood up, stretched, and headed off to the small meeting room where Madam Kos had been settled. He walked briskly to get the blood flowing and to clear his head. Chief Horvat followed, as did his assistant to take notes.

"Let's hope that this leads somewhere," he called over his shoulder. "If only all people were as forthcoming as this lady." Kovač smiled as he approached the room, determined to put the elderly lady at her ease.

Opening the door, Kovač smiled broadly at the lady and extended his hand in welcome. His lean, tall figure in a smart, plain, light grey suit, white shirt and blue tie and neat haircut made an impressive figure beside Chief Horvat. The now slightly crumpled appearance of Kovač's suit and shirt from his journey and long day did not detract at all from his appearance. Chief Horvat, on the other hand, was wearing his ill-fitting police-issue uniform, belly protruding slightly, forcing a small corner of his shirt to dangle down over the front of his trousers.

"Inspector Franc Kovač from the Slovenian Intelligence and Security Agency in Ljubljana. Madam Kos, I presume?" On seeing her nodded, nervous confirmation, he continued, "You know, I am sure, your local chief of police, Chief Horvat? And this is my assistant, Nina Lah, who will take notes so Chief Horvat and I can concentrate on your good self instead of on my handwriting."

Kovač paused to allow time for his humour to take effect. "Please, have a seat. I see you already have a drink, but please, if you require anything else, do let me know. I am extremely grateful that you came. Your thoughtfulness is a compliment to your family and society."

He knew that he was laying it on thick, but he had to get people on his side, and this lady would almost certainly talk once she left. He wanted positive messages to permeate through the town to both give confidence to others so they would come forward with information and also to start the process of putting people at ease with their own personal security and safety.

After they were all seated, Kovač immediately spoke to avoid any embarrassing silence, this was not an interrogation.

This was different, and he was at pains to put the elderly lady at ease and make her feel important.

"Now, I understand that you heard our broadcast message about an unaccounted for man following today's atrocity and you are concerned about someone staying at your guesthouse. Please, we would like to hear why you are concerned and who the young man is. I can assure you that no one will visit to look at your accounts for at least six weeks." On making that comment, Kovač gave Chief Horvat a fleeting, but meaningful look. This lady was not to be hassled over any failure to declare income from running her guesthouse, a practice the authorities knew well.

Madam Kos was wearing what was possibly her best dress saved for special occasions. Not surprisingly from her conservative attitudes, it was modest and plain, falling to midway down her calf, while still managing to accentuate her overall slim build. Over the top, she wore a matching jacket. The pale blue reflected her eyes and set off the grey, arguably silver, shoulder-length straight hair.

She briefly fidgeted and shuffled her behind slightly, making herself comfortable. "I really do not want to insinuate anything because he is such a pleasant young man. He arrived two days ago and intends to stay for another five days."

Such a long stay visibly made both Kovač's and Chief Horvat's eyebrows raise, so Madam Kos hastily added, "He's been to Predjama Castle and the caves there twice. He's an amateur photographer and has taken some lovely photographs. Such clever things cameras these days. Do you know that you can replay the photographs on a small television-type screen on the back of the camera? Very clever.

He showed my husband and me. Today he decided to stay here and visit our castle and caves. Tomorrow he is planning to go hiking in the hills and mountains for a few days." At this point, Madam Kos paused for a drink.

Kovač filled the silence, having listened intently and nodded occasionally. He smiled again. "That's very helpful background, Madam Kos, thank you. Please could you tell us his name, and also why it is that you are concerned? Presumably you saw him this morning."

"Absolutely, Robert, although he likes to be called Rob, was as cheerful as always this morning. He went for his daily run. I really don't understand why young people like running around so much these days. Anyway, he didn't stay for breakfast, he said hello and he went out. I can't really remember the time. He did say that sometimes he wouldn't have breakfast and would take a coffee elsewhere. Well, out he went, and I presumed he would come back because he was not as fully dressed or prepared as he usually is when he leaves for the day. Then, when I went up to his room to make the bed, the guide for the castle and caves was still laid out on the table with his camera and notes for what he wanted to take photographs of. Also, he had said he would dine with us tonight and show us more photographs. He was good at telling us his plans. Such a charming, and considerate young man."

She paused again but was not interrupted. Kovač recognised that while Madam Kos liked to talk, she was also perfectly switched-on and would not miss a beat. "Now, where was I? Yes, his name is Robert Krane. As I say, he likes Rob. He's English and says he's from London. Lost his job a little time back. I can't remember what it was that he did, something at a bank, but he stressed not banking, which is all terribly confusing. When he arrived he immediately asked where he could register. He said he'd do it himself and did not want to inconvenience us. Had time on his hands since he'd lost his job and said his habit was always to take care of the paperwork. But he did show me the registration receipt so I could relax about that."

Kovač noticed that both his assistant and Chief Horvat had both started scribbling. Since the man's name and nationality had been revealed, it would be easy to trace the records. The woman's nattering was testing his patience, but he knew she would clam up if he interrupted, and allowing her to talk in her own way was the best way to get information from this particular lady.

"I haven't touched anything in Robert's room, of course," she continued. "That would be improper. Other than cleaning and making his bed, that is. I'll be pleased to show you around if that would help."

"That would, indeed," confirmed Kovač. "If you could leave your address and telephone number with my assistant, someone will be in touch. It may be later this evening, if not too inconvenient. But please do call me straight away if Robert returns, or if you hear from him."

"Yes, of course. I will do that. I do hope he is okay. Such a nice young man."

Kovač stood and extended his hand. "Many thanks once again, madam. Most helpful. Now, if you'll excuse us, we will leave you with my assistant."

Kovač and Chief Horvat left the room and hurried back to the main conference room. "Chief, please pull this Robert Krane's registration papers immediately. I will contact MI5 in London. Whatever you do, do not speak to anyone else. I really do not want the reporters hounding us more than they already are."

There was nothing else for it but to press ahead. Rob ran his fingers through his hair and sighed. He had wanted a challenge now that he had no job, and if the truth be told, he was greatly relieved to be out of that place. Doing something to challenge himself physically had been appealing, but he had not envisioned anything quite as extreme as this! And ideally, he would have been better prepared with clothing, equipment, and stuff. *Stuff?* he laughed to himself. "Come on, Krane, what sort of comment is that?" he muttered with a shake of his head and stood up, stiff from his huddled position on the cold, damp ground.

It was approaching 5:00 p.m., and if he wasn't careful, Stephane would be returning. Rob wanted to have moved on by then and found some cover since it appeared he would be camping. Stepping forward, avoiding sticks and loose stones, Rob came to the edge of an area where the trees were more spaced out and the going became easier. Some two hundred metres ahead a rocky outcrop materialised from between the trees and towered above a small timber cabin. "Shit!" he whispered in alarm.

Rob immediately froze and then very slowly, very cautiously, and watching very intently eased backwards to the cover of some bushes and waited. Had anyone seen him? Could he have set any alarms off?

Idiot! He chastised himself for letting his attention lapse. *Very clever.* Scanning the area, he realised the trees had been cleared in a planned way, providing sight lines to the two paths leading up to the cabin, yet still providing a near-seamless canopy over the entire area. There were also two traditionally built timber barn-type structures, mimicking the design of the cabin, just smaller. *Invisible but for the most thorough inspection.* Sinking back to the ground, he checked reception on his phone. *Nothing.* Rob glanced at the rock face. *Maybe at the top of that.* Making his way up, careful not to dislodge any loose rocks or stones, it soon became clear that he was in the middle of nowhere. Tree-covered hills and the occasional rock face were all he could see. His hair had become matted to his scalp, and Rob scrubbed his fingers vigorously back and forth across his head before once again checking for a signal. *Still nothing.*

Dusk was approaching. It was getting dramatically colder, and he had to find cover. Optimism spurred him on and, as he thought about the area, he was convinced he was in the Notranjska region of Slovenia, famed for its networks of caves carved out of the generally limestone rock. Finding a cave to spend the night in had been part of his planned trekking. His incurable sense of adventure and fantasy distracted him from his perils and lack of suitable equipment. Instead, this provided a valuable fillip as he dreamed of discovering a previously unknown network of caves glittering with crystals and majestic stalactites and stalagmites. He knew the prospect of crystals was a pipe dream—the region was not known for crystals, but so what?

Once back down and having found a new vantage point, Rob systematically scanned the rock face and identified a suitable opportunity for shelter a short way up the rock face and with a concealed access route. While approaching the rock face, he heard a rustling sound near one of the two sheds and, to his amazement, saw the rear end of a young wolf reversing out of a hole in the barn wall. In its mouth it was carrying food of some sort. It then proceeded to wriggle back in and come out with some more food, at which point Rob had an idea.

Picking up a large branch and a couple of fist-sized rocks, Rob positioned himself, out of the cabin's line of sight, so he could launch an attack upon the unsuspecting creature when it next emerged. So startled by the onslaught of flying stones and Rob's manic charge, waving the branch wildly over his head like an over-excited sports fan during a tense match, the wolf fled.

Rob left the wolf-removed food where it was and peered through the gap in the wall. Spying a number of bags of food, he grasped a couple, pulled them through the hole, and rapidly transferred the contents into his back sack, scattering other items around in a haphazard manner. Acutely aware that he was both exposed and that the wolf might return imminently, he wanted out of there fast.

After another quick grab for food through the hole, he had a full back pack and could also carry at least one of the strong carrier bags in which the food was contained. He jogged quickly to the rock face and started to climb. His spirits were now about as high as he could ever think possible given the circumstances.

Not surprisingly, as he looked down, he saw the wolf had returned and was sniffing around the scattered food. As Rob inched closer to his cave, two men came out of the cabin, lighting cigarettes. Rob pressed himself into the rock, wishing it would absorb him to avoid being seen. His blood turned to ice, and shivers spread through him, the high of a few moments before evaporating like liquid oxygen in a furnace. He held his breath as the men turned, raised their arms to point, and started to yell. *Phew, they've seen the wolf, not me!* The two started to throw stones at the animal, which promptly turned tail and fled once more. All the other men came pouring out of the cabin, guns at the ready.

Rob recognised the boss-man as he demanded sharply, "Hey, what's going on?"

One of the men pointed to the rear of the shed, "A bloody wolf was taking our food, that's what."

A quick inspection over, the boss-man ordered, "Fix that hole and clean the mess up. I don't want more animals," before sauntering back to the cabin.

The men set about the task in a leisurely manner so when, nearly twenty minutes later, they had finished, Rob's fingers and arms were shaking with the exertion of holding himself against the rock for so long. Only once the men were safely back inside the cabin did Rob gingerly climb the last couple of metres into a small cave and collapsed in a heap, exhausted, on the rock floor.

After a brief rest, Rob sat up and tried to scan the cave, but to no avail. The light was negligible, so all he could do was to sit in the mouth of the cave to inspect some of the food he had captured and start eating. He was famished.

Once the light had faded completely, Rob had no choice but to wrap up in the smelly rug from the truck and settle down to sleep. He could not risk turning any of his gadgets on in case their light alerted someone. At one point, the night's peace was shattered with the roar of some quad bikes. "More people arriving," Rob groaned. He had just started to settle after the heart-thumping shock of the latest arrivals, when rain started to hammer down. However, after a while its hypnotic rhythm helped him drift back to sleep.

3

Dawn broke over the hilly, almost mountainous region of Notranjska. Rob, cold and tired, started massaging life back into his limbs. He was sore and stiff after an uncomfortable and disrupted night's sleep on the cold, hard and rocky floor of the cave. It was still raining and with such intensity that Rob immediately decided to stay put. From the cave mouth, he could just make out the area immediately in front of the cabin, so he would be able to watch any comings or goings.

Following a light, jumbled breakfast from the food he had purloined, all there was to do was to take an inventory of what he had. The range and quantity of food was a pleasant surprise. *At least this will last for a while*, he thought as he looked at the contents of his daysack: iPhone, iPad, various cables, a Gerber multi-tool, a lock knife, a Maglite torch, and a pocket tripod for his camera back at the guesthouse. *Hmm. I wonder how Madam Kos has reacted to my absence. She's probably informed the police. Oh joy! Oh well, not much I can do about that. I may as well explore this cave.*

At the same time, people in uniform and civilian clothes started materialising in dribs and drabs at the Kras Hotel and the main conference room, where Kovač had established his base for the investigation. Most of the arrivals had their hands curled around steaming cups of coffee as they made their way to their designated position to start work.

Shortly after 8:00 a.m., Kovač's mobile phone buzzed. "Hopefully good news," Kovač muttered on seeing Henri Simmonet's name on the screen.

"Ah, Inspector," the Frenchman started in an accent that attracts so many. "Evelyne Dubois. Not much I can say, sorry. Thirty-eight years old and from Vichy. Both parents died while she was young, and she was raised by her grandmother, who is also now dead. No siblings. Registered occupation is a florist and lives above the shop. Was reasonably successful by all accounts, but she is not the proprietor. No record of the daughter's father.

"No record of any trouble with the authorities, but she was flagged by her bank shortly after her daughter was born because a regular, second source of income started filtering in. Nothing substantial, simply unexplained. It was declared and tax paid. Too small to register as a priority for investigation, so appears to have been forgotten and not investigated.

"They travelled to Ljubjana two days ago, as you said, using a variety of modes of transport. Passports were issued for the first time six years ago. She's visited other countries, always with her daughter, some quite a few times. This was their first trip to Slovenia. The other countries were Austria, Belgium, Germany, Italy, Spain, Switzerland, and Turkey.

"There's no evidence she ever paid for any travel. Her lifestyle and the apartment's contents suggest that she was not extravagant. The photo albums contained nothing of interest. The financial assistance and travel are the only suspicious elements we've found.

"That's all so far, but I intend to keep looking; there are a number of intriguing elements that have caught my attention. I'll stay in touch, but please also let me know how you progress."

"Many thanks indeed, Henri. That's very interesting." Kovač had been listening intently, scribbling notes in a pad as he propped the phone between ear and shoulder. "My news is that a young English man appears to have disappeared. The guesthouse where he's been staying has not heard from him since yesterday morning." Kovač continued looking intently at his assistant, who nodded, confirming that Madam Kos had not reported Rob's reappearance.

"We think he is the unaccounted for person from the hotel. Name is Robert Krane, and had recently lost his job. He may have been a spotter for the bad guys, or simply been in the wrong place at the wrong time. A team is about to search his room at the guesthouse. I'm waiting for the English to wake up before I call MI5. Let's keep in touch."

"Many thanks, *mon ami*."

"My pleasure. Let's speak again soon, although I may have to ask my assistant, Nina Lah, to update you."

"That won't be a problem. I perfectly understand. Well, *au revoir* and good luck."

Kovač stabbed the red disconnect call button on his phone and looked over at his assistant. "Inform the team to search Mr Robert Krane's room please. Then, type up these notes and circulate them to our team and to the authorities of the countries listed. We want to know anything they've got on this Dubois woman, if anything."

Kovač was on a roll. Scrolling through his phone's contacts list, he soon found who he was looking for and punched the green call button.

"Gurning." Kovač was taken by surprise because there had been no rings.

"Steven, it's Franc Kovač from Slovenia here. Got a few minutes?"

"Sure. How are things?"

"Complicated, to say the least. Other than that, I'm fine, thanks. And you?"

"Not too bad. Bored of the ever-increasing administration. So, what's up, Franc?"

"I would be grateful if you could run some checks on one of your nationals for me. Robert Krane. He's been missing since yesterday morning and we think he was at the hotel at the time of the mass killings you've probably heard about."

"Sure, happy to run some checks for you. Yes, I heard about the incident, so anything we can do, just let me know. Do you think our boy was involved?"

"Not sure. Nothing is making sense. Everyone was killed except for this Robert Krane and a nine-year old French girl who has disappeared, presumed abducted, but her mother, Evelyne Dubois, was amongst the dead. Henri Simmonet is looking into her and has already found a few matters to investigate further."

Kovač quickly briefed Steven Gurning on his conversation with Henri Simmonet. He always appreciated his conversations with Gurning. The man was razor sharp, perceptive, and generally helpful.

"Any chance that our boy was with the girl and her mother?"

"No. He was busy chatting-up a waitress.

"Ah. Well, as always, my friend, I'll run some checks and let you know what I find. What I can say immediately is that this chap, Krane, is not currently on our radar—I just typed his name into dispatches."

Madam Kos was in turmoil. She was swelling with pride at being of such importance to the authorities, especially as all her neighbours were watching and fully aware of the situation, she had made sure of that herself. However, she was also beside herself—the team of police investigators had clumped in with wet boots and dirtied the carpets throughout the house. She understood their explanation that a criminal would secrete incriminating items all over, not only, if at all, in his or her room. But that did not assuage her mood at the prospect of so much cleaning! She was, however, relieved to overhear the team boss calling Kovač to report that nothing of any interest had been found. She acknowledged that the team had been careful and thorough, and it was the thoroughness that troubled her. What would she say to the nice young man when, or if, he returned?

Kovač wasn't concerned about the cleaning when he signalled for Chief Horvat, his assistant, and a few others to join him. "Nothing's been found at the guesthouse, absolutely nothing," he announced. "I will wait for a response from the British, but this Robert Krane should not absorb too much time. Do not, I emphasise, do not ignore him, but focus on other leads. Chief Horvat, assign a couple of men only to locate him. He is, after all, missing and therefore deserves consideration."

Rob would have been appreciative, had he known, but he was far too interested in what he had discovered. Having slithered along a short, narrow tunnel, he found himself gawping as the beam from his torch cut through the pitch-blackness of a cave the size of a large house. There was everything he had read about in the guidebooks, only this cave was not in those books. There were jaw-dropping stalagmites and stalactites at the edge while the floor of the cave was a pool of dark water with ripples of concentric circles flowing across it, caused by dripping water from high up on the cave roof. He thought of his camera back at the guesthouse and cursed his misfortune for not having kept it by his side at all times.

After heading back to where he had slept, Rob returned with a white bag to a mark his exit. He then gingerly set out around the pool to explore. Venturing into and back out of dead-end galleries and smaller caves, Rob lost track of time thanks to the marvel of nature and his discovery. He had even experienced a unique picnic. *A lakeside lunch with a difference*, he had called it at the time, wishing once more that he had his camera to mark the occasion.

As he turned back upon reaching what he thought was yet another dead end, he stopped in his tracks. Off to his left he could just make out a light in the distance. And, unless the sun had broken through the rain clouds, which was unlikely, this light was almost certainly manmade. Therefore, despite being disorientated from the dark and many twists and turns, he reasoned that the light had to emanate from the kidnappers.

Rob shone his torch and ran a hand around the walls and roof of the rocky passage. *Good. No cables, no lights, no frequent, if any, usage by these guys.* He then worked his way forward, turning his torch off as he approached an opening.

Wow! Rob was looking through an opening easily large enough for him to squeeze through. An up-stand of rock beyond hid his opening from sight for anyone in the cave below. Very cautiously, and as quietly as possible, Rob eased himself through to lie on the ledge behind the rocky up-stand. Looking down, he could see the backs of three men facing the man he now knew was Burak Demir and the girl. Both were slumped but awake on the floor at the back of the cave. One of the three was talking.

"…is not coming because of the weather. So, Mr King Pin, our discussion and your health check will have to wait. I have my tools to assist, and have been assured that your daughter will be well looked after in another room until such a time as I'm able to check on her health. Presumably Emilio has already told you of how well I care for my younger patients?"

Burak Demir, addressed as King Pin, nodded.

"Good. Until tomorrow then, unless I become impatient to start your daughter's health-check, that is." With that, the three turned and left.

A few minutes' silence followed the sound of retreating footsteps and the echoing clunk of a door being firmly closed and locked. Burak then uneasily raised his arms, hands still handcuffed, and placed them over the little girl and hugged her. She wriggled further into his body until she was comfortable. Rob watched, transfixed, yet embarrassed at his voyeurism during these personal moments for a father and daughter. He had no idea of what he should do now. The speaker had sounded very threatening, and the insinuations regarding the girl's health-check were extremely unsettling.

Frowning with confusion, Rob watched with intrigue as Burak's hands deftly slipped his belt off without disturbing his daughter's drowsiness, who was soon fast asleep. He noticed with equal puzzlement that tears were running down Burak's cheeks. Then, as Burak wrapped one end of the belt around each hand, Rob realised with horror that the man was crying because he intended to murder his own daughter! No doubt because he knew what the other man was capable of.

No! This can't be happening. My intervention is required—now or never. I can't let this girl be murdered, or harmed! Picking up a small stone, Rob lobbed it over to where Burak and girl were slumped. Although certain there was no one in the cave, Rob had no idea how sound would carry.

Time went into slow motion as Rob watched, petrified as Burak raised the belt towards the girl's neck, tears now streaming down his cheeks, and as the stone arced through the air, then landed, tinkled, and skipped over the uneven rock floor. Burak tensed and looked up and around sharply, the jerky movement waking his daughter. Burak also rapidly moved the belt away from his daughter's neck and concealed it to one side. When Rob stuck his head above the rocky up-stand, he could see their eyes opening wide in disbelief. Rob held his finger to his lips. The man nodded and promptly whispered something to his terrified daughter.

For a while Rob merely exchanged stares with the two from his vantage point. *I must be mad! This is crazy!* Then, with great determination, Rob pushed himself up and looked around before dropping down onto the cave floor. Hesitantly, he walked over to the captives. Looking down at the man, he said, "Burak Demir, I presume?" The man nodded.

"I wouldn't be here if it wasn't for your daughter. I don't want any part of whatever it is that you're involved with, so I'll help your daughter to get away, but that's it! I'm sure you've made arrangements so she'll be adequately looked after."

Burak shook his head sadly before responding. "That won't do any good. I'm a dead man anyway," he said in a thick accent.

The girl immediately burst into tears and continued sobbing as Burak added, "My daughter is only here to make me talk. Without her they know I won't talk, and consequently, you *will* be hunted down." He emphasised the word *will* with a strong finality about it. "And no, sadly it has not been possible to make arrangements for her yet. So, without me alive, Anja will not be provided for. I've been too clever in the past and have not been able to untangle matters sufficiently yet to consider my personal arrangements."

Rob, unmoving, frowned, not understanding, so the man had to plough on. "I'm sorry that you have to hear this, sweetheart," he said gently to the girl before turning back to Rob. "I have tried to keep my personal life a secret, although clearly I have failed. There are certain elements who resent my attempts at creating a distance between myself and those many aspects of my business operations that are of, should we say, a less-legitimate nature.

"One is not meant to settle down in my line of business. One is supposed to merely live for the moment and for fun. When I met Evelyne, Anja's mother, I came to realise the lack of fulfilment in my life and sought to change it. That has so far proved impossible. Therefore, young man, whilst hurtful, I can understand your sentiments, but the future security for my daughter is now inextricably tied to my well-being and no one else's."

Anja was still sobbing but more quietly and did not appear to be listening, but even so, Burak fixed Rob with a knowing look and shook his head. This was no place to address her mother's death. Burak then continued with such a finality of tone that Rob was momentarily lost for words. "Our lives are now inextricably linked."

"If I help you to escape as well, you will continue to live a privileged life, albeit tragic and threatened. And I don't think that's fair, nor is it just." Burak remained silent, so Rob blurted out, "Okay, I'll help you, but you must agree to transfer absolutely everything to me and I will then set up some form of trust fund for your daughter and sufficient for yourself." After a pregnant pause, during which Rob realised how silly what he had just said must have sounded, he continued, "Yes, yes, I know that's a naïve statement, but you just said that you wanted out, so why not? There must be a way."

Without waiting for a response, Rob strode to a table a few metres away, watched by a curious Burak and Anja. Rob picked up a pen and a pad of paper and scribbled:

I, Burak Demir, transfer all assets, businesses, possessions, shares, and everything to Robert Krane. I do so totally willingly. Robert Krane accepts such transfer and acknowledges that he will provide for Burak Demir's only daughter.

Signed ....
Dated ....

Rob signed, shaking his head at what he knew was a worthless piece of paper, but he was trying to buy time to think. He walked back to Burak and dropped the pen and pad on his knees, noticing for the first time how they were shackled to the cave wall. He then returned to the desk and searched the drawers. Ignoring the array of knives and other items, Rob collected keys, another three pairs of handcuffs, a handgun, a semi-automatic machine pistol, and a number of additional loaded magazines for each weapon. *I can be confident up to the point of the cave's exit, then matters will get interesting.*

Returning to Burak, he sensed that the man was trying to size him up. His appearance should be troubling the man. How could someone have followed the captors, evaded their sentries, and made his way into what must be the depths of their hideout? Had Burak recognised him from the hotel? He had no idea. Rob picked the signed paper out of Burak's lap and removed the pen from his fingers, allowing the man to glimpse the weapons he had left atop his back sack a few metres away.

Burak simply watched every move attentively and nodded when Rob released them. Picking up his belongings,

Rob said, "Follow me, preferably without scuffing the walls—that will show the direction of our exit."

With that, Rob climbed back up to his entry point and reached down to help Anja clamber up. Burak was up in no time, showing a surprising agility and signalling that he kept himself in shape. Wasting no time, Rob led them through the hole and, turning his torch on once more, through the maze of passages and caves to the originating entrance. Having ignored Burak's protests to remove Anja's handcuffs, Rob helped her when necessary, particularly around the underground lake. He had no idea whether her father had trained her at all, and consequently what the young girl may be capable of. *But caution is the best part of valour,* he reminded himself.

At the entrance to his little cave, Rob handed out some food, which was gratefully accepted. *Do we leave now, risking a dangerous descent in the wet, or wait?* Rob considered. *Nah, we need distance between us and this place. Who knows how soon the disappearance will be discovered?* "I know it's getting late, but we need to get going. It'll be wet and uncomfortable in the rain, but there's nothing I can do about that, sorry. I'll go first. Anja, you follow. Your dad will help you down the first part and then I will support you for the final part of the descent. Burak, I'm having to trust that you won't play any games."

"Young man, or seeing your name on the paper, may I call you Robert?"

"Rob's fine."

"Okay. Rob it is. You have my word. I accept you will be unwilling to trust me. That is natural. But for Anja, and I have to say, for your foolery for getting involved, I can assure you that I have no intention of playing games. My life has been all about Anja for a number of years, and I will not intentionally place her in any further danger. How you fit into all this will become clear at some point, but you don't appear to be associated with any of my businesses or the authorities. I'm simply relieved to let another lead and to have the opportunity for Anja to escape."

Looking Burak in the eyes, Rob saw a tired, broken man, but a dangerous one all the same and one who could not be underestimated. He had learnt the hard way not to underestimate his opponents, and on this occasion, the stakes—his own life—were the highest he had ever played for. "Okay, let's go. There's barely two hours of daylight remaining."

Swinging his legs over the edge, Rob clambered down the cliff, his feet slipping on the rain-slicked rock. Anja followed, Burak holding her by the wrists as far as he could before handing responsibility for her safety over to Rob, who steadied her ankles and continued to guide her down. Burak, again demonstrating a degree of agility that belied his appearance, easily followed them down.

"Sorry both of you, but please hold your arms out." Rob was holding the handgun he had found earlier. Obediently, both did as he had requested, and Rob handcuffed them together. "I know this will make the going harder and slower and I am sorry for that, but that's the way it has to be." Burak simply nodded.

The trio set off, staying tucked against the cliff face. When well out of sight of the cabin, they headed off downhill, picking their way around trees, bushes, and other natural obstacles. Dusk was falling fast as they passed another small cliff with a few potential caves that offered shelter, but Rob pressed on. As they skirted a fourth rocky outcrop, Rob, quite by chance, saw what he was looking for—a small opening in the rock behind some scrub and a small tree growing out of a fissure.

Signalling to Burak and Anja, he secured Burak to a tree using another pair of handcuffs before climbing up to the opening to check it out. Leaving the food, he returned, released Anja and gently helped her up the rocks. Finally, he returned a second time and accompanied Burak up the rock face and into the cover of the small cave. This one, Rob had discovered on his first trip, held no similar excitements as his previous cave. Rob handed out some food and then secured his two companions together once more, linking one of Burak's legs to the small tree before moving further into the cave himself to settle down for yet another uncomfortable night.

Anja was soon fast asleep, cradled warmly in her father's arms. In the darkness, Burak quietly cleared his throat, "You awake?"

"Yes," Rob replied cautiously.

"I do run legitimate businesses, you know. Really quite successfully."

Taken aback by Burak's attempt at conversation and not entirely sure where this could be leading, Rob hesitated a few moments before responding. "With an undercurrent of criminal activity as well, no doubt."

"Ouch and touché. I have been focusing on the legitimate a great deal in recent years. There are a lot of good people involved who are unaware of the, err, other activities—okay, criminal activities. There you go, I've said it. The first time ever."

Rob was relieved that he had been fiddling with his iPhone and had initiated voice recording when Burak had asked if he were awake. This was an amazing, if not surreal, conversation to be having.

"Evelyne, Anja's mother, without saying anything started an unexpected change in me. Anja's arrival, beautiful innocence, and innate excitement about life have reinforced my desire to change what I can, while I can. For years, all I've been is a dead man walking and my life was most likely to end suddenly. Now, if we are able to respect your crude piece of paper, I will have no wealth to enjoy. That leaves what I've come to realise is of greatest value for me personally: Anja. I don't know what you were thinking when you wrote down what you did, but I was mostly happy to sign. Removing the burden of running legitimate businesses and keeping my not-so-legitimate colleagues away from muscling in on those businesses has weighed heavily on me for a long time. While passing that burden on will be a relief, I am prepared to help from the side-lines. Mind you, being totally reliant upon someone else to live will be interesting, to say the least! I am therefore concerned how that will transpire, but I guess we need to extricate ourselves from this place first."

Rob wasn't quite sure what to say, if anything. This level of openness was not what he would ever have expected. Burak Demir was complex and difficult to read. His willingness to relinquish such an enormous wealth defied sense. It had been far too easy. Rob mentally acknowledged that the likelihood for future tricks, if they ever escaped, was both high and to be expected. Burak was wealthy and powerful, and had proved himself masterful at covering up his criminal activities. "You're right. All I want to do is get away from this place," was therefore all Rob could think of as a response.

"Unfortunately for you, young man, should your involvement with my escape ever become known, you will never be able to take your safety for granted again, wherever you may be."

With little that could be said in reply to Burak's prediction of Rob's future life, an awkward silence was established in the cave, and both men eventually drifted off into their own unsettled sleep.

Of the seven men in the cabin, five were playing cards. Another, the one who had been speaking to Burak in the cave, was lounging on one of the bunk beds lining the wall. The seventh man, the leader of the group, was sitting apart from the rest at a small table studying some maps while speaking quietly on a satellite phone and taking notes.

A single, heavy door with two substantial locks was set within a thick frame in the middle of the rear wall. There was a pair of small windows at each end of the cabin and another two windows on either side of the front door. The cabin was sparse, with few furnishings. A small counter with a camping gas stove, battered metal kettle, and a couple of equally battered pans served as a kitchen. Food-encrusted plates, goblets, and cutlery were strewn across the table where the men were playing cards.

The leader put the phone down gently and continued scrawling away on his pad. After a while, he turned his head, "Okay, let's go check on KP and the girl and make sure Kristin is still awake. Doc, Mauricio, you're with me."

Scraping the chair on the wooden floor, he stood up and crossed to the door, unlocked it, and led the way into the passage behind. The first few metres had been hewn out of the rock before joining a naturally formed small cave. Walking past a few doors, they came upon Kristin, asleep on his chair, head propped up against the doorframe behind him. The leader hooked his foot behind a chair leg and up-ended the whole thing.

"Idiot!" he yelled. He unlocked the door, leaving a dazed Kristin to scramble to his feet and follow the trio into the brightly lit cave, only to find it devoid of the expected prisoners.

The ensuing ruckus was messy. Forcing Kristin against the rocky wall, the leader promptly delivered a series of powerful blows to the man's face and abdomen, while yelling obscenities in his face. The leader eventually stormed off shouting, "Rip this place apart, and rip him apart as well if need be. Just find them, or we'll all be history. Doc, feel free to practice on him to make sure he was not part of the escape, or that there is nothing that he hasn't told us! This will be the last time he falls asleep on duty!"

Doc and another man dragged Kristin off to a side room while everyone else arrived and started a thorough search of the cave.

"Oh shit!" said one eventually, pointing up to the barely visible opening through which Rob, Burak, and Anja had escaped. "Someone's going to get a bullet!" Standing well back in the cave, he had stretched despondently, figuring the search to be fruitless, when he had looked up and saw the gap. Moments later one of the others had scrambled up and confirmed their worst suspicion. Someone had not surveyed the place fully.

"Toss you for who tells the boss," the first guy said, digging a coin out of a pocket.

"Tell me about what?" growled their boss, who walked into the room at that precise moment.

"Guns, keys, and handcuffs taken from the desk, and looks like the escape was through a previously unseen hole behind that ledge up there," Mauricio said, pointing. "I peered through, but we don't have any torches to explore. I can't figure how to explore without waiting until the morning to buy torches from a nearby village."

"Too right—we won't wait, nor go buy torches. It'd raise attention. Figure it out with the lighting in here, and check the sheds outside."

Gustov waited until their boss had left. "Stephane, you check the sheds. Mauricio and I can start on the electrics. Unless there's a heap of slack, this cable won't get us far."

It was four o'clock when Gurning called Kovač again. A few minutes earlier, he had tapped in his password for the Alerts Registry System (or ARS for short) on his computer. He then filled in the requisite fields so any mention or query on Rob's name by any of the UK's authorities would be immediately flagged.

Kovač was frustrated to say the least, and that came across in the tone of his voice, despite his attempt to disguise it. He had read all of the reports into the incident, forensics, ballistics results, and the reports of stolen vehicles which had been cross-checked against the tyre marks found at the scene. Gurning's report did little to help his temperament.

"Hello, Franc, Steven here."

"Steven, hi. I really hope you can tell me something helpful. The investigations at this end are going nowhere, and I'm taking a lot of heat."

After a slight pause, indicating that the MI5 officer was considering his words carefully, Gurning ran through his list of bullet points about Rob, all neatly set out on a single piece of paper placed on his desk. "Not sure if this helps in the way I anticipate you want. I would move Robert Krane to the low end of my investigations, or discount him altogether. Except, of course, you have the annoying obligation to find a missing foreigner. Born and still lives in London. Thirty-one years of age. Unexciting family background. Single. Clean record from all authorities, not even a flicker. Even no points on his driving licence. No political affiliations. No financial pressures identified. Made redundant recently, along with many others from some US bank. He was in a back-office support function when his department was shipped off to India and Hungary. Was highly regarded and popular, but vocal with his disagreement to the reorganisation. Various degrees and some charitable voluntary work. Talented amateur photographer who has exhibited, but not seriously or to any great acclaim. Now here's the interesting bit: he won gold a few weeks back at the European Combined Martial Arts and Unarmed Combat Championships. That tops and complements a lot of awards. Apparently, he has been very successful on that circuit for a couple of years now. When he tours, he nearly always arranges to speak to groups of underprivileged kids to inspire them into activities, whether work, artistic stuff, or sport. So to sum up, essentially one of those good, likeable people who excel at rather a lot. One of the girls here even tried phoning him a few times, but only got voicemail."

"Yes, I had been hoping for a lead, but that was too much to hope for considering how well organised the operation appears to have been." Kovač then added, with a heavy hint of irony, "No CCTV anywhere, of course, because serious crime doesn't happen in Postojna."

"I know the feeling all too well, I'm afraid. Well, I've tagged Robert's name so should anything come in, I will be alerted immediately. When do we inform his parents? We don't want this getting into the press first."

"Hmm. You're right, of course. Possibly best to inform them. Can you arrange that?"

"No problem. Will do. Story will be that he is unaccounted for and un-contactable, but that may be expected because of the nature of his planned holiday. Speak to you anon. Bye for now."

"Thank you, Steven. Good-bye."

Gurning sighed as he turned to gaze out over the River Thames from his office in Thames House. A pleasure cruiser was struggling to make headway against the strong incoming tide, churning the water up in its wake. He glanced at his notepad and the to-do list scribbled earlier while sitting in a dull meeting.

Call Franc Kovač

  Set up an all-systems flag against Krane's name, priority and alert for me only.

Call 6 (his shorthand for MI6)
Call Krane's family?
Boss?

He drew a firm line through the first two items on the list. Should he or should he not mention this to his boss? He was still not sure. Ordinarily the usual channels within the Foreign Office would manage these matters, particularly when nothing untoward was flagged. So why would he even consider troubling his boss, the DG or director general? Instinct was whispering madly at him. No, he had absolutely nothing, so he rapidly typed up a file note of his conversations with Kovač to circulate to the relevant parties. They could pick this one up. That way he wouldn't have to deal with awkward questions from the family and could avoid getting his peer, Graeme Spreachley, at MI6 unnecessarily engaged.

4

Rob awoke after yet another uncomfortable night and heard, yet again, the pattering rain on leaves. Burak and Anja appeared to still be asleep. He checked his watch. It was 7:30 a.m. and the dull, grey light had made its silent way into the depths of their small cave. He shook his thick and fuzzy head because of lack of decent sleep. He did not want to face the truth of Burak's comments from the previous evening, at least not yet. Looking at his companions, he was of two minds about whether to let them continue to sleep or to wake them and get moving. The imperative to keep moving and seek help made the decision for him.

"Come on, time to get going," he said loudly. Intrigued, he watched the different ways in which the child woke, as opposed to an adult who was always alert.

Passing out some food, less than previously because their supply was getting low, he commented, "At least the rain appears to be letting up."

"Won't make a jot of a difference for us," muttered Burak as Anja sneezed and sniffed.

Soon the bedraggled trio were threading their way through the dense trees and undergrowth once more. They paused briefly by a crystal-clear stream to drink and splash their faces from its refreshing waters before crossing. The cool water temporarily shocked any vestiges of tiredness from their minds and bodies, reenergising them to press ahead. Following an approximate parallel route to the stream, they headed downhill in the hope that it would lead somewhere worthwhile.

At last, as the rain ceased, that plan paid off as they encountered a small road. Having taken another drink from the stream and checked Burak's and Anja's handcuffs, Rob directed that they track the road while staying within the forest's cover. His heart was racing at the thought of potentially coming across signs of life and what he should do once they did. By late morning, they arrived at a steep cliff and lost the cover of the trees. "Let's have a rest before we continue on the other side," Rob announced. Gazing out across the valley below, Rob saw another valley opposite them where twinkles of light reflected on the windows of buildings and passing traffic as an occasional ray of sunlight broke through the cloud. His heart leaped at the thought of possible help, but also thumped at the prospect of having to explain what he was doing guiding a handcuffed man and small girl while also carrying a pair of weapons.

Michael Stanley! Why didn't I think of him before? He'll know what to do. But what to say? An e-mail will help structure my thoughts. Michael was something at the Metropolitan Police in London and trained with Rob at a martial arts centre in Wembley. They weren't so much friends as periodic drinking or cheap dinner partners after a training session. They would chat about anything and everything, except for Michael's work, about which he was always cagey. Rob had Michael's mobile number and personal e-mail address. So, given he had a signal at last, he settled down with his iPad and typed out an e-mail, with the words, "As per text message" written in the subject line. He would send Michael a text as soon as he had sent the e-mail.

Michael,
Hi. I'm in a spot of bother here in Slovenia and need advice and a lot of help. A few days ago, there was a shooting and kidnapping where I was staying. To escape, I hid in the attackers' vehicle, don't ask! Quite by chance, I was able to free the two kidnapped people and escape with them. I'm now wondering what to do. Photos of both are attached. The man is Burak Demir, who admits to being a criminal. The girl is his daughter, Anja. Signal has been non-existent, but I can see a well-used road in the distance, so presume signal should stay reasonable from now on.
  Help!
  Rob

Quickly scanning what he had written, Rob attached the photos, gulped at the thought of the likely reaction his e-mail would generate, and then tapped the send button. Checking that it had gone, he sent Michael a simple text.

URGENT! Please check your personal e-mail. I need help. Rob Krane.

If that didn't grab Michael's attention, nothing would. With that, he scanned an approximate track down into and across the valley towards the smaller valley opposite them that led to the barely visible road. "Okay, let's get going!"

Once they had crossed the road, Burak drew close. "Enlisting help?"

"That's right. Sent an e-mail and a text to a friend who will know what to do."

"I hope so and also hope it won't involve staying in this country. I doubt that would be very safe given how I was traced by my power-hungry cohorts."

Rob didn't reply but merely kept trudging onwards and downwards, watching his step as the terrain became steeper and keeping an ear and eye open for any traffic and a way of proceeding with as much cover as possible.

The *beep, beep* of his mobile drew Michael from his reverie while he was queuing for a sandwich in Scotland Yard's canteen. He wanted a distraction from the tedious report writing that necessarily followed the conclusion of an operation, even though nothing had come of it. He had to read the text twice for the contents to fully sink in. Rob had never been one for dramatics, so Michael quickly paid for the first sandwich he could lay his hands on and went in search of his boss for clearance to access an external and personal webmail account.

Kevin Barnes was where he nearly always was, in his office. Michael quickly explained what he wanted and received the requisite curt nod of approval and signature on the inevitable form to be handed to the tech guys down in the basement.

"Let me know what is so urgent, please," said Superintendent Barnes as the form was passed back across the desk. He knew of

Michael's friendship with Rob and, like Michael, was curious about what could fluster such an incredibly accomplished man to use such attention-grabbing words as Rob had in his text.

Fifteen minutes later Michael was back at his desk. "Strewth!" Michael exclaimed, far more loudly than he had intended as he read his friend's e-mail. *How the blazes did he get himself wrapped up with someone like Demir?* He forwarded the mail to his work account and logged off his personal account. As soon as the e-mail arrived, he printed it. Walking briskly down the bland, featureless corridor, he found himself once more at his boss's office, but this time, Barnes was in the adjacent meeting room with colleagues. Ignoring that, he knocked on the door and entered. "Sorry, boss. You need to read the e-mail I mentioned earlier."

Michael walked around the table under the incredulous stares of the six others sitting at the large rectangular table. It was littered with files, pads of paper, and cups of steaming coffee. Interrupting one of Barnes's meetings was not something one did lightly.

Barnes scanned Rob's e-mail very quickly. "Let's go next door. Continue without me," he said to the others as he stood and walked out. "Doris, please get everyone's work roster for me. I may have to rearrange workloads for young Michael here."

Doris, the battle-axe of an assistant who had been with Barnes throughout his career, gave the appearance of not changing a thing, but in reality she had deftly switched activities to what her boss had just ordered.

Barnes closed his office door behind them and gave Michael a wry smile. "Well, it appears your friend has got himself into a pickle. Have you registered this on the systems yet?"

"Not yet sir, no. It appeared to be of sufficient interest to come straight to you."

"Agreed. Right, let's see what we have," the superintendent continued as he opened ARS and started filling in various fields. When he had finished a minute later, he looked up to address Michael once more. "So, other than the fighting stuff that you two get up to, what can you tell me about Mr Robert Krane? That way I should be able to figure out who else to contact, if anyone."

"That's not very easy, sir, I'm afraid. While we've gone for a drink and/or dinner a few times, in reality, I don't know much about him. And vice versa, as you'd expect."

"I'd sincerely hope so," Barnes chipped in.

A few minutes into Michael's brief exposé of Rob, the phone rang. Barnes scowled through the glass panel of his office at Doris, who simply shrugged and mouthed, "Sorry, urgent."

Barnes hit the hands-free button of his phone and enunciated a pointedly sharp-sounding, "What?!"

"Inspector Gurning of MI5 for you. Said it had to be immediate."

"Okay then." He rolled his eyes skywards for Michael's benefit. At the sound of the transfer, he announced, "Superintendent Barnes." He winked at Michael with a sly grin, announcing an intended game of brinkmanship with this spook who had dared have the temerity of overriding his request not to be disturbed.

"Ah, Superintendent. About your ARS entry a few minutes ago—we need to speak."

All thoughts of any games went flying out of the window; their attention was well and truly grabbed.

"Go on," he said warily.

"It sounds as though you're on speaker. I prefer to know who is listening, and considering the potential ramifications of this matter, we may have to meet in person."

The superintendent mouthed "*smart-ass*" before replying, "I'm with Michael Stanley, who reported Robert Krane's contact and who also, I have the pleasure to add, whipped one of your boys at the inter-divisional martial-arts contest last year."

There was only the briefest of pauses before Gurning continued. "Yes, I remember that and will be pleased to work with Michael on this, presuming your agreement, of course. May I ask why you entered Robert Krane's name on ARS? Unfortunately, this has potential international and broad national security consequences, as well as political ramifications."

"Yes, Inspector, I'm coming to appreciate that, and apologies for the initial sarcasm." One of the things Michael really appreciated about his boss was his down-to-earthness and his humour, as well as his readiness to acknowledge when a comment may have been made out of place.

"That's okay, sir. The thing is, our Slovenian friends are investigating a mass murder in relation to the apparent and inexplicable kidnapping of a young girl in Postojna. Robert Krane, is currently unaccounted for and was known to be present at the time of the shooting. Information is needed to either discount him from the Slovenians' enquiries or tag him for being involved. The introduction of Burak Demir, as you noted on ARS, adds a level of UK national self-interest that cannot be ignored and may override other considerations, such as cooperating with other intelligence services. Demir's name will have started other alerts ringing, so I'll need to identify those and coordinate things. We should meet." After the briefest of pauses, he added, "Urgently. I will sort a room here at Thames House."

The superintendent simply raised an eyebrow. "As always, we're here to assist." His words were full of a blend of sarcasm and sincerity that Michael had heard before and could only marvel at. "Send Michael an inter-services message on where and when and he will join you. I had already anticipated that I'd have to relieve him of his current duties—at least for the time being."

"Much appreciated. Michael, please be here within the hour. Ask for me at reception. See you then. Not a word to anyone else. I'll ask the DG to sort out the political niceties and conflicts between the services. Oh, just one thing—when was the initial contact, and what is the expected follow-up, when, and how?"

"Not quite an hour ago and not stipulated," Michael replied, noting how neatly Gurning ignored the request for an inter-services message.

"Okay, thanks. See you soon."

With that, the line went dead, and Michael regarded his boss carefully. "Well, my lad, your friend appears to have ticked all the boxes for a right royal situation. You'd better hot-foot it over to Thames House, but don't let the allure of the intelligences services draw you away from where the real work gets done!"

Michael knew a few of his number had left their elite group for MI5 or MI6, but he had never considered it himself. Nor had he really had contact with those services before, so had not appreciated the possible allure his boss referred to. "Fat chance, sir. I'll keep you posted."

With that, he picked-up the e-mail he had printed and returned to his desk to close everything down before heading off to Thames House.

Barely forty-five minutes later, Michael found himself in a large, nondescript meeting room, similar to those at Scotland Yard. Gurning wanted to wait a few more minutes for people to gather. Those who had arrived were grouped in their own little cliques, having secretive, muttered conversations. The body language screamed that interaction with others was not welcome. Michael moved over to the windows and lifted a blind, hoping to look out over the river, but he was disappointed to find no view at all. They were overlooking an unexciting, grey light well. He let the blind drop again with a rattle and took a seat as Gurning called the meeting to order. *No allure here then,* he thought to himself as he took a seat, thinking back to his boss's earlier comment.

"Okay all, thanks for coming at such short notice. I've a very simple agenda this afternoon. First, to brief everyone here about the situation as we know it and take a note of vested interests and queries. Secondly, as an even smaller group, to establish contact with Robert Krane and agree next steps with him. Needless to say, everything discussed here today is to be treated with the highest confidentiality and sensitivity, so before you leave you will be required to sign another of those beastly Acknowledgement of

Restricted and Confidential Information Forms, so no onward dissemination of information. Your bosses will be brought into the picture as soon as they sign. Right, let me introduce Detective Michael Stanley from Scotland Yard, who received the initial contact and can brief us on all he knows. I'll then provide an overview of my conversations with the Slovenians. Michael."

Michael took less than ten minutes to finish his briefing and answer what questions he could, acknowledging that it was not much.

It was then Steven's turn. "Okay, myself and Laura Harding here are both MI5," he waved a hand at a youngish woman sitting opposite Michael. "We became involved when Inspector Kovač of the Slovenian Intelligence and Security Agency called me. Their current supposition is that the shootings were so well executed and unusually well-equipped that some form of terrorism must lie behind the inexplicable kidnapping. Robert Krane's unaccounted-for status potentially linked him to those thought-to-be terrorists, possibly as a spotter. MI5 will lead this case. We believe that Demir's activities and extensive networks have links to and/or fund and/or are associated with organisations that intend to harm British interests both at home and abroad. The latter, of course, being the reason why MI6 is here, represented by Graeme Spreachley." Gurning nodded in the direction of another man, neatly turned out in a light grey suit.

"The thing is, we also have reason to believe that Demir may be oblivious to his links to terrorism. As far as we can tell, he started as a petty, small-time criminal somewhere in Turkey. However, he was soon hitting the big-time in

Istanbul. While there, he also discovered that he was equally successful with legitimate business and at times was able to merge or blend the two. Inevitably, success in Istanbul soon tempted him to spread his wings further afield. His operations spread rapidly, both in scale and type of activity. This assessment has been corroborated with the National Intelligence Organisation in Turkey.

"Demir's criminal activities are known to operate across the UK. However, no direct links to Demir himself have been established, as shown by the failure of the French prosecution a few years back. In the room we have colleagues from the NCA and Scotland Yard, and to help tread the paths of the government's political relationships with Slovenia, we have our friends from the Foreign Office.

"We will keep everyone here briefed via e-mail. For those who know me, I don't appreciate unnecessary meetings cluttering up my diary. The key thing I want to establish today is that we do not engage with any of our Slovenian counterparts for the time being." Holding up his hand to wave off objections and attempts to interject, Gurning ploughed on. "Yes, yes, I realise that is awkward for all of us with relationships to preserve, not least political. However, there is a lone British national overseeing a man who evaded questioning when he walked free from that French court. We are desperate to get Demir to the UK and hold him for questioning. We don't want red tape, whether Slovenian or international, getting in our way. Okay, I can see a few of you are bursting to jump in, so ask away."

Fifteen minutes later, following much debate, Gurning brought the meeting to a close and invited all but four to depart. "Right, before replenishing our cups or breaking for nature, while I was talking I had the terrible realisation that Robert may well be using his mobile while we sit here cogitating. We need to put a stop to that. Michael, the honours please—by text. We don't want the Slovenians tracking him. Advise him that we will contact him again by e-mail."

Gurning, Laura, and Graeme, politely waited in silence while Michael sent Rob a quick text.

At the bleeping sound of a successful text transmission, Gurning continued. "Okay, as I see it, the questions we need to resolve are: One, how do we sensibly communicate with Robert without giving the Slovenians an opportunity to trace his location? Two, where is he? Three, how do we extract them in short order? Time is not on their, nor our side. Four, where do we keep them once in the UK? Five, how safe will Robert be if he returns to an unprotected life as normal? Any comments?"

"I can help with point three. We have a very able young lady based in Ljubljana. The country is quite small, so a pick-up should be possible with relative ease. My only concern is how to keep hold of Demir. By all accounts, he is a tricky and slippery character. I'd be so bold as to say that point two is easily answered provided we can overcome your first point, Steven."

"Agreed to that."

"May I make a suggestion to cover point one?" Michael asked.

"By all means," Gurning responded enthused. "At this stage, anything is a good start."

"Well, Rob likes his techie toys. He sent an e-mail whilst clearly on the move, and the photo he sent was not of standard scale, meaning he had cropped it."

"Yes, so go on," Gurning encouraged. "I'm a bit of a dinosaur when it comes to technology, so you'll need to explain."

Michael caught a glimpse of Laura's wry smile at her boss's frank admission. Michael placed Gurning in his mid-fifties with grey, silvery, and receding hair. His face was, however, virtually ageless, no doubt helped by a healthy and physical lifestyle, evidenced by his trim physique and easy movements.

"Of course. Depending upon what Rob has with him, we could either exchange instant messages or even hook up through Skype or similar Internet video and/or audio conferencing application."

"You're kidding me! Laura, please fire up the computer over there," Gurning pointed to the credenza along the far wall. "We could certainly give that a go. You sure it can't be traced?"

"Actually, sir, it can, but only if you are specifically monitoring for that type of Internet traffic, and it takes somewhat longer because of the nature of the technology. I'll text Rob stating that's what we intend to do. If you're anything like Scotland Yard, however, authorisation will be required to use the necessary app."

"Oh grief, more techie protection. It's necessary, but so tedious to deal with. Laura, you've always said that you know someone. I will approve the request."

While Laura navigated through MI5's various systems, Michael sent Rob a text, adding that he would send another text when they were ready to start communication. Barely two minutes later Michael slid his phone across the table for Laura to review Rob's response. She quickly completed the electronic authorisation form and submitted it. Gurning then logged into his own system to validate the request.

Laura then went through the rigmarole of logging back onto her own system, downloaded the same video- and audio-conferencing application that Rob used, and established the settings. Eventually, she searched the contacts for Rob's pseudonym, '*fitnessman*'.

At the back of the meeting room, Graeme had been speaking quietly on his own phone while the others were sorting out the technology. Now, as Laura waited for the excruciating egg-timer to disappear from the screen, he said, "I've put our Slovenian agent on standby to support whatever action we deem appropriate. She will await further instructions."

A muffled bleep and buzz emanated from Rob's back sack, alerting him to a text. It was a reassuring sound, making him think that just maybe life could soon return to normal. But checking the message would have to wait a few minutes; they were currently in the open and Rob wanted to get to the cover of more trees before checking his phone. He hoped beyond hope that it was Michael. It had been a couple of hours since he had sent his text, and while he knew a meaningful response would take time to sort, simply knowing that people were acting would provide an immense boost to his ragged spirits.

Their journey had been strenuous, and while not of particularly great distance, it had been steep. Anja had struggled so much, in large part because of her inappropriate footwear, that Rob agreed to separate her from Burak and helped her as much as he could. Rob's greatest concern had been the distinct lack of cover and the topography was not conducive for walkers. Those facts, coupled with their dishevelled appearance, were more than adequate to make a passing motorist suspicious.

Burak had been equally wary. "I agree that we don't have any choice, but we should think about our actions and response should a car come along and we are spotted," he had advised.

Rob had agreed but immediately quashed Burak's first suggestion that they try to wave the vehicle down, kidnap the occupants and take the car to make a break for it. As far as Rob was aware, he had not done anything illegal and did not want to start! They had eventually agreed on progressing sufficiently far from the road that their appearance would hopefully not attract attention and that Rob would give a cheery wave. Burak was not thrilled, but accepted the proposal, mostly because he had little choice. He could also appreciate the wisdom of the decision from Rob's perspective, and his admiration for the young man had increased further.

"Rob, we should have a rest," Burak called from behind him.

"Okay, no problem. That makes sense. We'll soon be under cover of those trees ahead of us. We can rest there."

"Okay."

Anja was once again handcuffed to her father as a precaution against anything that Burak could possibly contemplate. As a result, Rob matched his walking speed to theirs and had to contain his impatience at both wanting to know who had sent him a text and wanting to reach cover. It was late afternoon when they reached cover of the trees and could sag down onto a damp, fallen tree trunk. They were all hungry, but had no food left.

Rob moved away a few metres to check his text. Wiping his hands on his jacket to clean away the grime before using his gadgets, he opened up his bag. The sudden rush of blood as he read Michael's first text, coupled with his hunger, made him feel weak and dizzy. Why hadn't he thought about it himself? At least someone was thinking on his behalf, and he was grateful for the warning not to use the mobile phone because of the potential for him to be traced. *Hopefully, my calls to mum and dad's answerphone and my voicemail weren't sufficient!* He had left quite a lengthy message for his parents, and there had been quite a few voice messages for him. Could either or both calls have been long enough to be traced? He had no idea.

After sending his text in reply, Rob did as directed and turned the signal for his iPhone off. That left his iPad, through which his friend could contact him by e-mail and/or by web-conferencing. He shook his head in amazement that Michael had recalled their conversation some months before that he had the iPhone and iPad working off different connections.

Swapping devices, Rob flipped open the cover for the iPad and waited, feeling some of his tension ease at last. Having swapped an instant message with Michael, an e-mail from Laura Harding with "from Michael Stanley" in the header appeared. It was a very simple one-liner asking for a response when ready to connect. Before sending the reply, Rob rummaged around in his bag to dig out an earpiece with built-in microphone—this was one conversation he did not want Burak to hear.

Relieved that he was thinking rationally again, Rob adeptly tapped through the menus on the screen, and with the benefit of Google Maps, he pinpointed their location. The collection of buildings they had seen and decided to head for was Podgraje, a small village in the neighbouring valley and close to a road that connected with a the main road that ultimately crossed over into Croatia, which was less than five kilometres directly south.

After a deep breath, he replied to Laura's e-mail confirming he was ready, switched to his conferencing application, and waited with great trepidation, nerves tingling and butterflies in his stomach. How were things going to turn out? Who was Laura Harding, and who was he going to be speaking to?

5

The soft *duh-buh, duh-buh, duh-buh* gongs of the conferencing application soon flashed on Rob's iPad. Burak had been watching Rob curiously ever since Rob had inserted the earpieces. Rob stood and pretended to stretch as a forefinger tapped the accept button to acknowledge and start the incoming video conference. He ambled a bit further away, leaned back against a tree facing Burak and Anja, and said, "Hello" in as nonchalant a manner as he could.

Four faces stared up at him from the screen. Thankfully, one was Michael's, who waved. "Hello, Rob. It appears that you've got more of an adventure from this holiday than you'd bargained for! First up and before any introductions, you obviously got my text?"

"Yes, I did, but unfortunately, not before I'd left a message for my parents on their answerphone and listened to my voicemails." Anticipating the obvious next question, he continued, "The first, for my parents, was less than a minute. The second was probably a couple of minutes as there were quite a few messages, including from the landlady at the guesthouse where I've been staying. There were also two from different policewomen whose names I couldn't hear properly. The numbers they gave were different, although I didn't have paper or pen to write them down with."

"Okay, thanks for that. Don't worry about the policewomen, they are known. We'll have to keep this brief and quick in that case. It's doubtful that the first call could have been traced. It's a given that the Slovenian authorities will have tagged your phone by now. The second call, on the other hand, was almost certainly of sufficient length to get at least a partial fix, depending upon where you are. The more rural, the fewer masts and therefore the harder to secure a good fix. I don't suppose you know where you are, do you?"

"As it happens, I do. I checked before replying. We're in the neighbouring valley to the east of a place called Podgraje, just north of the Croatian border. I'll spell it: P-o-d-g-r-a-j-e. Appears to be a small village."

"Great. Laura here will just call it up on another screen for us while we talk. Now, with me we have Steven Gurning and Laura Harding, both from MI5, and also Graeme Spreachley from MI6."

Rob blanched at hearing those organisations' names. *What have I got myself involved in?*

"Rob, are you okay?"

He nodded once and muttered, "Yes."

"I guess hearing that MI5 and MI6 are involved is somewhat disconcerting. It's because of Burak Demir, who you mentioned is with you. Is that still the case?"

"Yes. He's with his daughter. I can see them both now, and they're out of earshot. He's not looking this way, except for the occasional glance. He's mostly focused on his daughter, so I'm confident that there's no lip-reading going on, although I suspect he's guessed that I have contacted the British authorities. He knows that I know who he is."

"Ah." The four people on the screen all looked at each other, clearly concerned about the potential implications for Rob's safety.

"I've handcuffed them, both individually and then together." An undisguised look of startled, impressed surprise was evident from all four.

"Good man," Michael responded with feeling. "I think it's safe to say that we're all impressed. How that came to be and the story of your involvement and escape will have to wait. The key thing is to arrange a pick up and get you back to the UK. Graeme will send your location details to an MI6 operative in Slovenia. Crucially, we really don't want the Slovenian authorities involved, and therefore you must continue to stay as inconspicuous as possible. As far as you can tell, could you have been seen by anyone?"

"Not that I'm aware of, no."

"Good. That's something."

"I've found you." Laura suddenly interjected. "That's great. I suggest that the pick-up be at the first junction up the hill as you travel towards Podgraje. We'll send you an e-mail with details of type of vehicle and who, possibly also a photograph," she said with a sideways glance at Graeme, who simply nodded. "The reasonably good news is that being in such a rural area, it is very possible that if anyone is tracing your calls, they would not have been able to place you accurately, thereby necessitating a time-consuming and labour-intensive search. Be aware of airborne surveillance as well please, so do stay under the cover of trees as much as possible."

"Not a problem. We are under trees at the moment, and there'll be tree cover all the way to the meeting point. We can get there and take a rest. We'd possibly have to start looking for shelter by then anyway—it'll be getting dark in a few hours."

"Damn good point, Rob," chimed in Michael. "We'd better let you go now. We don't want to attract attention, even though this will be far, far harder to trace. Oh, I don't suppose your technology can also show us your captives without giving the game away can it?" Without saying anything, Rob tapped once more on the screen to provide his audience with a zoomed-in shot of Burak and Anja.

"That's Burak Demir all right," Gurning said. "Had no idea that he had a daughter though."

"Okay, thanks, Rob," Michael added. "We'll drop connection now and hopefully see you in a day or so. Good luck." With that, the connection closed, and strangely, Rob felt incredibly lonely all of a sudden. Paradoxically, at the same time, he was relieved to know that people were mobilising to come and help.

Looking at his watch, they had only been at the rest stop for thirty minutes. "Let's take another thirty minutes before making tracks," he said to Burak as he sauntered back to the fallen tree trunk and sat down with a sigh.

"No news, then?" Burak enquired casually, looking up from Anja and sideways at Rob.

"Nothing noteworthy yet, no."

"You make a lousy liar, Rob. You'll have to work on that. A good poker face for commercial negotiations, I suspect, but a lousy liar. There are subtle differences, but I'm sure you can learn."

Somewhat taken aback, Rob merely humphed, to which Burak commented, "Such responses only serve to give you away further. Let's hope that we won't have to rely on verbal reasoning to get us out of this place!"

Rob stifled a yawn and leaned back against another tree, looking at the way they had come. *Still no vehicles.* With a slight shake of the head, he thought about how isolated this region must be and the consequent challenges to receiving help.

Some two and a half hours later, it had become really quite dark beneath the trees, exacerbated by the east-facing nature of the hill up which they were walking. A few rays of the setting sun were catching the higher hills on the opposite side of the valley. Rob, becoming a little blasé about their remoteness, was about to leave the cover of the trees to cross another road when he caught the sound of a car. Quickly signalling to the other two, they lay on the ground as a car raced passed unseen. If they could not see it, the theory went that they in turn could not be seen, so long as they weren't hiding ostrich-style with their heads in the sand!

Now, as they approached the designated meeting place, Rob became concerned to see another set of headlights twinkling between the trees travelling along the road they had followed earlier that day. Two cars in the space of a few hours. Was that possible in this remote area? Of course it was, but…

He let the thought hang as he watched Burak, who was now carrying Anja on his shoulders. Somehow, he had swung her up without a word or a request to remove the handcuffs that held Anja and himself together. Could Burak really be genuine in his desire to hand everything over and focus on his daughter? It appeared highly illogical, but if actions were to be believed, maybe. Rob really could not figure this man out.

The distant revving of a vehicle's engine echoed dimly and hung in the air. Was that the one he had just seen or another car? There was no way to tell, but as they drew closer to the pick-up point, Rob became extremely nervous. Surely seeing cars was to be expected. It was, after all, evening, and people would want to head home.

Fifty metres ahead Rob saw the fork in the road where the meet was to be. Certain that Burak could not see the junction from where he was five or six metres behind, Rob announced, "Okay, let's have a break before looking for somewhere to spend the night."

Anja required no further motivation, she almost fell from her father's shoulders to collapse on the ground, promptly falling asleep. Burak looked down at her with a fond, loving smile, muttering, "Probably for the best." Looking up from his crouched position next to Anja, he changed his tone, "So what next?"

"Let me find out" was the easy reply as Rob also dropped to the ground. "That position looks mightily uncomfortable," Rob commented, noticing the forced position Burak was in from still being handcuffed to Anja. Standing up, he walked over to undo the handcuffs linking father to daughter. Rob then returned to the spot he had found for himself and checked his emails in the eerie silence of the forest. Rob's stomach muscles immediately tightened; there was another e-mail from Laura giving him the news he longed for.

Yasmin Gorski will meet you at the designated junction at 6:45 p.m. She will be driving a medium-sized blue van with a logo of three trees on each side. See the attached photo. She is medium height and build. Don't worry about language, she speaks fluent English. At the junction, she will slow down, pull over, get out, and open the rear doors. She will then sit in the rear under a light eating a couple of sandwiches for a maximum of ten minutes before leaving. Please confirm receipt of this e-mail so we can let Yasmin know to proceed as planned.

Great! he thought looking at the mug shot. *That could be a million and one women except for the fact she'll be here in the middle of nowhere.* The photograph showed a woman with short, straight brown hair and stern features.

Rob sent his confirmation and he sat back to wait—it was already 6:30 p.m. A fifteen minute wait was not too bad, except that his nerves were already stretched to their limits. *At least I can justify waiting that long since Anja is asleep.*

Burak had repositioned himself to place Anja's head on his lap. Impressed by Anja's stoicism, Rob marvelled at the unlikely relationship and the caring that Burak, a man with no doubt a horrendous history of violence, was displaying. *Hopefully there will be no long-term consequences for her mentally.*

As Rob's thoughts wandered, the minutes ticked by rapidly, and soon the sound of a vehicle shifting down a gear to address the road's gradient could be heard. Both men looked about warily and at each other.

"This may be our ride," Rob announced. "You stay here until I can verify it."

Burak simply nodded his acknowledgement.

Less than two minutes later, a dark-coloured van with the three-tree logo pulled up on the other side of the road. As per the e-mailed directions, the driver got out and sat in the rear with a light shining down upon her as she ate a sandwich. Rob glanced between the woman and the photo numerous times to make sure. There was no doubt in his mind, and he returned to say as much to Burak, but he was gone!

What had happened? Anja was still there. Rob was at a complete loss. "Sod it!" he cursed to himself vehemently. Looking at Anja, he knew he had to take her with him but was thoroughly shocked that Burak would desert her after all the loving attention he had shown her. *Maybe a leopard can't change its spots after all!* he thought miserably.

Picking the girl up as gently as he could, Rob walked over to the rear of the van. "Yasmin?"

The woman looked up. "Yes. And who are you?"

"I'm Rob, and this is Anja."

The woman stood and scrutinised the area with a sweep of her eyes. "I was told to expect three of you. Where's the other man?"

"I think he did a runner while I was checking you out. I'm sorry. I really didn't expect him to leave his daughter. I have no idea what he's thinking—he's still wearing handcuffs."

"Well, we can't wait, he'll have to look after himself. Everyone is surprised that he hasn't tried to kill you, handcuffs or no. Get the girl into the back and strap her in securely. Then you. I'll close the doors behind you once you're all done."

Anja hardly stirred as Rob followed the first set of instructions, thoroughly deflated that he had come so far and failed. With Anja in place, he got out of the van. "Please, may I have a moment to look for him?"

"No! The girl is still attractive for the kidnappers to use against Demir. We need to get going. Please, get back in."

"Oh come on. A couple of minutes won't hurt."

"No!" came the very firm response.

Deflated, he turned and started to climb back in.

"Go, go, go! We've got company!" It was Burak, yelling loudly at them as he crashed out through some bushes on the opposite side of the road.

Rob leaped out of the van as the woman spun round, removing a handgun from her jacket. Burak skidded to a halt at the rear of the van, breathing heavily. As he started to strap himself in, Burak explained, "Standard procedure. Tail reports ahead and then drops back so not to be seen nor heard. Attackers, usually the police for me, move into position silently, often with an electric or hybrid car. I went ahead to scout it out." Suddenly, four armed men emerged through the bushes fifty metres away and were closing the gap.

Yasmin immediately opened fire, as did the men. Everyone's shots were wild, missing their intended targets. Rob, while aware of the weapons tucked into his trousers, relied instead upon instinct and training. He rolled across the road, narrowly being missed by a burst of bullets that spat pieces of the tarmac into his face. He then leaped up for a close-quarters fight, which was his preference. By doing so, he unsettled his opposing combatants, who tried to keep their distance to use their guns.

As Rob mingled between the four men, varying his

kicks and punches, it became too dangerous for anyone to use their weapons. Either the attackers risked hitting one of their own, or Yasmin risked hitting Rob. Yasmin moved to one side, seeking a clear line of sight, but by doing so, she exposed herself. As Rob turned his attention to one of the others, the assailant closest to Yasmin twisted round and squeezed off a number of rounds. Two bullets ripped into her, one slicing through the upper leg, the other just catching her in the side, sending her spiralling against the van before falling onto the tarmac.

Rob kept himself in the middle of the four who were now circling him, trying to either shoot or attack with their more basic fighting skills, but they were outclassed. Rob smiled to himself as he thought of them as a group of gangly adolescent boys prancing around a dance floor trying to impress the girls! He comfortably ducked a swinging right-handed punch from one. A glancing blow immediately followed to his right shoulder from another's gun barrel. However, Rob used the momentum of that to spin around and deliver a forceful, straight-armed punch into the chest of yet another. In the ring, he knew that punch would fell most of his competitors. To his amazement, however, the man simply stepped back, apparently unfazed and only slightly off-balance. The man was tough!

Half-crouching, Rob realised his predicament and that this fight would be no pushover. He needed another ploy. These guys might not be able to fight well, but so far they were completely undeterred by what he had thrown at them. He kept moving, parrying their lunges and immediately counterattacking, trying to disable at least one of them to even up the numbers.

The standoff lasted quite a while until Rob spun, dropping to his hands and lashing both feet into the nearest man, one foot to the solar plexus the other into the nose. A high-pitched shriek and gush of blood followed the scrunching of nose cartilage. The man's handgun scuttled across the road out of harm's way.

Rob followed through, landing on his feet and lunged forward, catching a second man totally by surprise. They spun briefly, struggling to maintain balance. The man got an arm around Rob's throat. Rob feigned a collapse, forcing the man to adjust his position and grasp and in doing so, lessened his grip slightly. Rob immediately spun round to bring the man down onto his back with Rob on top. He sprung back up and stood over the man before pummelling him in the chest and face, feeling both a great satisfaction and a stupendous revulsion at his intent to hurt, or even kill. After a couple of twitches, the man became still.

The remaining two circled Rob, Yasmin groaning in the distance as she tried to stem the flow of blood. Rob kept himself between them to avert the use of firearms. After a while of noncontact circling, Rob suddenly and swiftly struck out at the man nearest him with a sharp jab to the throat as he dropped into a crouch. The man dropped like a sack of potatoes with a grunt. Rob rolled behind the man as his comrade fired, killing him instantly. Rob pulled one of his own weapons from his waistband and squeezed off three rapid shots. One found its mark, spinning the man. That gave both Rob and Yasmin the time they required to line up their respective shots. They hammered the man multiple times, sending him staggering backwards into the roadside bushes.

In great pain, Yasmin called, "Quickly, into the van! There will be others, and the authorities will be close behind!"

"Are you okay to drive?"

"Yes! I'll have to be. Get in!"

Yasmin steadied herself on the front of the van with one hand before stumbling around the front, dragging her hand along the bonnet for support before clambering into the driver's seat. As Yasmin was moving, Rob ran to the rear, checked Burak and Anja were securely strapped in, slammed the doors closed, and then ran round to the front passenger side, slamming his door closed. The engine roared into life, and the van lurched forward, Yasmin groaning with pain.

"I'm changing the plans," she said simply.

Rob leaned to one side to look back in the wing mirror. One man was lying on the road speaking on a radio. "Blast! The injured one is reporting in. We'll need to be ready."

From the tone of the engine and the ease with which it accelerated, Rob deduced that this had been customised, no doubt for situations such as this. A few minutes later, a single shot echoed through the valley, clearly distant, so it was not aimed at them.

They looked at each other. "It appears they don't look after their injured." Rob's shocked expression was enough for Yasmin to add. "You're clearly new to this, despite your abilities."

"Yes."

"We need to hole up to patch me up. I won't be able to drive for long. We also need to switch vehicles. I know a place nearby, we use it when receiving or preparing for crossings into or from Croatia."

Driving hard, flinging the van around corners, they careered between the trees on either side of the road. Five minutes later, lights could be seen ahead at the village of Podgraje. Yasmin slowed, picking her way through the backstreets of the village. At one corner they passed a middle-aged couple, who stopped and watched their progress.

"Is it to be expected that people stop and watch around here, or do we stand out?" Rob asked.

"Generally, yes, they will watch. This van is known, so, unless they saw the bullet holes, we should be okay … provided no one asks specifically for this van, that is!"

Yasmin spoke in a very matter-of-fact way that Rob decided was normal and had nothing to do with the pain she was in. He glanced sideways at her. Her brown hair was now dishevelled. A thin brown leather jacket, soaked in blood, covered a light blue shirt and worn jeans. As they headed out of the village, they passed a car driving in the opposite direction. Silently, they charted its progress into the village in the wing mirrors. Fortunately, it continued without even a tap on the brakes.

When another car approached, Yasmin pointed the van towards the main north-south road along the valley, as though to join that carriageway, but as soon as the other vehicle disappeared, she swung the wheel round and took once more to the country lanes, turning the van's lights off in the process. Sirens could now be heard in the distance. "Don't worry, they won't come this direction. We're okay."

Upon entering the forest again, Yasmin reduced their speed to a crawl to navigate the narrow lanes and sharp corners. "It's not about speed now but about not being seen so whoever is after us will have to cover a wider territory in search of us," she said in acknowledgment of a glance from Rob. "You were pretty useful back there. I was expecting to be alone if a fight broke out. If you hadn't helped, I doubt we would have made it, so thanks."

"No problem." Rob tried to sound unconcerned by what had just happened, but the truth was he was sickened at having killed some people, even if they had threatened his own life.

After a short time of silent driving, Rob gasped and held on, expecting a violent, bone-wrenching crash. Yasmin had veered off the lane and drove straight at and through a group of trees. They drove ten metres like this with branches scraping the sides of the van, the twigs screeching on the metal, before they emerged on a narrow track. After two minutes, they arrived outside a couple of small huts nestled between trees.

"Please, open the doors to the one on the left," Yasmin asked. Rob obliged, grateful to be outside and fill his lungs with fresh air. Yasmin had opened her window so the cold air would help keep her awake, but even so, the smell of drying blood had been unpleasant. The doors swung open easily. Barely giving Rob sufficient time to jump out of the way, Yasmin drove in and parked. "Let our passengers out, and then come and help me over to the other hut," she called, and Rob started to do as requested.

The other hut's interior was sparse, but pleasantly and surprisingly warm. By the time Yasmin hobbled in, supported by Rob, Burak and Anja had settled themselves on a mattress in a far corner. Rob guided Yasmin to a chair, where she sat down, shaking slightly from the shock. "You'll find medicines in the cabinet over there." She pointed to the far wall and a row of cupboards. "Please bring all that you find. I'll need your help."

As he walked over and rummaged through the cabinet, Rob asked, "I don't suppose that there's any food here as well? We haven't eaten for quite a while."

"Yes there is, in the cabinets over on the side wall. Help yourselves."

"Burak, please take a look and see what you can put together for us while I help out here." As Burak got to his feet, Yasmin dropped her handgun onto the table within easy reach and with a loud thump. Burak regarded her momentarily, nodding an acknowledgment to her unspoken warning not to try anything. Injured she might be, but she was still very alert.

Rob set about helping Yasmin. He cut her trouser-leg off to cleanse the leg wound before wrapping it with gauze, padding, and bandages.

"Please, some morphine," Yasmin asked as Rob looked towards her side. He found a couple of pre-prepared syringes and jabbed one into her arm. He then gently removed her jacket and eased her shirt off to get to the wound. Grimacing at the sight, Rob followed Yasmin's instructions to finish patching her up.

Once finished, Rob joined Burak and Anja sitting at the rickety table in the centre of the room. As he ate, Rob looked over at Yasmin, trying desperately to keep his eyes on her face and not her shirtless chest. "Want any?"

He was taken aback that Burak had not prepared anything for her. However, Burak replied, "Not a good idea. Food on top of the shock her body is going through will exacerbate the situation, quite possibly making her vomit, which would weaken her further. Drink is all that she needs." Rob didn't argue, sure that Burak knew a lot more about such matters than himself, and took her a cup of water instead.

As they ate, Yasmin sent a series of texts, while keeping a watchful eye on Burak.

Franc Kovač was not happy as he dropped the phone into its cradle. He was back in his office in Ljubljana having realised that there was little more he could do in Postojna. All forensics and other evidence had been bagged, tagged, and sent away for assessment. All the witness statements were the same—no one saw anything and only heard the noise. He was frustrated beyond belief and under pressure from all sides: his boss, the local police, politicians, and the media. And now there were reports of more gunfire not far from Postojna, but in the middle of absolutely nowhere! It would therefore take time even for the local emergency services to arrive at the scene, let alone his teams. In this case, the word *local* was clearly an inappropriate euphemism!

"Nina," he barked at his assistant, "contact the locals with respect to the latest shootings. I don't want anything disturbed until our guys have assessed the situation on the ground themselves. Nothing! Then mobilise the team; they need to get there fast!"

This latest set of shootings was bound to heap further pressure on his team, whether linked, or not. Kovač's instinct was, however, that they were linked. The coincidence that the shootings were not related would be too hard to swallow. With his limited resources, it had been necessary to share the intel that Robert Krane's mobile phone had been used twice—not far from where these latest shootings had occurred. He had hoped that Krane would be found quickly with lots of people watching out for him.

He was infuriated that it was already dark so little could be done until either the morning, which was most likely, or mobile lighting arrived. What could have happened to prompt further shootings though? Krane must be involved, but how? The Brits were adamant that there was no reason why he would pose a threat. Something just did not stack up. Why was the girl so important? There had to be a key piece, or pieces, of information missing.

When the first phone call came through from the local police at the scene they sounded nervous. Kovač could hear the talk in the background, as well as the comments from the caller. He learned that there had been both armed and hand-to-hand combat, leaving four men dead. None fitted Krane's description. One appeared to have been executed with a single shot to the head. Dark tyre tracks suggested that someone had left in a hurry.

The execution of one man worried him. That didn't happen when someone was in a hurry to leave, which was suggested by the tyre tracks. So what had really happened there? Something did not make sense, unless, of course, someone had already followed up to ensure no one could talk. If that was the case, this matter had taken an even more macabre turn.

6

As day four dawned, there was a hive of activity around the latest fight site. Police, the Slovenian Intelligence and Security Agency, crime-scene specialists, and, of course, the media were all there. Detailed notes and measurements were taken together with hundreds of photographs.

"We've found four bodies, as you know sir," the senior on-site investigator was telling Kovač. "Three died from bullet wounds, one appears to have been executed. The execution shot was from an entirely different weapon than any of the others used. Not only was the calibre different, but there is also no casing, whereas there are dozens of cartridges lying around from the other weapons. The bullet is buried in the road surface and will be retrieved. We will see if we can get any useful forensics once we've recovered it. The fourth man died from blunt force trauma. Judging by the marks, it was hand combat.

Possibly Krane, thought Kovač, immediately acknowledging that a great many people were suitably skilled in such combat. But all the same, it was a bit too much of a coincidence.

The man paused for breath before continuing. "The execution, together with some other factors, suggest that a clean-up squad may have come after the fact to ensure that no one was left alive who could talk. It is possible that the executed man had used his radio at some point. The body is in the centre of the road facing the direction in which the fleeing vehicle went."

Kovač continued listening patiently to the briefing, contemplating whether he should fly down. "Have all doctors and hospitals have been alerted, as well as the Croatian border guards? You are, after all, less than ten kilometres away from the border."

"Yes sir, all have been notified. We've also alerted the Croatian authorities in case the suspects already made it across the border. Border CCTV footage is also being reviewed."

"Good, well done. Keep me informed."

Ten minutes later, Kovač received another call with a further update. Even as the update was being relayed, he could hear further excitement in the background. The same investigator was saying, "We followed tracks through the woods directly to an unclaimed and unregistered car found a few hundred metres further up the road. The vehicle has been seized for a forensic search. It also appears that a planned surprise attack was foiled because a set of footprints, not matching any of the deceased, was headed in that direction before doubling back at a run."

This was an intriguing find, but it did nothing to help solve who everyone was. As Kovač listened, a series of whispered messages were relayed from an out-of-breath colleague to the reporting investigator. "Sir, we have just found where three people were apparently waiting for a period of time, quite probably for a pick-up. Again, none of the footprints match any of the deceased. One set could belong to a child. A team is following the tracks back to see where they came from. However, those tracks do not head toward the vehicle, the fight, or anywhere. They simply vanish. We've started a thorough search of the area in case the child is in hiding, although it is possible he or she was carried to the vehicle."

A child! Yes! Kovač felt vindicated. His instinct that the girl was somehow involved was correct. *But why? Why are so many people dying for this young girl?* Three days had passed, and there had been no reports of a ransom demand and no one had come forward concerned about her. Ordinarily one would expect a ransom demand within the first twenty-four hours—that is, of course, if the purpose of the kidnapping was for ransom. *If this isn't for a ransom, what could all this be for?* Kovač shook his head in bewilderment. *What's more, if the girl was there with someone skilled in unarmed combat, that must be Krane. He has to be involved; he was at the hotel at the time of the kidnapping and is unaccounted for. It's all too coincidental. But it's unlike Gurning to be covering up for something, unless it is very big.* Kovač was bewildered. His own investigations on Krane drew a similar conclusion to that of Gurning's, that Krane was an innocent. But his instinct said otherwise. What didn't make sense was why Krane would now be with the girl when he had apparently been a part of the kidnapping. Kovač's head began to spin with all of the unanswered questions. "Thank you," he said as the briefing ended. "Nina, please ensure that the photographs of both the girl and Krane are circulated again. They may or may not be together, and emphasise to all border controls to be on alert." With that, Kovač sat back in his chair to think.

✦✦✦

In sharp contrast to Franc Kovač position, life at the MI6 hut in the middle of the forest was very relaxed. Rob awoke first, his mattress across the front and only door. Yasmin was between himself and the other two, at her insistence. Burak and Anja remained fast asleep. A cord had been tied around their handcuffs and linked to a buzzer to alert Yasmin should they move, despite being securely tied to the hut's corner post.

Rob watched the gentle heave of her chest beneath a light blanket and was relieved that there was someone on his side and with him. What was it that made someone place their life at risk for the sake of another? And why for the interests an entirely different nation? Rob had no idea, but as he watched her, he was extremely grateful. There was no way he would take the security forces for granted again.

Yasmin's phone vibrated, and she answered groggily, Rob presumed in Slovenian. Upon hanging up, she announced, "We have a visitor. A good visitor." Moments later there was a buzzing of alarms in the hut, immediately followed by the screeching sound of branches on metal—another vehicle was arriving.

Rob pulled his mattress away from the door and a young, skinny-looking youth came striding in. He slumped down on a chair, completely at ease in the place, and appeared completely unfazed by Yasmin having a gun trained on the door, just in case. He then lobbed a parcel on to the table.

"Rob, please could you look through the parcel and hand me the set of clothes most suited for me? I hope they are obvious. The other clothes are for you three once we arrive at the safe house and you've had a chance to clean up. There will also be some toiletries in there for you all. Ignore my glum colleague; he doesn't like getting up early."

Rob did as requested and then politely turned his back on Yasmin as she changed, somewhat taken aback that the new arrival did not. Once Yasmin was ready, she said, "Right, all of you get yourselves into the transport. It won't be comfortable—you're going to be hidden beneath the floor and whatever load we've been given on this occasion."

The nameless, skinny youth, Rob, Anja, and Burak trooped outside, closing the door behind them, and started the laborious process of unpacking the van to slip beneath the false floor. The youth then repacked the stacks of boxes and furniture into the van. Eventually, they moved off.

Gurning, Laura, and Graeme were huddled at one end of another internal meeting room on the fourth floor of Thames House, beakers of steaming coffee in front of them on the table. They were all bleary eyed from a restless night wondering what could have gone so wrong that the pick-up had been compromised and ambushed. Elsewhere in the meeting room, alongside a map of Slovenia and its neighbouring countries, there were pictures of Rob, Burak, and Anja all pinned on the wall. At the opposite end of the room, a white board, covered with Laura's neat jottings, stretched the full width of the room.

The silence was broken by the audio conference equipment *bing-bonging* noisily, its lights flashing. As Gurning leaned over to answer the incoming call, Laura jiggled the mouse that was next to her, and a large, wall-mounted screen flickered into life. Yasmin's voice filled the room in strong, strident tones that belied the reality of how she felt.

"Gregory has arrived and taken our friends outside to settle them into their transport," she announced, her language cautious despite using a secured satellite link. "The journey to the guesthouse should not be too long, nor too strenuous. They will be well looked after when we arrive. Rob will be available for conversations later in the day. You should be able to stream the footage from the van's cameras now."

Laura clicked on the pre-established icon for secure sharing of files or other material. The three watched intently as Yasmin described the events of the previous evening and consequently the need to change plans. When the film clip had finished, Yasmin said quickly, "I should go now. I heard the transport doors close, so my passengers are waiting for me." With that, she simply dropped all connections.

"Wow," Gurning said. "Your girl doesn't waste words, does she, Graeme?"

"Apparently not. I guess she simply wants to get to the safe house in Piran. We've already arranged for her to receive medical attention there. Some folks are heading over there from Italy." Holding up a hand to prevent any comment, he added, "They're using a very different route to that planned for the extraction. Laura, are you sure you still want to participate?"

"Absolutely," she replied, possibly a little too eagerly, as she eyed the pictures of Rob on the wall. If her eagerness was noticed, neither of the men commented.

"Okay, no problem. In which case, as planned, you fly out this afternoon. We'll keep you updated on events. A cover team has already arrived, and they have the safe house and general area under observation. They have already reported an increase of police activity and tightening of border controls, so the operation will be a challenge. You'll meet Stefano Cassini, typically Italian as far as I'm concerned and a really great guy. At the moment, we still intend for you to meet Yasmin for a briefing at the Skocjan Caves, but clearly, depending upon her condition, that plan may have to change."

"Understood. Before that, I suggest we review the footage again and try to get identifications for the four attackers. Then we can try to establish their connection to Burak Demir and why they are targeting him. While I am sure he has many enemies, this is the first time on record that he has been threatened, so what has changed?"

"I agree," Gurning nodded. "And Graeme, I suspect that you need to touch base with our Slovenian friends to show an interest in the recent events and find out if they have anything to connect Robert Krane to all this. It would be great to keep him out of this as far as possible until we really know the extent of his involvement. Then, if feasible, he could disappear back into the daily world of anonymity."

"I'll do that and see what I can learn."

The creaking of the van's doors opening alerted the three dozy occupants in the under-floor compartment that they had stopped and something was happening. It was hard to distinguish from the muffled voices whether they were at their final destination, or if this was something more sinister. Burak whispered urgently and quietly to Anja not to move and to remain silent. They were all now wide awake, senses straining to hear what was happening, heartbeats sounding like bass drums in their ears. The muffled voices continued, all male. Then the sound of grinding and sliding against the wood floor was heard as some of the furniture was moved. Could this be a good or a bad sign? The muffled voices continued. Tapping along both sides of the van was the first sign that this was not what was intended.

The van had arrived at a checkpoint, and police were separating cars from all other vehicles. All vans and lorries were pulled over for questioning and possible inspection. That Yasmin was asleep and her companion, Gregory, had refused to wake her had roused irritation with the police, who, for the time-being, respected his wishes—Yasmin was clearly unwell. This was fortunate, since the wound in Yasmin's side had started to bleed again! Instead, the police decided to give Gregory a hard time and give the van a thorough going over. Gregory tried to balance being reasonable with being suitably challenging of their approach, giving rise to occasional animated and loud disagreements.

When a couple of policemen started tapping the sides of the van with small rubber mallets, Gregory's protestations increased to being incensed. He made out that the little marks created would cause trouble for him with his boss, making the police laugh and find other cosmetic aspects to wind Gregory up, distracting all but one from the purpose of the checkpoint. The one was shining his torch into the rear of the van and tapped the floor. He then tried to shift some of the furniture to get a better look. Gregory came back round to the rear and pushed the man aside, rummaged around, and emerged with a can of polish and rag cloth. He then started vigorously polishing a couple of marks at the rear, disrupting the one diligent policeman, who had to cease his exertions to address the belligerent driver, the ninth of the still-young day.

Their exchange, now twenty-five minutes since the van was stopped and five since the search started, was interrupted by a ruckus near the end of the queue coming in the opposite direction, distracting the attention of the four policemen surrounding Gregory and his van. Seven of the eight police working that side were headed down towards the disturbance, watched by their colleagues on the other side of the road, while the eighth was trying to prevent vehicles from moving off prior to clearance. Soon, the seven proved insufficient as impatience and anger flared among numerous drivers and passengers up-and-down the queue. As a result, all police from both sides left their stations to quell the multiple outbreaks of disturbances before matters escalated too far. This allowed other drivers, including Gregory, to simply drive off without their checks being completed.

Yasmin, who had not been asleep, immediately sat up once they were underway. "Okay, guys, keep it up for a few minutes longer. We're moving and almost clear," she muttered into a collar microphone. As they moved well beyond the police checkpoint and any potential for the police to wave them down, she said, "Right, we are clear. You can let matters ease, and many thanks. A great diversion."

"That was close," she said to Gregory. "I'm glad that I called in for the support early. Otherwise, it may have turned out very differently." Gregory merely nodded, kept his eyes facing front and drove on, wiping the sweat off his brow. "I just hope they don't get into too much trouble and that it doesn't occur to the authorities, or anyone else, that the outbreak was a diversion to get us through."

After a nerve-tingling ten minutes, they took an exit off route 111, heading into Portorož and joined the coast road, passing the smart hotels in the centre. A few minutes later they pulled over into a small dockside complex of long, nondescript sheds. Gregory leaped out to open the roller-shutter doors, drove into the space beyond, and then closed the doors behind them. After much strenuous effort, Rob, Burak, and Anja staggered to their feet into the semidarkness of the warehouse, partially full of old, cheap furniture stacked and labelled as though it was an official storage unit of some sort or another. Two mid-range and inconspicuous Slovenian registered cars were parked to one side of the van.

As the three wandered around the unit, getting life back into their cramped and stiff limbs, Gregory helped Yasmin out of the van. He then guided her into the driver's seat of the lead car, leaving the door open. Yasmin called out, "Rob, Mr Demir. Please take the wash bags from Gregory and freshen up a little, as well as shave please. Mr Demir, you will need to help your daughter. The objective is to be sufficiently normal and presentable to be everyday passengers in a car. We don't want to draw attention to ourselves. The next stop will be the safe-house where you can fully wash and change clothes. Gregory will show you the way. Please be quick. Rob, you will have to remove their handcuffs for this part. Gregory will guard the outside of the door and there is no window, so no need to worry."

When they emerged, they felt far brighter. Gregory handed Rob and Burak a pair of sunglasses each as Yasmin said, "Mr Demir, you are with Gregory riding in the front passenger seat. He will not talk, but has the potential to be extremely violent if attacked. Rob, please handcuff him again. Mr Demir, you will kindly keep your jacket over the handcuffs, as casually as possible. I should add that the doors have been modified so you won't be able to open any of them. I have a close proximity autolock key. Rob and the young girl will travel with me. Rob, you're in the front, as though we are a family. It's not far, although we shall take different and circuitous routes. I'm trusting that there won't be any, but are there any questions?"

After a short silence, Yasmin simply said, "Okay, everyone to their respective positions." Burak gave Anja a hug and whispered something before walking over to the second car. Once Rob and Anja were settled in the lead car, Yasmin continued, "Ordinarily I'd be happy to talk while driving, but not today."

Gregory opened the roller-shutter door once more, and they drove out. Yasmin dawdled sufficiently to watch as Gregory got out of his car, closed the warehouse door, and drove off in the opposite direction. Anja could not help but turn and watch her father disappear. She was watched in turn by Yasmin in the driver's mirror. "Don't worry, little girl, you will be back together again soon," and Yasmin drove off.

The two cars drove through the narrow streets of Portorož and eventually the short distance to the eastern outskirts of Piran. They then headed towards the predominantly wooded neighbourhoods on the northern, less-populated side of the peninsular and pulled into the driveway of a medium-sized house. Yasmin, Rob, and Anja arrived first to find a man and two women waiting for them inside. Immediately, the two women took Yasmin off to the rear of the house, one carrying a medical bag. As they went, Yasmin threw her handbag to the man, "The proximity device to open Gregory's car doors is inside. They should be here soon."

Rob collapsed into a comfortable sofa to wait. Anja, on the other hand, trotted over to a window to watch for her father's arrival. She didn't have to wait long, but as she instinctively moved to the front door, she was stopped by the man, who pointed to a chair, "Wait inside."

Rob spoke for the first time in a long while, "It will be okay, Anja. Your dad will be inside very soon. All this is for everyone's safety, as I'm sure your dad has already said."

The little girl nodded while keeping her eyes glued to the open front door. An audible *thunk* of locks preceded the opening and closing of doors. Burak entered the house moments later, still carrying the jacket over the handcuffs. Anja ran over to give him a hug and he draped his arms over her head.

Gregory and the other man spoke in lowered tones for a few moments before Gregory departed, leaving the parcel of clothes and toiletries behind.

"Hi, I'm also Gregory for the purposes of our acquaintanceship," the man said. "This house is fully secured, as is the perimeter. You will find fresh clothes in this parcel, along with toiletries. The bathroom is down that corridor there on the left. Robert, you first please. Once you're ready, there are some people who want to speak with you. We can then have something to eat."

With a little shove of his foot, the parcel slid across the wood floor to where Rob sat.

Upon emerging, Rob exchanged places with Burak and Anja. Gregory II, as Rob had decided to refer to him, nodded towards one of the women sitting on the sofa.

"The nurse will check you over quickly. Layla, over there, is my partner for looking after you while you're here. We've taken over from Yasmin and Gregory."

After the quick medical exam, Gregory II motioned to Rob to follow him. Opening a door, they descended into a well-lit basement corridor and entered a small room. A table in the centre had a bottle of water and a couple of glasses on it. The two chairs faced a video conferencing screen. Gregory II motioned for him to take a seat. "I'll leave you now. The conference will start automatically. I'll know when it's finished and come to collect you." Turning to go, Gregory II paused and added, "Yasmin says good luck and thank you for your intervention with the attackers. You saved her life, which deserves the thanks of us all." With that, he left, locking the door behind him.

Moments later, the screen burst into life, with Gurning and Spreachley filling the picture.

"Afternoon, Rob. Although no doubt still exhausted, we hope you feel slightly brighter now you've freshened up. Laura Harding, who was with us before, is on audio. She's travelling at the moment, so is unable to join us in person."

"Hello, Rob," she said, announcing her presence. She was actually at home and grateful that none of them could see her as she packed for the next few days.

She was excited at the prospect of foreign travel again, but she knew she would miss her modern two-bedroom flat on the tenth floor of the St. George Wharf complex overlooking the River Thames at Vauxhall, in central London, a fifteen-minute stroll from the office. Laura stopped her packing and looked out over the Thames, enjoying the view as she concentrated on the conference call. She had been able to buy the flat with the legacy left by her grandparents some years earlier and was delighted that she had done so.

"What about Michael? Where's he?" Rob asked.

"Michael's back on normal duties. I appreciate that he's your friend and that is why you contacted him in the first place, and we all agree that was a decision of inestimable wisdom. However, we decided that friendship could affect decision-making and did not want to take the risk, even though with Michael that would be extremely unlikely. I hope that you understand." Rob merely nodded. He had welcomed the sight of a friend and the reassurance that had come with it.

"Good. Well, plans to bring you home are well advanced. Follow the directions when given by your hosts. You're in good hands. For now, though, we'd like to ask a few questions. We can cover the full detail once you're back. Importantly, we need to understand what, if anything, Burak Demir has said during the few days you've been together. Please think carefully, even a passing comment that may appear inconsequential to you may hold a greater meaning for us. We're also interested in why he appears to have been so willing to come with you. Okay, you had him handcuffed, but has he tried to escape? Was he ever out of your sight?"

Rob took the sudden silence as an indication that he was expected to talk. He took a deep breath and heaved a sigh. "Personally, I think he was not expecting any of this. At one point he commented that he had tried to keep the relationship with the murdered lady and his daughter a secret. He said that on meeting Anja's mother, and then particularly once Anja was born, he realised how much more there is to life. He started trying to distance himself, as much as possible, from his criminal activities and focus on his legitimate businesses. However, this created issues with his criminal associates, who guessed something was going on, although Burak has not told them about his legitimate business interests."

"He openly admitted to being a criminal?" Laura jumped in, querying Rob's phraseology with an amazed expression in her voice.

"Yes, he did. I remember it well. I was fiddling with my iPhone at the time and started recording our conversation."

"So you have recorded him admitting to being a criminal?" Gurning asked incredulously.

"Yes, that's exactly what I've just said," Rob responded, slightly frustrated.

"Just checking that we understood you, Robert. Please, I'm sorry if at times we come across as infuriating, but in our business we have to be absolutely precise. Presumably, you don't have your iPhone with you at the moment?"

"No, I don't. Sorry."

"Oh well, next time please bring it with you."

"Sure," Rob replied in a non-committal manner.

"Did he ever comment on why he thinks his associates were trying to kidnap him or worse?" Laura prompted to re-gain the focus that had suddenly lapsed.

"Oh, he's sure they were going to kill him, but they needed to know the details of his networks. At one point he commented that he intentionally maintained many separations in his activities but did not elaborate. He also said that he'd take that information to the grave instead of letting some chap called Emilio pull the strings, and Emilio knows that. That's why they kidnapped his daughter—she was their leverage to get him talking."

"Hold on," Spreachley interrupted. "Sorry, but you mentioned Emilio. Who's he?"

"No idea. Nothing was said about him. Burak simply mentioned his name a few times."

"Okay. So you were saying why he was kidnapped."

"Yes. Burak acknowledges that his apparent changing of allegiances to other matters could be perceived to place his associates and their operations at risk, that he was going soft. Time with Anja and her mother started to change his values, away from only himself, away from the hard loyalties of the network and making money in any way he could. However, he is sure that his associates would not, could not understand that. Burak said that in the past, he also looked on similar changes in people as them going soft, placing the network at risk through split loyalties. He acknowledges that, which is why he kept his relationship a secret, or at least thought he had. Ideally, he would completely split the two, legitimate from criminal, and has started to do so, but there remains a lot of overlap."

Rob paused for a drink, hoping for questions since he had no idea whether what he was saying was helpful. With no questions forthcoming, he ploughed on. "In many cases he built the legitimate businesses on top of the criminal activities to help hide the criminality. More often than not, the legitimate businesses are unaware of their reliance on criminal proceeds. To simply cut that link would be massively detrimental and bring the businesses to their knees, impacting innocent people, which he does not want. That's what he's been struggling with for a number of years. He says he's now worn out with trying. It's also why he is willing to hand everything over to me."

"He what!" Gurning blurted out, almost shouting.

Spreachley simply slumped dramatically, shaking his head in disbelief. "It had been going so well."

"I've no idea what prompted me, but while he was still trapped there in the cave and I had to decide whether to leave him and/or Anja, I thought I wanted something for the risk. I'd read how wealthy he is, so I wrote on a piece of paper that he had to pass everything over to me and asked him to sign. I expected some degree of negotiation, but instead he simply signed. Only later did we discuss why he had done so, and that is when he admitted that he is tired of his current way of life. All he wanted was an assurance that Anja would be looked after."

"I can't believe this," Spreachley said, shaking his head again. "It's the height of naivety. Demir must be scheming, and therefore, the fact that he's still with you suggests that this is all part of his plan. What on earth possessed you, man?"

"As I've said," Rob commented in a tired manner, "I've no idea what possessed me, and yes, after the fact I also considered my actions to be naïve and that the likelihood of Burak living up to his side of the agreement as being zero. Only time will tell." He finished with a shrug.

A faint fuzzy buzz sound from the conferencing equipment filled the silence that ensued, each mulling over the exchanges that had occurred.

Laura broke the silence. "Actually, this has potential."

"You must be joking," Spreachley said sharply. "I always gave you more credit than this, Laura."

"Graeme," Gurning said quickly, knowing how Laura would leap at the chance of a sparring match with Spreachley, which was something he really did not want in front of an outsider. "I suggest we listen to Laura's reasoning before leaping to a conclusion. I asked her to join this case precisely to be insightful and consider the possibilities and angles in ways you and I rarely do."

"Humph!"

"Well, clearly Demir could well have been playing Rob all along, but first, he wasn't to know that Rob would come riding to the rescue and second, it would be an incredibly cynical thing to achieve at such an emotionally charged time with his daughter's welfare and life in the balance. So…"

"Ah, that reminds me," Rob interrupted. "I didn't say that Burak was about to murder Anja when I intervened."

"What!" the three exclaimed.

"This is simply unreal," muttered Spreachley.

"Another man was in the cave when I arrived. Along with two others, he was speaking to Burak, and the innuendo was dreadful for what he planned for Anja. It was clear that Burak knew what that could be, so he was about to murder her to avoid her being put through whatever this other man had planned. I could see tears streaming down his face as he prepared to kill her."

"Oh my word," Laura gasped in response to Rob's revelation. Gurning and Spreachley were struck silent.

"That leads to my supposition," said Laura after a moment to compose herself. "Maybe, just maybe, Demir *is*"—Laura stressed the word *is*, paused, and repeated the word—"*is* looking for a way out and found a way in the face of his death. Whether truly through Rob or using his agreement with Rob as the signal of his intent, we can only find out, but we should, I suggest, give him the chance to prove it."

"So why didn't he put his hands up with the French a few years back?" Gurning countered before Spreachley had the chance to dig a larger hole for himself.

"Fair point, but my instinct is that Demir doesn't want his conversion, so to speak, to be public. He wants to do it his way. He's a man used to being in control, so he tried to do it his way. Now that opportunity has gone. For us to get him out of Slovenia, it has to be covert, and who else would Rob enlist other than the British authorities? Bear in mind that we are one of the most respected security authorities the world over for our treatment of people. Demir would know that. Once he is sure he is out of reach of the Slovenian authorities and fully in our hands and before we have the chance to go public with his capture, he will have the opportunity to declare his intentions."

"Why not public?" Spreachley asked.

"First, in order to protect his daughter and possibly himself. Second, if he goes public, his associates will have the chance to counterattack. Also, if he went public, his associates would know to reorganise. That could jeopardise Demir's attempts to protect the legitimate businesses, which would then fail. To achieve his goal, he needs help and a lot of it. Quite by chance, this could provide the route to his dream. Okay, okay, it sounds far-fetched, I know, but what if, just what if?" By now Laura was pacing around her flat, waving her arms around animatedly.

"I buy that," said Rob. "In my view, he's a broken man. I saw it. He fell hard—I mean *so* hard and *so* quickly. He saw the woman he loved shot in front of him, and then the mere threat of harming Anja must have nailed it for him. So when I materialised, why not? He just went for it. He had absolutely nothing to lose and everything to gain."

Another silence played out while all four thought about this. On screen, Rob could see Gurning and Spreachley fidgeting as they tried to get their minds around the unlikely possibility and if even partially true, the potential ramifications, of which he could not even hope to imagine.

"Fine," announced Gurning. "Let's play this out. Flush him out. Give him every opportunity. Robert, please, we need to trust and rely on you not to breathe a word of this to anyone, not even other members of our teams, and especially not to Demir. Only the three of us please."

"No problem. And by the way, drop Robert please and call me Rob. Everyone else does."

"Good. Well, let's get to it. And Rob?"

"Yes."

"Great stuff. I'm looking forward to meeting you."

7

Later that evening, Laura's plane touched down at Marco Polo Airport outside Venice. Stefano Cassini watched as the passengers disembarked, noticing and nodding approvingly as a young, slim woman with short, fair hair tied back in a ponytail walked down the steps with athletic ease, her cream blouse and tan linen trousers flattering her female curves. He knew from photographs that she had hazelnut brown eyes. Stefano walked away from the viewing platform, elegant in his flannel trousers and lightweight, pale blue shirt accentuating his olive tan, to wait for Laura in the arrivals area.

"Miss Grahams," he called, using her alias, as she came through the sliding doors. Stefano gave a polite bow and held out his hand. "Welcome to Venice. May I help you with your luggage?"

"Thank you. Stefano, I presume?" she replied, scrutinising his facial features to compare to the photograph she had been given.

"At your service. Come, you must be hungry. There's a pleasant restaurant not far from the harbour that I know. A table is booked with a view you'll adore—the sea, the boats. The only thing missing is the sunset, but we'll have that tomorrow in Piran."

Laura smiled at his charm—she had been warned of Stefano's flattery and was prepared. She enjoyed his eloquent, smooth talking in the knowledge that, apparently, it was all show. His commitment to his wife and family was legendary in the Services.

An hour later, once Laura had dropped her bags at the safe house, they were seated, as promised, overlooking the Mediterranean and tucking into a fine Italian seafood dish accompanied by a crisp, dry, white Sicilian wine.

"So tomorrow we will sail to Piran," Stefano said in perfect English. "It should take five hours or so to get there, so there's no need to rush the morning. We can swing around Venice and enjoy the sights and see the route to our friends' house should they be available the following evening."

Laura was only too well aware that this was business and Stefano was talking about their plan B should they decide that, upon their return, it would not be safe to return to the same port as their departure.

As Stefano continued to speak, Laura marvelled at the way he was briefing her on their planned schedule in public by turning it into some sort of romantic foray. She joined in by asking pertinent questions about their friends' house in Venice, about Piran and the Skocjan Caves. As she did, she relaxed into the evening, and their conversation soon moved on to pastimes, hobbies, holidays, and dreams, just like any courting couple. It was, therefore, a wrench to share a last grappa with the restaurant owners, who knew Stefano well, and head back to the safe house in Porto di Piave Vecchia, which was close to the small harbour where the motor yacht was moored.

✦✦✦

The fifth day since the kidnapping was calm and relaxing for Rob, Burak, and Anja and mostly so for their protectors. Gregory II and Layla were vigilant at all times and regularly talked on their mobile phones.

It was not until lunch, while Layla was serving dessert, that Gregory II provided an update. "I know it's frustrating, but please stay indoors and away from the windows at the front. Continue to rest and regain your strength. Tomorrow we will smuggle you all out of Slovenia and to England. I won't answer any questions, but I do want you to be aware that the trip, at least the first part, may not be as easy as we'd hoped. We won't leave until the afternoon—unless plans have to change. Unfortunately, that is very possible, so please ensure that you are ready to go at a moment's notice.

"There is a very heavy police presence at all Slovenian points of entry/exit. The one thing that benefits us is the presumption that you are operating alone. Now, enjoy the apple pie. As you'll have already realised, Layla is an excellent cook."

✦✦✦

Stefano and Laura, meanwhile, were enjoying the sun while speeding across the wide-open Mediterranean. It had been difficult to concentrate during the trip around Venice to learn the way to the plan B safe house. This was her first time in Venice, and she marvelled at the place. Stefano had quickly realised that and kept testing her every time they turned left or right to make sure she knew the landmarks, so she could recognise the route should she need to without his assistance.

Laura couldn't believe she was doing this courtesy of her work. *No small wonder Stefano loves his job, I could get used to this as well.* She had walked around the 17.5-metre motor cruiser a couple of times already, just to absorb the experience. Stefano kept it immaculate, so the age did not show other than for the few aspects of styling he had not been able to change. It was pure white, sleek, low-lying, and oozed opulence. The thought that James Bond would be impressed sprung easily to mind.

As they set off on their voyage, Stefano had explained that the boat had been confiscated following a huge drug seizure six years earlier by a British naval vessel just inside international waters. Then, while waiting for London bureaucrats to decide what to do with it, he had taken it out at a moment's notice following a tipoff and had been able to prevent the kidnapping of an influential British businessman at sea. Shortly after that, and another tipoff, he helped the Italian authorities bring down a smuggling ring by posing as a potential smuggler. With those two results in the bag, Stefano had successfully persuaded London to let him keep the craft, and many subsequent success stories could also be recounted—plus, he added with an elaborate shrug, a few not-so-successful episodes!

Late that afternoon, throttling back on their speed, Stefano called over his shoulder, "We're approaching Piran. It's worth a look. I love the approach into this small harbour."

Laura joined him as they cruised into the harbour. Stefano's approach was intentionally slow for Laura to take in the Venetian Gothic architecture surrounding the harbour, dominated by the bell tower of the Church of St. George. She loved the market town–type busyness of the place and the colourful, small fishing boats.

"It's wonderful, amazing. Will there be time to just wander about, nose in the shops, and explore some of the streets?" she asked.

"Absolutely! Don't forget that we're on a romantic trip and I'm out to woo you." He glanced over at her, winked, and grinned mischievously. "All part of the cover."

She couldn't help but return the smile. "Great for the first part, although I'm going to be very hard to get!" They both roared with laughter.

Soon after mooring, security arrived to check their papers.

After a perfunctory search and check of their papers, they were left in peace. Stefano went below decks and extracted what looked like a mobile phone. Laura immediately recognised it as a portable electronic bug detector. The screen flashed green. Stefano grinned and said softly, "We can't be too careful on this trip, but it does help being a frequent visitor!"

For the next hour or so, they meandered through the streets, soaking up the atmosphere and blending in as the tourists that they were for the evening. As they did, they became very aware of the increased police presence. Dinner at Tri Vdove was everything and more than Stefano had promised. They sat on the terrace as the sun set with glorious food and ambiance and the sound of gentle waves on the rocks just a stone's throw away.

✦✦✦

The next morning Laura emerged from her cabin amid the tolling of church bells and to the aroma of fresh bread. Stefano was busy in the galley. "We'll be busy today, so we'll require all our strength," he grinned. "Anyhow, breakfast is the best meal of the day. You'll need a warmer outer layer for when we get to the caves. Do you have anything because otherwise I will lend you something?"

"The bread smells divine. And yes, I do have an outer layer with some robust lightweight walking boots. Thank you for the thought and the offer."

Forty-five minutes later, they hailed a taxi that had just disgorged the previous occupants, who were clearly tourists. "Probably from a nearby hotel coming to look around the old town," whispered Stefano in Laura's ear, pretending to be romantic.

"Skocjan Caves please," Stefano called through the window.

The journey was uneventful and mostly quiet, both looking out of the window. From time to time they would point something out to each other, using expressions such as, "Oh look, darling," to give credibility to their cover story of a romantic weekend away just in case the police questioned the driver at some future point.

Much to Laura's amusement, Stefano was playing the gallant gentleman brilliantly as he bought the entrance tickets for the caves and insisted upon carrying all the extra items in his back sack. They opted for a short tour and joined the queue. Another couple soon joined the queue immediately behind them and they soon started chatting. Thus, introductions already made, by the end of the tour, the four tourists agreed to have a drink together and sat apart from everyone else in the sun.

Layla introduced one of the scouts who had been monitoring activities in Piran, and seeking an appropriate spot to make the exchange, passing Rob, Burak, and Anja into Stefano's and Laura's care.

As the scout said, "It'll be far too risky for the exchange to occur within the city limits," the others responded with lots of nodding and laughter, as though he had just cracked an excellent joke. "I recommend a water-borne exchange close to the northern coast line of the peninsula. There is a good stretch of wooded coastline west of the only holiday resort, where we can hire some small boats. Pick-up could occur without attracting attention two hundred metres west of the pier. There'll be plenty of cover and nothing unusual to have people exploring the coastline. We'll just make sure that no one else has the same idea," He added with a grin and a wink.

More laughter by all ensued before Laura asked, "And how are our friends?"

"They're all fine," Layla replied. "The girl, Anja, has a bit of a cold but is otherwise okay. Nothing to be concerned about that changes the nature of the pick-up."

"Good," Stefano said. "And what time should we be making our sweep? I'm tempted to leave earlier, swing past the Italian border, and then come back for the pick-up. That way we'll be able to review if we're being shadowed."

"Good idea," the scout replied. "Presumably we'll all have our mobile phones to keep in touch?" Following more laughter and nods all around, he continued, "So I suggest we swap our false identities and contact details as though we intend to stay in touch and call it a day."

So with polite handshakes and hugs, they exchanged scribbled bits of paper and parted. Stefano and Laura headed back to the harbour and found a café for a late lunch before cruising off under the watchful eye of the authorities.

Returning to the safe house, Layla changed her appearance with a wig, makeup, and some padding in various strategic places. She then turned her focused on Anja, who loved the attention and dressing up, particularly the new hair styling. The two chatted about their ideas for the new look, and Anja giggled at the additional padding given to her, increasing the appearance of her age. Rob and Burak were mere spectators and left to wonder about themselves.

After a light lunch, they were led through an internal door to the garage and a large, family-type car. Layla opened the trunk and motioned for both Rob and Burak to get in and lie down. It was a tight fit for the two men, but they made it. Layla draped a lightweight sheet over them, dumped a few groceries on top for good measure, and partially pulled the roll-top cover over before closing it once more.

Their journey was short and uneventful. Having found a remote track off the coast road, Layla left them with Gregory II, and drove off. They threaded their way through the trees and made their way down to the rocky coastline, staying just inside of the treeline and out of sight.

After what seemed an age, two sailing dinghies scrunched onto the stony shore, and two men got out. Gregory II immediately hustled his three charges towards the new arrivals. There was no sound from any weapon, but they heard the sudden whine of bullets flying through the air. Gregory II and Burak felt the full impact thudding into their sides, sending them sprawling onto the rocks. Anja screamed and faltered as she saw her father fall. Rob quickly picked her up in one arm—they had to keep moving and he wanted to shield her from danger. He then reached down and grabbed Burak by the scruff of the neck and hauled him to his feet, pushing him to keep running. Gregory II rolled once before regaining his footing and continued running.

The two new men strafed the trees with their own silenced machine pistols. Both sides had clearly had the same idea—use suppressors to avoid unnecessary noise that would alert the police and security forces. While Gregory II, struggling with pain, bundled them into the dinghies, another salvo of bullets smashed into the surrounding rocks, sending pieces flying in all directions, shredding the lightweight fabric of their shirtsleeves and stinging their arms. The two men shoved the boats off the rocks and jumped in as a further salvo of bullets struck the fibreglass hulls. The two men returned fire as Rob and Gregory II took charge of their respective boats and started to sail out to sea, towards a white motor cruiser that was approaching at speed.

With Laura at the helm, Stefano shouldered a rifle to provide covering fire. With maximum reverse thrust, the water frothing up as though a saucepan boiling over, Laura brought the cruiser to a standstill between the shore and the dinghies. The motor cruiser was now taking fire and Laura rushed to throw ropes and a ladder over the side for Rob, Burak, and Anja to climb up.

Stefano kept shooting, trying to spot and eliminate their attackers. Although it felt like an eternity, the exchange continued for an intense twenty or thirty seconds before coming to a sudden and silent halt. Laura helped haul Anja on to the boat as Rob manhandled Burak over the side. The man's face screwed up in pain from having taken the earlier hits.

Once everyone was on board, Laura yelled, "All clear, let's go," and Stefano rammed the throttle to full speed, steering directly out to sea and leaving those in the dinghies to fend for themselves.

The intention had been for Gregory II and his companions to stay out sailing, but that was not possible—they were sinking! They were going to have to swim ashore and confess to stupidity and a collision!

Stefano's motor cruiser was riddled with bullet holes, but fortunately nothing that would impede their passage. As Laura checked on Burak, he groaned and muttered that he would be fine and was glad for the bullet-proof vest Gregory II had insisted he wear.

"I need someone up here to spot. Should be Laura. All others keep out of sight," Stefano yelled.

When she arrived by his side on the flying bridge, she saw that, having been hit by fibreglass splinters, he was bleeding.

"We're going to have to adopt plan B," Stefano called into the rushing air. "The bullet holes will attract far too much attention in Porto di Piave Vecchia. I've steered away from the coast—we don't want the Slovenians getting an easy view. We need to get to the Italian side as quickly as possible."

A few moments later he added, "Clean my face, would you, and look as though you're enjoying yourself!" He winked mischievously. "If the authorities decide to take a closer look because of our speed, we need to be looking our best, but I don't want to slow down in case the other side have a speed boat and decide to give chase. We won't be hard to track!"

The headland was not far away, but the minutes seemed to drag before they were able to change course for Italy and pass the promontory. As they rounded the headland and looked back towards Piran, there were only a few yachts milling around. "Nothing out of the ordinary," Stefano yelled over the noise of the wind and the waves crashing against the bow. "Please keep watching, but as though you're enjoying the scene. See any motor boats travelling fast and I want to know. You'll need to keep a watch for the entire trip with greater vigilance for anything remotely suspicious once we approach Venice—those waterways are busy."

"Understood," Laura replied, her heart beating fast from both the adrenalin of the fire fight and the nervous expectation of a potential chase. "I'll go down and check on our passengers. Then I'll keep watch with the binoculars from the windows; that will give me cover should the Slovenians be watching."

"Good idea for now, but I'll want you up here as we approach Venice. There'll be far too many boats, and you'll need the 360-degree view afforded by being up here."

"Okay, see you in a few hours, unless you'd like a drink and something to eat?"

"Just a large glass of water, please."

With that provided, each settled in for their high-speed journey. Laura reappeared at Stefano's side as he throttled back to cruise past Porto di Piave Vecchia and towards

Venice. The sun was setting directly in their eyes, making them both squint. Stefano carefully navigated around the Venetian islands and various channels, occasionally doubling back until they arrived at the boat yard to be used as plan B. A colleague waved as he swung a pair of timber gates open, leading to a large shed built over a short inlet, all designed for boat maintenance. The sound of the gates rattling shut brought a wave of relief to all on board, but afforded no rest. Stefano immediately leaped into action, calling out instructions.

"Guido, get the work boat to take us to the land transportation. Laura, give these passports to our passengers. Rob is your husband, Anja your daughter, and Mr Demir your father. You take after your absent mother," he added, noticing her sceptical look. "Please make sure that they all understand their respective roles. As soon as Guido is back with the work boat, we leave. A people carrier is waiting to take us to the airport, a private plane is waiting to take you all home. The boat may have been tracked, so I don't want anyone hanging around."

The exhausted group sat in utter silence at the stern of the workboat as they were ferried across to the mainland, where they piled into a people carrier for the short drive to the airport. At the private terminal, Rob and Laura shared a couple of nervous glances over Anja's head as their driver exchanged more than a minute's worth of quick-fire repartee with the guard. Eventually, and with an exuberant display of grudging reluctance, the guard waved them through, glowering through the windows. Their driver muttered to himself in rapid, expressive Italian as they drove through—but only once the windows were firmly closed.

A few minutes later, and after a perfunctory passport check at passport control, they headed for an isolated private jet near some outlying hangars. Once out of the vehicle, and as they walked towards the plane, Rob, as nonchalantly as possible, commented, "I hope there won't be any of the dramatics we frequently see in the films." Laura smiled an acknowledgment, noting that Burak had also heard and was sweeping the area with his eyes.

"My thoughts entirely," Burak muttered, regarding the heavy-set men on either side of the steps with unease. "So this must be what they call rendition!" he quipped as he passed them by. Laura found it hard to suppress a smile as the two heavies bristled, but held their position. They all had strict instructions to bring this man back to Britain without arousing attention. That Burak still had the presence of mind to crack such comments was impressive, at least as far as she was concerned and, from Rob's smirk, his as well!

Once airborne, they settled back for a light dinner, after which they all dozed for the remainder of the near four-hour flight. It was approaching 1:30 in the morning when they were gently shaken awake by one of the heavies. "Ten minutes to landing," he said in a monotone voice. "Strap in."

Bleary-eyed, Rob asked Laura, who was sitting next to him, "Where are we landing?"

"Northolt in west London."

"How come we're able to land there at this hour? I thought that there were restrictions on aircraft over London at this hour."

"There are," she replied, smiling. "A restriction is what it implies—simply restricting such landings or take-offs. That provides suitable flexibility to occasionally—well, ignore them, I suppose."

"Oh well, whatever. It's just good to be back," Rob said, looking out of the window at the lights below. He then turned back to Laura, "I would like to get my belongings back from the guesthouse somehow and say thank you to Mrs Kos." He paused, adding with a sigh, "But I guess I am now persona non-grata in Slovenia, and there were still quite a few places I wanted to see."

"Don't worry," Laura replied. "We've already thought of that. Once everyone's safely on British soil we intend to start the process of fully restoring your excellent reputation. How the Slovenian authorities respond will take some tactful politics and will depend on whether we inform them about Mr Demir!" Laura had nodded her head towards Burak as she was talking.

8

The chilly morning air of the westerly breeze hit them fully in their faces as they more stumbled than walked down the steps that had been pushed up against the side of the plane. If they hadn't been fully awake, they were now as they instinctively started shivering—their thin summer clothes providing little protection against the typical British climate.

Laura stepped forward to greet their welcoming committee, speaking to them in hushed tones. Waiting for them, engines still purring, were two nondescript cars and a small minibus with blacked-out windows. Laura waved them to the minibus. Anja stayed close to Burak, who held her hand and guided her to the back seats. Anja, struggling with exhaustion, snuggled up against her father, who quietly looked about him.

Rob hesitated at the front of the minibus, wondering where to sit. He also wanted to be at the back and put distance between himself and the two heavies from the airplane, but he didn't want to be seen aligning himself too much with Burak. He therefore opted for a seat two-thirds of the way back, leaving a couple of rows of seats between himself and Burak.

Several minutes later, they joined the westbound carriageway of the A40. Rob couldn't see the two cars anymore, but knew that they had been with them as they left the airbase, one ahead and one behind. At first Rob stared blankly out of the windows marking off the various landmarks that he knew well from his own use of the A40, but gradually drifted off into a light sleep.

When he woke up, Rob realised they were stationary and dawn was breaking. The engine was still running so the heater could continue to blast warm air into the cabin. The driver had disappeared, but the two heavies remained seated at the front. Glancing over his shoulder, Rob noted that Burak and Anja were still fast asleep. One of the heavies ambled over to him and whispered, "If you go into the house, you'll find the facilities on your right under the stairs or the kitchen straight ahead. I know it's still early, but there's a good breakfast and strong coffee ready. Alternatively, head up the stairs and find a room with your name stuck to the door. You could lie down again if you feel like it."

While the man's tone was pleasant, it was clear that he was expected to leave the minibus and head inside, so Rob obliged. Stepping down off the minibus, Rob looked about himself, blinking in the cool air. It was a good few degrees cooler than at Northolt, and the only sounds belonged to the birds and the minibus engine. He walked towards the house and the front door that stood ajar, ready for him.

Nice, but very isolated, he thought to himself. *Must be the Cotswolds judging by the architecture. Must cost a fortune.* The two cars from Northolt were also in the driveway, as were another two. *More people*, Rob thought, sighing inwardly.

"Rob, we're in here," Laura called as he pushed the front door open. The smells of a typical home-cooked English breakfast were hanging in the air and very appealing. He wavered momentarily between taking the stairs and finding a bed or responding to Laura's hail and heading to the kitchen. With a sigh he relented, knowing what was expected of him. As he entered, Rob recognised Steven Gurning and Graeme Spreachley from his video calls. He shook hands with the two men, who were dressed casually, unlike the suits he had last seen them in, as Laura placed a plate laden with food and a steaming mug of coffee on the table, ready for him to sit down.

"It's good to have you back in the UK," Gurning said to Rob. "You've been an immense credit to the country, and we will work with you to help return your life to a semblance of normality, as well as getting your belongings back."

"Thank you," Rob mumbled, mouth stuffed with oozing, juicy food.

"I expect it will be a good couple of days before you can consider going back home. During that time, we will want to meet with you and go over as much as possible. We will also be talking matters through with Mr Demir."

"What will happen to him and to Anja?"

"That hasn't been decided yet. We would like Mr Demir's input into that, although I suspect we will try to have Anja fostered to give her a life away from her father's criminal activities and the consequences thereof. Almost certainly we will need to give her a new identity, which for one so young should not pose too many difficulties. We'll also make sure she gets whatever counselling she needs."

Rob nodded before looking up to say, "I'd like to say good-bye to them both before we head in our separate directions."

"Of course, we'd expect that, and there will be plenty of time for that as well. We'll keep you all together until you go home. After your exertions, we expect that a level of connection has developed between you all."

Gurning held his hand up as Rob jerked his head up with a look of alarm. "That is perfectly normal, and I am not insinuating anything at all, Rob. You were simply in the wrong place at the wrong time and got caught up in a terrible mess—you acted brilliantly by saving people's lives. More than once, I might add."

Rob briefly lowered his eyes, uncomfortable at the praise. "And what about Burak? What will happen to him?"

"In part, that depends on him. We hope to get information from him that will both break his various criminal networks and also some terrorist activities. No, he's not a terrorist," Gurning countered quickly on seeing Rob's troubled expression. "But that's why we're involved. Whether he knows it or not, there are terrorist links to his criminal activities."

The radio lying on the table sprang to life. "Our other two guests will be with you shortly."

"Okay, thanks, Jim. Once they are indoors, please secure the front door, and then you'll be free to head home. Thanks for all your help," Gurning replied.

A few moments later, a buzzer sounded in the kitchen, followed by the closing of the front door. Laura stood and went to greet Burak and Anja. As they entered the kitchen, Laura said, "I'm sorry we didn't really get the chance to be properly introduced. I'm Lisa Grahams." She gave Rob a kindly, but pointed look as she said it, hoping he would understand she had to use a cover name in front of Burak. "Rob you know, of course, and these are my colleagues, David and Adrian," she continued, motioning to Gurning and Spreachley.

As Burak shook hands and introduced his daughter, Laura laid the table for them. "I hope this will be okay for now. We can discuss likes and dislikes later in the day before I go shopping."

"This is fine. Thank you," Burak replied politely.

"Now it's just us," started Gurning. "I'll fill you in with our more immediate intentions and how the next few days will pan out. First, after breakfast we will leave this place and head to somewhere new. Given your status, Mr Demir, we prefer to be ultra-cautious. The next safe house is known only to our director general. The house is nicely secluded, with a walled garden within far larger grounds, enabling guests to spend time outside without risk of being observed. This is, of course, for your personal security, as well as for our benefit of being able to converse with you undisturbed in relaxed and congenial surroundings. We don't know how long you will be there. The objectives, very simply, will be to debrief and discuss future cooperation before deciding upon the future. For Rob, clearly we anticipate him returning home and being provided with support to return to a normal life, if ever there is such a thing."

"I'm not sure of how possible that will be," interjected Burak. "I've promised and signed away my entire wealth to him. So, unless he wishes to relinquish that, Rob is tied in. I intend to honour that promise, so it's entirely his choice."

Everyone's expressions revealed their surprise at Burak's comments. "Surely, Rob, you didn't think I'd renege on that?"

"I don't really know what I expected," admitted Rob, "although I had informed our friends here."

"Okay, let's finish up here," said Gurning, "and get ready to head out in fifteen minutes. Mr Demir, your daughter and you can continue to eat. That's not a problem, there's no hurry. The new house is not far, so your lengthy journey is close to an end. Adrian and I will be driving, and as we leave, I'd ask that people keep their heads below window level. That way even our spotters won't know you've gone until much later. We'll be swapping cars as well after a short distance."

An hour later, they were comfortably ensconced in the living room of the new safe house. Anja was upstairs fast asleep, and their new hosts, William and Jessica, had provided more coffee as they explained they were protective hosts with ready means to ensure their safety. Gurning and Spreachley had left, and Laura had stayed.

Burak broke the silence. "Rob, do you mind if Lisa listens in?"

Rob glanced cautiously at Laura before answering, "No, not at all. It may be helpful in the long run."

"Good point. Look, I'm serious that you are welcome to the complexity of my wealth. When I signed your piece of paper, I was prepared to renege on the deal as I simply wanted to save Anja. I am confident in my ability to judge character, and I'm confident you will manage any wealth that you gain wisely. Having thought it through these past few days, I do think it best that I withdraw from what I was doing. I should warn you that there is a lot of unpleasant baggage that comes with it. I therefore suspect that Lisa and her colleagues will insist on helping with that baggage, as am I. I can't see any objections to you receiving my clean wealth. Much of the clean wealth is unfortunately reliant upon the criminal, so you'll need help with the overlap as well.

"Anja is all that matters for me now. My life is effectively over. How Emilio thought he could take over I have no idea. I always kept the many strands of my network separate—and he knows that. No other person has an overview of my network, although a number were clearly aware that my reach went well beyond their own particular strand, simply because of the way I could assist their operations when they required.

"One thing I want to make clear from the outset is that it will take time—years—to unravel my operations in a way that prevents them from scattering and re-emerging later, restarting on their own accord, stronger and wiser for the experience. That is what I want—them to be closed down for good."

From Laura's expression and the phraseology of that last remark, Rob was certain it was meant for her ears. It came across as being genuine, even though it could easily be interpreted as a way for Burak to keep the upper hand, and Rob was sure that was also the case.

Burak was still talking, so Rob quickly re-focused. "I don't want to put you under undue pressure, Rob, but we need to agree on how to proceed really quite quickly. If the leaders across my network don't hear from me soon, they may assume I'm out of the equation and scatter anyway. It's important that I retain a semblance of control to provide Lisa and her colleagues with the time to close in and take operations out without them fragmenting.

"Lisa, which part or parts of the British security services do you represent?"

"Both David and I are MI5. Adrian is MI6."

Burak scowled in surprise. "Why are you involved? I was expecting you to say one of the agencies interested in serious organised crime."

"I take it from that remark that you are unaware of how some of your network either source, transport, or pay for their merchandise and how some have expanded their activities and relationships."

"Generally, that's correct. I establish the lines of business and take an overarching coordination role, leaving the daily activities to others. I don't like the idea that my network is supporting terrorism, which is intimated by your involvement. Terrorism operates at an entirely different level from me. I don't like what I am hearing at all."

"You know what, Mr Demir?"

"Burak, please."

"Burak, I actually believe you on that point. But the reality is that potential terrorist and espionage activities have benefited from your network, and we can evidence that. The problem is that we cannot fully trace the linkages, or we do not have adequate intelligence or evidence to act. This applies in many countries, so we expect many requests to extradite you once it's known you've been apprehended. We are absolutely certain that through you we can disrupt terrorist and espionage activities both here and abroad, as well as nailing a substantial amount of seriously nasty criminal activity."

"Damn it! This casts a very different complexion on the situation. Of course I will help."

Again, Burak came across as being genuine, but only time would tell. From their exchanged glances, both Laura and Rob were clearly thinking the same thing. Rob was intrigued. In part, he wanted to know more and be involved. On the other hand, it all sounded quite scary. What should he do?

9

After two days of intense planning, Kovač and his team were ready.

Gurning had invited one of Kovač's men to Britain to interview Rob as soon as possible after the initial debriefings, and they had pored over maps for a few days, together with aerial photographs taken by reconnaissance helicopters.

It had been part of Gurning's plan to reconcile himself with his opposite number. Understandably, Kovač was furious when he was informed that the British had undertaken an operation on his patch and prevented him from the potential glory of fully resolving the incidents.

Only time would tell if it would work, and for that to happen, Kovač required a breakthrough of some kind to show for all his efforts. Gurning really hoped that would occur. Otherwise Kovač had been very clear that he would have to inform his political masters of what had transpired, and both agreed that was far from ideal. If that happened, details would inevitably get to the world's press that Britain had worked against Slovenian interests, and that would be a tough one to quell without mentioning why. Gurning appreciated Kovač's position and the competing tensions of their profession and their ruling politicians.

Despite their best efforts Kovač's team had come up empty-handed and needed a break to restore faith in their service. Finally, and surreptitiously, a couple from Kovač's team had set out on a 'camping and photography holiday' around the area identified by Rob. It had taken three days of apparent fruitless meandering before they came across the scattered leftovers of human food eaten by a wolf and a rocky outcrop visible in the distance through the trees. Staying well back, the couple surveyed the scene, easily identifying the place against Rob's description. This time they were prepared to face the gauntlet of calling in. This time, they would turn the tables on their many colleagues who jibed them for being a couple in love and on holiday together. This time they had results.

Kovač and the raiding team approached from the valley without a path. Timing could not have been better. The couple, as they had become known, had informed him that a quad bike with a trailer had arrived during the night. Although they had not seen anyone during the day, the quad bike was still there, and Kovač was therefore eager to proceed and not let whoever was there slip through his fingers.

As they approached, the team split into three groups. Two sections approached the main cabin from opposite ends of the rocky outcrop. A third group was sent to identify and guard all cave entrances. He did not want anyone escaping from him in the same way that Rob had slipped Demir away from under his captors' noses!

They held position as one man from each section approached the two outbuildings, each staying out of the line of sight of the main cabin's windows. Each man extracted a flexible cable camera from his back sack and, through one of the many holes or cracks that were evident, slipped it into the hut.

"Clear," came the first whispered report over the radio. "As described and expected, a food store but little remaining."

"Clear," came the second report. "There's another quad bike but partially dismantled. Appears to be under repair. Otherwise, bits and pieces, various tools, etc., as you'd need to be self-sufficient out in the mountains."

"Understood. Proceed to disable the quad without it being obvious, just in case an escape is attempted. Everyone, prepare to move in."

The second man shuffled along on his stomach through the grass to the quad in front of the cabin. Arriving at the quad bike, the man quickly identified the location of the fuel pump and switched it off. He then drained the tank into a plastic container. They had strict instructions not to damage or destroy anything of value that could be sold to generate revenue for the Service. With that, he too returned to his team, ready for Kovač to give the word and storm the cabin.

"At least it isn't raining," Kovač said to himself as he cast his eyes around, appreciating the quiet beauty of the space, the fresh smell of the trees, as well as the isolation. "This would be the perfect spot for my dreamed-of get-away-from-everything cabin." Dragging himself reluctantly back to the moment, he considered the time. With luck whoever was inside would either be preparing lunch or already eating. It would be a perfect distraction as long as he, she, or they did not look out of a window. So far none of his spotters had indicated any sign of activity in the cabin, and a final check confirmed that continued to be the case. The blinds remained down and had not moved.

Kovač gave the signal to move in.

Cognisant of Rob's warning that there could be alarms, they approached with caution. One man buzzed his radio briefly, the signal that an alarm had been found, and they all froze for precious seconds while the individual marked the area with aerosol paint and crawled around the danger area. As soon as the teams were in position the lead man inspected the door before comfortably smashing it in with a handheld steel battering ram. The door splintered and fell into the space beyond with a thud as it hit the floor. Even before the door hit the floor, the lead man and two colleagues threw some flashbang stun grenades into the cabin at differing angles to cover the entire space. They waited for the near-immediate blasts and then stormed inside, masks on, weapons at the ready.

Kovač watched from a distance, tensed up and waited for the sounds of gunfire, but none came. His radio clicked. "Clear," the leader called. Kovač would now have further anxious minutes of waiting as the team worked their way systematically through the place and whatever tunnels and caves lay beyond. The element of surprise was now surely lost.

"Sir," started the team leader, "the cabin is clear. There are obvious signs of current life—an overnight bag and food ready to be eaten. There is also a substantial supply of cleaning materials and solvents. Whoever is here must be inside the caves that the British reported."

"Understood, proceed."

Having thoroughly checked the cabin for trap doors or other concealed areas, the men took up positions on either side of the only other door in the back wall of the cabin that was built against the rock face. This door presented an entirely greater challenge. The two locks, a third of the way from the top and bottom, were firmly fastened, and the door opened towards them into the cabin, making battering it down far more difficult. By placing a strong piece of thick wire into each lock in turn, they determined that the key was in place on the other side.

Surely, Kovač thought, *this must be a good sign. Someone has to be on the other side—unless, of course, there is an exit we have yet to discover.*

Methodically and swiftly, Kovač's men rummaged through their sacks and in seconds extracted five flat squares of flexible explosive. They fixed one above each lock, the door handle and both hinges, set the fuses, stood back, and pressed the handheld detonator. The blast blew the windows out and rumbled through the forest, sending birds squawking into the air, flapping their wings noisily in agitation at the disruption to their usually tranquil environment.

The door remained where it was momentarily before falling forward onto the floor. The residue of smoke billowed out across the room before dissipating in the breeze that emanated from the door and now-open windows. Kovač cursed. "Why didn't they open the windows?"

Mercifully, the lights were on in the passage beyond. There were was a closed door on either side of the passage and another, open door five metres further along. Impenetrable, silent darkness faced them through the open door. The infrared scopes on the team's assault rifles revealed nothing. This was not the sort of tunnel you wanted to be caught in partway along.

One man, back as flat against the wall as he could get it, inched along the tunnel while covered by three colleagues, two kneeling and one standing in the cabin's doorway. The passage's walls of bare rock almost rippled, casting shadows all over from the bare bulbs overhead. As the first man reached the first doorway, a second man slipped along the passage to join him.

With one man on either side of the door, the second man tried the handle. It turned, and the heavy door swung open silently on well-oiled hinges. The men gagged at the sudden stench that flowed out and at the sight that met their eyes. They barely gave themselves adequate time to scan the room before they hurriedly closed the door. No sane living person could remain in there for long. The door, thankfully, provided a good seal.

They gave the signal that the room was clear of life and that they were about to change sides. Hesitantly, they swung the opposite door open, identical to the first. Gagging once more, even though they were prepared, they rapidly made their way back to the cabin and outside for some fresh air. The room had been the same. Nothing was said as they passed—all those at the entrance to the tunnel shared all too clearly the smell of death as the cooler tunnel air was sucked out into the relative warmth of the cabin.

"Okay," the team leader started, keeping his voice low as he spoke through the radios incorporated into their helmets, "Time to find this sucker. As before, three cover from one side of the passage. The rest will hug the opposite wall. I'll lead. Once close enough to the furthest door, we'll throw a couple of flash bangs into the area. Then we take the space at speed. Ready?"

All affirmed their readiness with a sharp, "Sir!" before taking up positions.

"And we take him alive. The boss has made it clear anything less is unacceptable. Got it?"

Another sharp chorus of, "Sir!" echoed through the radios.

The leader then led the way, covering his advance with his assault rifle constantly at the ready and one eye firmly against the infrared sight. On reaching the point from where he wanted to throw the flashbangs, the leader scanned the space ahead through his sights. There was nothing to signify life of any form—all he could make out were some cold chairs, a table, and packing crates. "Cover!" he ordered and then lowered his rifle to prepare the first flash bang. Suddenly, he grunted loudly as two bullets slammed into him, one in the chest and the other in his throwing arm. The report of the firing weapon followed the shots, echoing around the cavernous room and tunnels.

The team leader was thrown back into the next man in line, making both men stumble. He also dropped the flashbang, which promptly went off at their feet, flipping the two men up with the blast and onto their backs. The flashbang also thoroughly disoriented the others who were close to it, despite their body armour. More bullets followed, thumping into the next two men, knocking them off their feet. More bullets ricocheted off the tunnel walls, bouncing around off the rock with terrifying twangs and sending splinters of rock flying into the men's faces.

In the confusion, having identified where the bullets were emanating from, the three men at the far end opened fire. Desperate to move their fallen comrades and get back to safety themselves, Kovač's men in the passage shouted for the shooting to stop—they did not want to be hit by friendly fire! It was mayhem. Others, aware that to retreat could be disastrous, stormed forward through the chaos, oblivious to their personal danger, opening fire as soon as they were clear of their colleagues. As soon as possible, they lobbed more flashbangs into the area beyond to try to disorient and disable their opponent. As they entered the dark space beyond the tunnel, they spread out, seeking whatever cover they could.

Another man fell, taking a couple of well-placed bullets in the chest, leaving him to curl up into a protective position to minimise the unprotected areas of his body, hoping desperately that his body armour would continue to protect him. The remaining two lobbed more flashbang stun grenades in the direction of the shooter, wishing they were the real thing. They rolled aside once more as the flash and boom caused glass from the darkened overhead light bulbs to come sprinkling down upon them like a short, heavy rain shower.

Cautiously, with rifles raised, they rounded either side of the pile of packing crates. Midway between them was a young, plump, fair-haired man with at least two days' stubble. He was sitting up, back against the wall, watching them through night-vision goggles. His guns lay at his feet, poking through the crates. In his left hand he held a detonator, but the men could not see any explosives in the dark. He smiled sadly.

One said, "Put it down slowly. You've caused enough harm. No more is needed, and you can live."

His reply, loud enough to be heard by all the others over their radios, sent a chill through their spines. "I suppose you've seen inside the other rooms? That'll happen to me if I leave this place without my job done."

These men had not seen inside those rooms, and they started to feel glad that was the case; only their battle-hardened colleagues had, and they had left for air without reporting any detail. Nevertheless, they did not want to die in an explosion with this man. "No it won't," one said confidently.

"There's no way that you can keep me safe. They get to anyone they want, anywhere."

Knowing the best ploy was to keep him talking, they did just that. "Who are they? Tell us and we will help you."

"No you won't. Not forever you won't, and Emilio says that W has long tentacles and a longer memory. It was W that ordered us to do those others in for letting the prisoners escape. Doc enjoys that sort of stuff."

"So there you go, people do escape from these guys. With our help, so can you. We can get you out, as though one of us. Then we create an explosion and report that an unknown person was left inside. We can then remove a fake body, just to preserve appearances."

The man was clearly mulling this over, so the officer pressed his point home. "I can call for an extra suit now if you like. How about it?"

So far it had been the same person speaking, keeping the young man's attention. The other was merely keeping careful watch from the other side.

Kovač was pacing around outside, listening to the conversation, extremely concerned at the turn of events, the injuries sustained, and the tone of the conversation. As a precaution, he ordered as many men back as he feasibly could. He wanted to call those on point back as well; he loved these men, but he knew he could not. They all knew and accepted the risks.

Instead, he listened to the team chatter with one ear as they planned how to save those inside from almost certain death. With the other ear, he listened to the dialogue between his man and the unknown defender.

As their plan approached its execution phase, Kovač prayed silently to any god that would listen and paced back and forth under the trees, scrunching the dry leaves and twigs, not bothering anymore with their previously intended silence. The lives of his men were threatened and at stake!

The silence of the dark cavern was shattered with a single, deafening shot. Another team member had silently positioned himself a few metres behind Kovač's man who was not speaking and had taken the shot while the defender's head was turned towards the speaker.

The young man screamed and howled as his left wrist disintegrated in an explosion of blood, skin, and bone. A large-bore, hollow-point bullet had been used; the shot was accurate and virtually took the young man's hand off at the wrist. The detonator skidded across the floor, and the nearest of Kovač's men scooped it up carefully. They all then waited. They waited for the fizz, then the rumbling and subsequent explosion of noise that would announce their death and send them to meet their maker. But other than the constant howls of pain from the young man, no sound came.

Permitting themselves just a few seconds of personal space to appreciate their success and immense relief, they informed Kovač of a successful disarm. The three men then set about giving the young man some necessary medical assistance while waiting for their colleagues to arrive with a stretcher. A couple of helicopters had already arrived and were waiting to deliver doctors and medical supplies, as well as to take the injured to hospital.

Kovač met the team upon their exit, receiving them warmly and heaping on his congratulations.

As one team left, having done their job to secure the area, another two teams arrived, one to guard the place and the other to forensically search it. As the yet-to-be identified young man was whisked away by the medics, Kovač emphasised that he expected to interrogate him as soon as possible, no excuses. In his opinion, no one involved with atrocities in his country could expect any sympathy, merely the basics of what human rights afforded them. He was prepared to sail as close to the wind as he could on this one to get results. His country had been thrown into turmoil and fright because of all these atrocities, and he wanted to get someone and make him pay!

Kovač waited for the forensics team to make an initial assessment before donning his own specialist overalls and shoes to venture inside for a first-hand experience of the place. He wanted to see for himself before returning to head office and reporting to his superiors and the British. Taking on board the recommendation of his team, he left the 'slaughter rooms', as they had been called, to the end.

The cabin was nothing exceptional. Fairly basic, no comforts at all. The single tunnel had been carved out of the rock well, almost professionally, but without regard for the finish. *How could this have been done without anyone knowing,* he wondered, *and where did they dispose of the waste?*

At the end was a large open space behind a heavy wooden door, reinforced with steel bands. This was where the young man had holed up and met his comeuppance behind the packing crates. Also, judging from the steel hoops inserted into the rock face and various chains along the floor, this must have been where Demir and his daughter had been held. Looking up, he saw the opening through which Krane had spirited the pair from under their captors' eyes. *What an exceptionally lucky break for all concerned,* he thought. Kovač was keenly aware that had Krane not intervened, then Demir and his daughter would very possibly have disappeared for good.

Kovač had seen enough, and it was time to go, but first, to see these so-called 'slaughter rooms'. He opened the first door, feeling confident that his men had been teasing him; they were all hardened, emotionally tough men after all. He had been surprised that those who had looked in had been so affected. Again, and sadly, they were hardened to that, or as far as he was concerned should have been. *Maybe their training needs to get toughened-up*, he thought as his hand fell onto the door handle.

He swung the door open, half-nonchalantly, and immediately knew why his men had reacted as they had. He froze. He wanted to gag, to retch, but was too shocked. It wasn't the stench, although that was bad enough. He understood why they had used the expression 'slaughter rooms'. Three men were hanging on poles facing each other, severely beaten and mutilated, definitely tortured. A pile of extremities lay at the base of each pole, fingers, toes, feet, hands, ears, nose, kneecaps. There were pools of dried blood at the foot of each pole. Kovač could not imagine the warped, demented mind of those responsible, nor the horror faced by those subjected to the brutality, nor the torment for those witnessing the brutality, knowing they would be next. He could imagine that the perpetrators inflicted their sadism on one man at a time, leaving the others to watch what awaited them.

There was no need to go inside. Kovač closed the door and looked briefly into the opposite room, anticipating what he would see. There were three poles but two men, so five dead in total. At the base of the unoccupied pole, he could see from the age of the floor that the poles had been there for quite some time, so there was no telling how many people had been subjected to such horrors, right here in his own country, the security for which he was partially responsible.

Whoever these Emilio, W, and Doc were, he wanted them badly, desperately even. There was now no doubt in his mind. He would help the British, despite the embarrassment they had caused by sneaking Demir out from under his nose. He acknowledged that Demir was of far greater importance to the British than to his own organisation. He now also accepted, reluctantly, what he had known since Gurning's call informing him of their operation to extract Demir and Rob. He would have done precisely the same thing in Gurning's position.

Kovač closed the door and headed off, back to his office. As he walked briskly downhill to the waiting car, he took deep breaths of fresh, mountain air and tried to focus on the scent of the pine trees. He gazed around at the beauty of the countryside, searching for wild animals, for flowers, for anything to counter the horrific images that kept working their way back into his mind. He knew he would be haunted by this day for years to come, until the culprits were caught, or killed.

In the car he called Gurning to brief him, particularly in relation to W and Doc.

"I've no idea who they could be," Gurning said, "but will certainly ask Demir if he knows their identities. I do seem to recall either Rob or Demir mentioning a Doc, as you express it, so it may be the same chap. Let me know how you get on with the cleaner."

"I will do. Good-bye, Steven, and thank you. This should satisfy my political lords and masters, and the media. I will respect your secrecy over Demir."

Kovač sat back and pondered what sort of person the young man in their custody really was. There could be no doubt he was a cleaner—someone coming in behind the perpetrators to clean up their mess and leave no evidence. Hopefully he had not been able to clean too much so Kovač's own forensics team could come up with something.

10

Several days later, a plan was emerging. At times the discussions had been fractious, at times genteel. There had been many harsh words, threatening at times, but the underlying message throughout was loud and clear—Burak was not going to tell them everything in one go. He intended to keep a strong grip on how and when his network would be dismantled. That it would be dismantled was beyond dispute. That Burak was prepared to participate and support its dismantling was also not in question. Gurning and Spreachley were clearly frustrated at being thwarted and not being in ultimate control. Burak was convinced that he knew best, and handing control over to the authorities in one go would be a huge mistake because they would not proceed appropriately.

The number of overnight stays at the safe house became more numerous than they had ever expected. Initially they had been extremely reluctant for Burak to contact anyone associated with his network, but after two days, they had relented, recognising the logic in Burak's argument. Listening in with Rob and Laura, they had marvelled at how Burak handled the explanation of his temporary absence to his network leaders, instilling confidence and loyalty once more. The only person within his network Burak did not contact was Emilio, for obvious reasons.

They were all terribly uncomfortable as Burak discussed future criminal activities and helped formulate the plans, but they acknowledged that unless he did, the game would be over. They became even more uncomfortable as they reluctantly accepted that they would have to let many of the activities occur, whether in Britain or not, because by intervening, the game would also be over, and they just did not have the resources available to jump in and disrupt everything. The scale of his network was far beyond anything they had expected. Despite his criminality, a high degree of respect for Burak's intellect and acumen had developed.

Burak was clearly in his element. Enjoying and treasuring his time with Anja, he relished his regular engagements with Gurning and Spreachley and seeing how they came to accept that their initial expectations of simply milking him for all his information and to come crashing down on his network to close it down had been utterly misguided. Lengthy briefings back at MI5 and MI6 were taking their toll, and the two men were visibly exhausted. The pressure for results was immense, and so the euphemistically titled debriefing sessions became more intense.

One mid-afternoon a week later, Gurning and Spreachley therefore met with Laura and Rob to discuss what they had gleaned and what their options really were. They sat outside at one end of the walled garden bathed in sun, sipping their chilled drinks and watching Burak play with Anja at the far end, enjoying the little girl's regular bursts of laughter. It was, Rob mused, really rather surreal considering the topics of discussion just completed and about to be embarked upon.

"Okay, so who wants to summarise where we stand, if we are, that is?" Gurning asked sardonically.

Without hesitation Laura jumped in, riffling through her notes while Spreachley watched, his eyes fixed intently on the young woman, his hands clasped with his two forefingers stretched upright and pressed against his lips. Rob and Gurning, on the other hand, were relaxed in their chairs but no less focused. "We have a far broader criminal network than we ever conceived. It ranges from money laundering, drugs, and the smuggling of people, antiquities, gems, and other valuable commodities. He's into bribery, protection rackets, dubious construction and public works contracts, gambling, prostitution, and controls local and regional gangs involved with petty and organised crime and intimidation. You name it, it's there and frequently coupled intimately with his legitimate businesses, the managers of which appear to be completely unaware of what's going on. His operations are geographically dispersed, although primarily in the wider definition of Europe and neighbouring countries."

"Yes, but what bothers me is that Burak's still holding all the cards, and he knows it. We need him. He appears to have an almost encyclopaedic memory, committing everything to memory instead of to paper or computer, or so he says," Gurning commented.

"And I have to question how much control he really has," Spreachley added. "He openly accepts that he leaves operational matters to others. This Emilio chap has clearly gone rogue, so it's very possible others have as well."

"True, but that doesn't change the fact that he has the inside track, and we don't!" Laura countered. "The thing is, the scale of his network is such that, as he says, it's unrealistic for us to even contemplate taking the thing down in one go!

Therefore, until we act against a particular strand, I, for one, agree with him that unless he remains involved to hold the network together, in all likelihood, it will simply fragment and we will have lost the opportunity!"

"Yes, yes. I see the logic, but what I don't like is that he wants to dictate when we act and on which strand of his network!" Spreachley complained.

"Do we have a choice? At least he's willing to help. And does it even matter, so long as we take the network down?" Gurning questioned. "Don't forget that we've had very little success against him so far. Maybe he does know best!"

"Hmm. I suppose I do agree with his reasoning to strike this Emilio Arroz chap quickly. He will be too busy reacting to protect himself from a counter attack to restructure his activities and disappear." Spreachley conceded.

"Good," nodded Gurning. "Because this does provide an amazing opportunity to make a huge dent in organised crime and disrupt terrorist funding and activities. I also like his dedication to his legitimate businesses. It's a clever model that he's developed—launder as much of his criminal proceeds through his own legitimate businesses to keep the money within the family, so to speak."

"That maybe so, but without that revenue flow, many of those businesses become unviable and will collapse." Rob added, joining the discussion.

"And that, young man, very neatly brings us to you. Are you prepared to join this venture with us or try to return to your previous life?" Gurning looked at Rob, but held up a hand to ward off a response. "Before you answer, please be aware that if you do join us, there will be risks, and above all, you won't be able to disclose a thing, let alone discuss matters outside of a pre-cleared group of people. You'll find us supportive whichever way you choose. Life on our side is unusual, to say the least! Many can't adapt to it, so we won't think any less of you if you say no."

There was a silent pause as the enormity of Rob's decision weighed heavily on each of them. "I presume that I can't use the 'call a friend' option," Rob replied eventually, referring to a television quiz show.

While his comment had broken the tension in the air by providing a little joviality, the decision would not go away, and he was acutely aware of that. After a few more moments to build the tension once more, he said with a wide smile, "It's a no brainer, of course I'm in. I wouldn't miss it for the world. I abhor much of Burak's life, but I totally respect what he wants to achieve for his legitimate businesses, and it'd be a great honour if I can be the man to deliver that."

The subsequent and immediate chorus of, "Wonderful!" from the others was genuine and heartfelt.

"This does mean, of course," Rob continued, "that I will have to be involved with all matters pertaining to the network, both the legitimate businesses and closing down the criminal elements that impact those businesses. What's more, my involvement will be as an outsider running the businesses. I will not be a member of one of your Services. I say that because I want to work for the benefit of those businesses, and not be subject to whatever conflicting policies and procedures your respective organisations may have in place!"

The others were stunned, and it was left to Gurning to break the silence. "Well, well. It would appear you've given this a lot of thought, and clearly enjoyed the moment to boot! I have to say that while your proposal will make life awkward for us, I do see the sense in it."

"The only thing is that you will be excluded from the planning of our operations. Our internal requirements are for confidentiality," chipped in Spreachley, somewhat aghast at the prospect of someone not wanting to join the Service.

"Oh, I doubt that," Rob countered confidently. "I'm sure there are many times when you need to involve external people in your operations so they don't unintentionally upset matters by, for example, turning up at the wrong time!"

Gurning's and Laura's pinched smiles could not hide their admiration for Rob's punchiness and pluckiness, nor the fact that he was spot on and had blown Spreachley's argument to pieces.

"I'm sure that settles the principles then," said Gurning to cover Spreachley's embarrassment. "There will, of course, be plenty of bureaucracy to complete, but we're essentially there, and I am delighted to have you on board, Rob."

"I echo that," chimed in Laura.

"May I join you?"

They all looked up to see Burak approaching. "Of course," replied Rob. "Our conversation had petered out, so good timing."

"Well, from the laughter, it certainly sounded a jovial ending, so I trust that is a positive sign?" Burak paused only fleetingly since he received no reaction. "As you can see," he continued, gesturing towards Anja with a smile, "my daughter has found a new interest." Anja was skipping on the terrace and singing in time with the rhythm.

"So it would appear," Gurning smiled. "I've heard friends say that young children have a short attention span."

"Absolutely," Burak agreed with feeling. "No children of your own, then, if you don't mind me asking?"

"Not at all. No, no children. My wife and I weren't able, and we have very happily filled our lives accordingly. While we often wonder about family life, we established a lifestyle totally unsuited to children long before we even discussed having a family, only to then find out we weren't able!"

As Gurning spoke, Rob saw a strange expression on Laura's face, one he couldn't quite place. Leaving Gurning, Spreachley and Burak to talk, Rob and Laura wandered over to Anja and joined in her play.

Later, when Rob and Laura were alone on the terrace, he asked, "Remember Steven's comments about family life?"

"Yes" she replied guardedly.

"Well, you had an expression that I couldn't place, and I'm just curious, I guess."

Laura smiled appreciatively. "It is rare to get a glimpse into Steven's personal life, so I was surprised. I guess it was one of those moments when circumstances conspired to put him at ease." At Rob's questioning, furrowed forehead, she explained, "Well, we were all delighted that you want to work with us, we had shared some laughs, the sun was shining, we were relaxed, and Anja was skipping and singing. You could almost say that the atmosphere was akin to a being at a friend's house, so the conversation slipped easily and comfortably along. It's a positive reflection on all of us, and I'm sure Steven appreciates that. I have the distinct impression that he likes you."

"That's good to hear. And he also appears to like and respect you."

"Yes, I've been very lucky. While I've had to move around various departments for experience, I always came back to his team. He's a great boss, looking out for his people. He still picks up a few operations, despite his seniority. The Service wants the benefit of his experience and wisdom across the board, but he insists on running some ops to stay fresh."

"Good for him. Why did he get this one?"

"Oh, that's simple! First, his Slovenian counterpart contacted him enquiring about you. Then once you made contact and mentioned Demir, well, it was a slam-dunk. Demir is so high-profile, and the implications for the UK alone are immense. Add the complexity of the international piece as well and there could only be one choice—Steven."

"Ah, I'm with you."

"By the way, I think you've been very shrewd in not joining the Services to retain an element of independence. Just don't let anyone know I said that!" she said with a broad smile and a glinting twinkle in her eye.

Later that evening, having put Anja to bed, Burak suddenly became serious as they ate dinner. "I've had a few ideas of how to disrupt Emilio. I would like to test my thinking with you and discuss the implications, particularly how to keep the legitimate side of the businesses running afterwards. I'd suggest that there is value in keeping them running because other strands of my network and not just Emilio will use them. I've also got some thoughts on how to stage the handover to Rob."

"That sounds positive," mumbled Gurning, chewing on his food, "but best to wait until the morning when we'll be fresh. I don't want any misunderstandings occurring as a consequence of tired discussions. So, does anyone know when the next Formula 1 race is due?"

The next morning, whilst their hosts entertained Anja, they gathered in the dining room, a digital voice recorder in the centre of the table as usual and pads of paper and a glass of water beside each chair. Coffee, milk, sugar, and bottled water had been placed on a side cabinet, together with a plentiful supply of biscuits and fruit.

"I trust everyone slept well," started Gurning. "Following Burak's welcome remarks last night, I'd suggest that we get right down to business. But first, it's been agreed that from now on we adopt our real names. In doing so, Burak, I hope that you realise you will be effectively muzzled for the rest of your life, so before reintroducing ourselves, I just want to check that you fully understand."

"Yes, yes, I do and it comes as no surprise."

Following a round of introductions, during which they joked that Rob's name had not changed, they settled down to hours of tough discussion. Burak started to sketch out parts of his network, neatly demonstrating that it would take time to compile sufficient evidence to bring compelling convictions against the leaders of each strand to his network. He also outlined how they could strike at part of Emilio's operation across Britain. The toughest part for Gurning and Spreachley was accepting that they would have to knowingly allow criminal activity to continue without arranging an intervention—that would be a tough concept to sell to the MI5's political masters!

"Don't forget the positive messages," Rob interjected. "You may be able to appease the politicians a bit by emphasising the protection of the legitimate businesses and all those employed by them."

"Spoken like a true businessman," Laura smiled.

"Well," concluded Gurning, "I think we all know what the three of you have to do over the next few days. We need sufficient material to create a suitable briefing for our masters, one that contains a plan of action". He looked at Laura, Rob and Burak. On receiving confirmatory nods from each, he continued, "Burak, I'd like a separate conversation with you once the others have left about both your and Anja's futures."

Taking the hint, Spreachley, Laura, and Rob left the room, Spreachley pulling his cars keys from his pocket whilst mumbling something about having to get back to the office. Laura and Rob headed outside to sit on the terrace with a couple of cold Cokes taken from the fridge.

"You haven't mentioned a special friend to telephone and provide some assurance to while you've been here," commented Laura casually as they went to sit outside on the terrace.

"Oh man, thank goodness I split from Jemima before I went to Slovenia. She'd be impossible at the moment, driving my parents crazy. I guess this lifestyle must play havoc with your personal life?"

"It does, yes, hence no man in my life at present. Mum keeps badgering me to settle down and have kids. Thankfully, Dad keeps her in check as much as possible and tells her to leave me alone, so I only get hassled when he's out. Dad is great. He's really cool about things, and I am sure he's guessed what I do. Mum just doesn't have a clue."

"What do you say to them?" asked Rob curiously. "I guess I'm going to have to come up with some cock-and-bull story as to what I'm doing."

Laura laughed. "Oh, I'm a travelling representative supporting cohesive communities for the government. Mum thinks that's absolutely great. Dad thinks it's funny. I'm sure he saw through the story immediately, but decided to play along. How about your parents?"

"They're wonderful and loving. I'm very fortunate. They are very concerned that I don't have a job, but cool with me taking time out. Yeah, yeah, there's a bit of a contradiction there, but that's them. They know that I saved enough to be comfortable for nearly a year, even allowing for holidays. They've even said that I could rent out my apartment in Vauxhall and move in with them if money becomes an issue."

"Vauxhall!" exclaimed Laura. "That's where I live!"

"Wow! I'm in a converted vinegar factory, of all places, just off Fentiman Road."

"Oh, I know. That's on Rita Road, isn't it? That's a lovely development. I'm in one of the blocks at St George Wharf."

"I bet that's convenient for where you work! Do you ever go to the Fentiman Arms, or frequent any other place around the area?"

"I've heard of the Fentiman Arms but never been there."

"Oh, you should, it's a great gastro pub. I often eat there when I'm feeling lazy, which is also quite often!"

Laura laughed. "Well, when we eventually get away from this place, you can introduce me."

At that moment Anja rushed up to Rob to give him one of her regular hugs and burst into rapid chatter, telling him all she had been up to.

11

"Okay, everyone, listen up. First, please can anyone who has not signed the register or the additional confidentiality forms please say so now."

Gurning looked around the crowded meeting room in Thames House at the expectant faces. Sunlight periodically broke through the clouds sending sparkling rays through the windows making people blink and squint. It was an unusually civilised hour for such a briefing, and Laura had overheard various mutterings that the pleasant time must either come with a catch, or something really big was going down, making her smile inwardly.

At the lack of response, Gurning smiled. "Good. Welcome. We have colleagues from all the various organisations participating in this matter. Laura will pass round the briefing as I speak. Each document is named and has to be signed for. The report's rear section details your own particular involvement in this series of ops. I say 'series' for good reason. A major crime lord is currently in our custody and has been for a couple of weeks. He is cooperating almost beyond expectations, and today we start to dismantle his criminal empire. Unfortunately, I cannot divulge his name for security reasons. In any case, his name is unimportant because he successfully kept himself anonymous as far as those operating from each location are concerned."

Gurning waited patiently as murmurs rippled around the room, noting a mix of satisfaction that a crime lord had been caught alongside mild irritation that the name had been withheld. When the hubbub had died down, he continued. "Nothing about these operations is to be discussed beyond those in this room because future operations could be impacted. Before anyone asks, no, it is not possible to take the whole thing down in one go. We have looked at that in detail—the breadth of operations is far too extensive and can only be taken down over time. This afternoon we start the surveillance on part of just one strand of this network—some money-laundering and drug operations. However, we must be aware that one, or all of these locations could also be used for other purposes, including terrorism, hence my team's involvement."

Gurning then looked to Laura, who continued the briefing. "We are focused on four locations for this operation, two in London and one each in Bradford and Leicester. We expect raids on peoples' homes will follow as dealers are also identified. Please remember, in large part the target locations are legitimate businesses that have simply been hijacked for other purposes. We understand there is a concealed room within the roof of the primary Leicester building where the splitting, dilution, and packing of drugs takes place."

"Thank you, Laura," Gurning continued. "You are required to study your briefing document immediately after this meeting and then attend the separate meetings as outlined in your packs at the times stipulated. Forthwith, your other work will be reassigned. Questions should wait until you've read your personalised briefing packs and attended the follow-on briefings. Okay, that's a wrap. Please could the core team remain; I have some news."

Gurning waited until only Laura, Spreachley, and Rob remained. "I thought you'd all be interested that I have some news from my Slovenian counterpart."

Rob glanced at Laura once again. Previously, throughout the briefing, when he had looked at her, it had been respectful of her as a woman, and he had been pleased to receive a warm, friendly reciprocating smile on more than a few occasions. This time was different, however. This time he was concerned, and from Laura's expression, she was equally in the dark.

"Yesterday, our Slovenian colleagues stormed the hideout where Burak had been held. It may not make the media here, so thought I'd let you know. Some of Inspector Kovač's team were injured, but the operation was a success. They captured the cleaner and they hope to interrogate him soon. They found five bodies in the process, all of whom were blamed for letting Burak escape. So, in other words, Rob, most of the guys you would have seen participating in the kidnap. One thing the cleaner has said is that someone called W required their deaths at the hands of the Doc and Emilio.

"As you know, it is part of Emilio's network we are targeting now. How this W person connects with Emilio we don't know, nor does Burak. While Burak doesn't know the Doc's true identity, he does know his reputation as one of Emilio's principal sidekicks. It sounds as though he's a really nasty character. Kovač wants this guy—well, all of them, in fact—so he's joining the queue. Well, that's it and good luck. Let's all keep in touch. Watch how you go."

As they left the room, Laura whispered to Rob, "Lunch at the Tate Britain. It's a great place." He simply nodded imperceptibly and walked on.

Laura re-read the briefing pack she had prepared for the surveillance team prior to meeting them. Then she left her desk in the open plan fourth-floor office for the meeting room that would double as a dedicated and secured 'war room' where their progress meetings would be held and the information gathered analysed. Her heart was pounding as she approached the meeting room—the excitement of playing a leading role in bringing one of the world's largest criminal networks down was palpable for all concerned. Trying desperately to keep her nerves in check, she took a deep breath as her hand took hold of the door handle and she opened the door.

"Morning all," she said brightly as she surveyed the room of familiar faces. "Good to see you all again."

Shortly after two in the afternoon, Rob's phone beeped. His usually placid face wrinkled in puzzlement as he read Laura's text: *Sorry, can't make lunch. Something's up. Speak later.*

Rob's response belied his apprehension: *How about dinner at the Fentiman Arms? I can wait. Let me know when convenient.*

With his mind preoccupied with what could be happening, Rob struggled to find things to do while he waited. It was therefore a huge relief when, at nearly 8 p.m., his phone beeped again: *See you there in 20. :-)*

Smiling at the friendly nature of the text, he quickly got ready. He dearly wanted to know what the afternoon had held.

Twenty-five minutes later, Laura walked into the pub and Rob waved to her from a corner table. "Hi. Sorry I'm a little late," she said jovially, kissing him briefly on the cheek.

"Evening. Good to see you," he replied, rather surprised at her friendly welcome. "Fancy a drink?" he asked, heading to the bar.

"Oh, a rum and coke please."

Rob returned a few minutes later with one rum and coke, a gin and tonic, and a couple of menus. "So, is there anything you can recommend? Also, how was the Tate?" Laura asked whilst studying the menu.

Having ordered, and managed to avert a long conversation with the friendly landlady, Rob asked, "So, how did the briefings go?"

Laura laughed gently, sipped her rum and coke, and teased him, "You mean why couldn't I make lunch?"

Rob feigned shock. "Not at all, well, maybe! But I am interested. Presumably something occurred? I know it happens, it frequently did at the bank."

"I will look forward to hearing about your work there one day—chapter-and-verse. In the meantime, our presence has generated some interest." Laura nodded surreptitiously towards the bar.

"Let me guess—there's been a steady stream of people materialising behind the bar, looking over at us, and then disappearing again."

"Spot on. How did you guess?"

"I'm reasonably well known here, mostly dining by myself. My success at the Martial Arts and Unarmed Combat Championships has caught their imagination. They even get me to autograph photos of me whenever I win a podium position and they've hung them on the other side of the bar. That's why I sit over here. It's flattering, but odd all the same. Anyway, you can't get away that easily from telling me about your afternoon, however hard you try to deflect my train of thought."

They both smiled at each other as the landlord this time brought some olives and the wine over, bowing politely to Laura as he poured.

"Hmm, nice," Laura said appreciatively as she tried the lightly chilled wine. "Surveillance starts tomorrow and the guys were having a spot of difficulty identifying apartments overlooking the subject addresses where we can install people around the clock. The good news is that the briefings we put together for our political lords and masters were accepted and will be submitted. Steven was really quite complimentary, and having got to recognise my style, he quickly identified those sections you had written. I'm sure he'll tell you himself, but he did say you've the makings of a good agent!"

"Yeah, right, as if compliments are enough to entice me. No chance!" Rob said with a wink and grin.

The conversation stopped briefly when their meals arrived and they tucked in.

"Delicious. I can see why you come here."

"Pleased you like it. As the menu doesn't vary that often, I'll have to introduce you to some of the other places around here, and you can introduce me to those places you know and like. That should keep us occupied for a while!"

Laura laughed again, relaxed after a long, tiring day. "Sounds like an excellent plan. By the way, the firm's legal team is working on ways to transfer all matters firstly into the Service's hands, through some circuitous routes, and ultimately on to you. You need to think how you will manage everything. It's going to be complex."

"No doubt! I've already been thinking it through and rather fancy a private equity type approach." Rob paused while the plates were removed. "That's to say, simplistically, to have a few really good people taking an overseeing governance and guidance type role, leaving the daily functioning to those at the coal face and who are already running the various businesses, unless, of course, it's determined that they aren't able. The issue is who and how to set it up." After a thoughtful pause, Rob added, "You know, it's truly bizarre to be talking like this. I know I need to be thinking this way, but to have such wealth thrust upon me is, quite simply, weird!"

An hour later, Rob held up his hand for the bill. "Let me walk you home. I suspect we've a busy day tomorrow."

Rob hardly saw Laura the next day. Instead, he spent his time with Jed Milligan working through all the detail necessary to transfer Burak's holdings. Jed had left one of the big law firms a few years earlier, where he had been a highly successful litigator. After one successful case working with MI5, Gurning persuaded Jed to join the Service and he soon became one of Gurning's few fully trusted inner circle.

Late that day, after the most intense meetings of his life, Rob headed for a nearby café, head pounding. Jed had been tough but uncompromisingly fair, and Rob thoroughly respected the man.

Sipping an iced coffee in a quiet corner, Rob pored over some of the papers he had been given. That he was—at least initially—a puppet for the government and its agencies was neither here nor there. He easily recognised and accepted the fact comfortably. Burak had spun a huge spider's web of a network and he knew it was only fair that he cover some of the costs of dismantling it—he was, after all, about to become immensely wealthy with the transfer of Burak's businesses! Recruiting the right team to help could be a problem, but he had agreed on some names to approach with Jed—some would be appointed through MI5, others by himself. Rob also realised the team would need a base to operate from, ideally close to Thames House.

Rob quickly typed up some notes to capture his thinking on an e-mail, and sent it to Gurning and Jed. He needed a drink, something stronger than the iced coffee he had been drinking. Looking at his watch, it was nearly six o'clock. Maybe Michael would be able to join him.

When Michael had reluctantly declined a drink, Rob realised that all he really wanted was the comfort of his parents' home and the pampering that would come with it. Too much had happened in too short a period of time, and

Rob now wanted, and needed, some space, so there was no place like home. As expected, his parents were delighted. They were also exceptionally concerned when he couldn't tell them much, as required by the police. After a while, they grudgingly accepted this state of affairs and settled into making a fuss of him, which ordinarily would have made him flee back to his flat, but just now the comfort of their proximity far outweighed anything else.

Two days later, Rob and his parents were having afternoon tea in the garden. The conversation had finally moved from Rob to their plans for reshaping the lawn to make room for more plants when Rob's iPhone bleeped. It was his first in many days and gave both Rob and his parents a surprise. Before his holiday, he received nearly a hundred texts or messages a day, but that had since dropped off.

"Now that's one thing we haven't missed," his mother commented, smiling. "That said, we have both been surprised."

"Probably something to do with not having told everyone I'm back," he replied, looking and feeling a little guilty. "I've been so wrapped up with sorting matters out and helping the police that I haven't really had the time." He thumbed in the security code on his phone and glanced at the text. "Ah."

"Well?" queried his father after a good twenty seconds, during which Rob had neither said nor done anything other than to look exceedingly puzzled.

"It's Laura. She's asking if I want to join her for a couple of days checking out some places up north, leaving tomorrow morning."

"Well, darling, I'm sure that would be lovely, a break with a friend would do you good. Are you going to introduce us at some point?" his mother asked as innocently as she could.

"Well yes, she said she's in the neighbourhood and will be here in a few minutes to give me a lift home…" Rob broke off midsentence, realising the direction of his mother's thinking. "Aw, Mu-um, it's not like that. Laura is—well, police," he stammered, blushing as he realised how it must have come across.

"Why would a policewoman want you to take a trip with her?" his mother countered, probing.

"Look, you have to take this at face value. There is nothing, absolutely nothing, going on between us. I am continuing to help with their enquiries," he added, suddenly realising that the denial probably made matters sound even worse, but whether from the police side or the insinuated romanticism he wasn't quite sure.

"Rob, come on—you need to tell us something," his father jumped in. "We are simply concerned for you. If you have a new lady friend, that's fantastic, whether she's police or not. If this is simply a police matter, please help us to understand. They held you for goodness knows how long on your return, and now you expect us to believe that you are willingly going on some trip around Britain to help their enquiries when you were an innocent caught up in something we don't know about in another country! I'm sorry, it doesn't make sense!" His dad's voice had risen, not to the angry stage, but clearly exacerbated.

The doorbell saved him, and his dad got up, fixing Rob with a hard stare. Moments later his father re-emerged. "Rob, it's for you." Then, after a pause for effect, he continued, "It's Laura."

Rob squirmed in his chair, completely lost for words and totally unsure of what his suddenly spinning mind and churning stomach meant. Was it confusion or excitement? Or, was it the prospect of an imminent adventure, or for Laura being at his parents' house? All Rob knew was that his inward groan had sounded so loud that the entire village must have heard it! Not forgetting his manners, however, he stood to welcome the smiling Laura, recognising his parents were sizing her up, a matter that was clearly not lost on Laura.

"Mr and Mrs Krane, I do apologise for barging in unannounced like this. I'm with Her Majesty's Government and assigned to the case Rob has been helping us with so brilliantly. A few things have cropped up for which we'd welcome Rob's further assistance. Knowing he came out to visit by train, I thought I would come to meet him and make the return journey simpler."

"Not at all," his father said smoothly. "Much to our frustration, he's not told us anything, but we're delighted he is of help. Although," he continued with the slightest of hesitation, "Rob intimated that you are with the police?"

Laura smiled again. "Yes, I suppose I am. That's the best description. You could say we are a branch of the police, dealing with specific types of crime. We usually disassociate ourselves with the word *police* because of how people usually relate to it. Snobbishness I suppose. Apologies if that's caused any confusion."

Rob felt relieved—Laura had been so smooth, so immediate, so compelling that he hoped his parents accepted her at her word. From their countenance, his mother clearly had, but he wasn't so sure about his dad.

As soon as they drove out from his parents' driveway, Rob virtually leapt down Laura's throat. "How on earth did you know where I was, and how dare you intrude like that!"

"Rob, I'm really sorry. Steven has assigned a protective squad for you so they followed you. I did tell him that you should have been informed, but—"

"Too damn right I should have been told!" Rob interrupted angrily. "And why do I need protecting?"

"A fair question. It's precautionary. Anyhow, that's how we knew where you were, and I came to meet you so we could chat while I drive. I need to bring you up to speed on the last couple of days. Personally, I'm pleased you had the opportunity to relax for a couple of days. It would have been best to let us know that you intended to leave London, though."

"What! I thought I'm a free man?"

"Of course you are. Please, we really appreciate all you've done and have promised to do. You have been and still are brilliant. We just don't want anything untoward to happen, and until matters are nailed down, we don't want to take any risks, which leads to our intended trip, assuming you still want to actively participate?"

"You bet I do," he replied, his tone softening from aggressive to interested.

For the rest of the journey, Laura briefed Rob on the surveillance of the four locations. Eventually, to lighten the tone, Laura informed him that his belongings had been returned from Postojna. As they approached London, Rob recognised that his earlier frustrations had subsided and his intrigue and excitement for the imminent trip had taken a firm grip.

✦✦✦

Later that evening, Rob called his parents to apologise for both the intrusion and having to rush off so unexpectedly. As always, his mother, who had picked up the phone, did most of the talking, and, as was often the case, he partially tuned out for much of it. However, he was suddenly listening intently again as her tone shifted perceptibly.

"Well, it was lovely to see you again, looking so fit and healthy. And Laura seems to be such a pleasant young lady, attractive too."

His mother had paused, clearly expecting him to respond and mental alarm bells started ringing in his head. "Mum, I've already said, there's nothing going on between us. We simply met because of the Slovenian mess."

"Well, give it time, darling. Even if it's inconvenient at the moment, as you say, things will settle down. Both your father and I noticed how the two of you looked at each other. We do know you."

"Oh, mum," Rob sighed.

"And darling, we are both concerned that all this Slovenian business is distracting you from finding another job. Don't underestimate how long it will take."

"You're right, mum, but don't worry, I'm already working on something. I don't want to say anything about it at the moment because I'm not sure how it will turn out yet."

"Oh, that's wonderful, darling. You father will be pleased."

"Anyway, mum, it's getting late, and I have an early start tomorrow."

"Of course. Well, love from us both. Goodnight."

"Yes, goodnight, mum. Love you both lots."

12

The buzzer was shrill in the early morning quiet of Rob's flat, announcing Laura's arrival and yes, Laura would appreciate a coffee before they set off. Rob quickly scanned the apartment, closed the doors to rooms into which Laura would have no need to see, and rapidly tidied up his breakfast things and the pile of post he was still working through. With a final satisfied glance around, he was pleased with its reasonably tidy, lived-in appearance, as opposed to the museum-like neatness of his parents' house. Moments later he opened his door to welcome her in, feeling slightly awkward from her kiss on the cheek.

Over coffee Laura ran through the planned itinerary. Leicester that day and the next, followed by Bradford for a day and finally down to cover the two London locations. Gurning was keen for matters to progress. An early and successful conclusion to this first op would place Burak under pressure to reveal more.

Shortly afterwards they set off, Laura having insisted upon washing up despite the presence of a dishwasher. She gave her opinion by saying dirty cups should not be left for such a long time, leaving Rob feeling suitably chastised, and he wondered if Laura had been speaking to his mother!

Laura guided her car across Vauxhall Bridge, along Park Lane, and out to the A40 before joining the North

Circular round to the M1 motorway heading north. Rob slept during the journey, lulled to sleep by the monotony of the tyres thrumming on the roadway. He woke as Laura turned off the motorway and navigated through the centre of Leicester towards their objective on the west side of Belgrave Road. Having hit the morning's rush hour traffic, the going was slow. As they arrived, Laura pointed out their dual objective and commented on why Leicester had proven more interesting than expected—both premises were on the west side of Belgrave Road, opposite each other across a side street. One was a money exchange, complete with a recently freshened-up facia board, and the other was a carwash.

"Abdul will explain once we are in the flat," she commented.

"Welcome, welcome," a young man announced, opening the door to a small flat overlooking both objectives. He showed them into the living room, where another man was perched on the edge of a rickety chair taking photographs through a gap in the old, yellowed net curtains. "Hey, Stu, our visitors have arrived. Stop pretending you're busy. I'm Abdul, by the way," and he shook hands with each in turn. "Coffee?" he called over his shoulder as he disappeared in the direction of the kitchen. Rob surveyed the apartment, recognising the musty smell and poorly looked after condition of the decorations as being very studentesque, which was logical considering the large student population in Leicester.

Half an hour later, as they took turns viewing the scene through a camera, Stu explained the set up. Abdul had rented the flat and set up a temporary home, with the rest of the team paying regular visits to support the surveillance and Abdul's training. Abdul was the newest and youngest member of the team and had found a part-time job locally to help him integrate into the local community.

The carwash appeared to be a hive of activity, and Stu thought they had identified three targets were, while the rest, including the owner, were merely innocent bystanders, unintentionally caught up in something they had no knowledge of.

Their targets appeared to receive a phone call to inform them of which car to engage with for either a pickup or drop-off. The car would arrive, and the targets would emerge to converse with the driver. Then the driver, as happened with many customers, would enter the unkempt building at the rear of the forecourt to wait while the valets completed their job. On one occasion, a member of Stu's team had managed to time his car's valet with a suspect's arrival, and, while waiting inside, he had watched the suspect driver enter the washroom carrying a heavy bag, followed by one of the targets. When the driver re-emerged, the bag was clearly not as heavy—presumably having completed a switch. They also could not be certain, but were reasonably sure that the targets were up to something inside of the cars. Otherwise, why else would they take personal charge of the in-car valet?

Sometimes, cars were taken inside for the more expensive, full-blown inside-and-out valet, known as "the Extensive." Another of Stu's team took his car through that service and was amazed by the sparkling result. The problem with that service, however, was that the vehicle was out of sight inside a workshop, so any exchange, regardless of size, was invisible to the watchers.

What had become equally obvious was that the trio, as they had become known, did no work unless they had received a phone call. Therefore, when the trio performed the Extensive, it was presumed this was because an exchange occurred—most likely one that could not be disguised in a bag or two. Coincidently, when the trio were involved with the Extensive, there had either just been an intensive period of standard car-washing activity, or one followed immediately afterwards. Later, if there had been a presumed money drop, one or more members of the trio paid a visit over the road to the money exchange-cum-launderer.

"But guys," Rob queried, "the money laundering doesn't make sense. There's all this cash. Surely the money exchange chap has to account for it?"

"Fair question," said Laura. "We don't know in this instance, but very probably the money launder will be a hawala dealer. Before you ask, hawala is widely used by various communities, often Middle Eastern or from the subcontinent, to transfer money around the world. Hawaladars are a network of trusted hawala dealers, often with family connections, or long-standing regional connections. Rarely does the physical money pass between the hawala dealers, thus confounding our concepts of the financial system, particularly because they rarely write things down in ways our investigators are able to understand.

"In this way, money can easily pass throughout a country and across borders, with the hawala taking a nice cut at each turn. We suspect that dirty money will pass through the hands of many hawalas before ending up, thoroughly clean, in the hands of the intended recipient, whether here or in some other country, and whether as cash or as an investment in some construction or other project. The thing is, these guys—and they are guys—can operate wherever with little more than a notepad in which they scribble their own personal code. Here it may be as part of the money exchange, but more often than not it is in the back room of another enterprise in a very informal manner. Some countries have made the practice illegal or have tried to regulate it, although as far as we can tell, to little effect. We haven't come to grips with it in the UK, and if truth be told, I doubt we ever will.

"Steven hopes for a positive consequence from this operation and that this hawala stays in business, but is brought into the fold, so to speak; that he learns to distinguish between the outright criminal and the occasional bit of dubious dealing for a poor family trying to help relations back home. That would be a major result for us."

"Wow," responded Rob. "And I suppose you are referring to the guy over there running a business that is or will become mine and that somehow or another either myself or someone who will work for me needs to persuade him?"

"Spot on," Laura replied, smiling broadly.

"Great, no pressure then!" he said, smiling before returning his gaze to the activities across the road. The next day and a half passed in an expected and uneventful manner, except for a couple of possible exchanges.

Rob was buzzing as they climbed into Laura's car late afternoon on the second day to head off to Bradford. They arrived at yet another anonymous, cheap hotel in time for dinner. Laura had scowled at Rob when, in Leicester the night before, he had suggested that he cover the cost for higher quality lodgings. At that point, Laura had patiently explained that they wanted to blend into everyday life and not draw attention to themselves, unlike James Bond, leaving Rob more than a little deflated.

The next day Laura drove out to Leeds Road Hospital in Bradford, and parked in the visitors' car park. They then walked back, twisting through a variety of residential side streets towards Leeds Road. As they meandered between other pedestrians, Laura initiated a mundane conversation typical of young couples working through the teething problems of starting out life together. She was relieved that Rob easily caught on so no one paid any particular attention to them. On reaching the memorised address, Laura linked her arm through his to guide Rob to the correct doorway and rang the doorbell for a flat above a parade of shops and diagonally opposite the subject travel agent.

Ranjeev answered the intercom, inviting them up to a small but comfortable flat. The setup was very similar to that in Leicester, except only Ranjeev was present in the flat, looking very tired. Recognising Laura's quizzical expression, he sighed and admitted that his partner was unwell and the local branch had not been able to find a replacement to join him. Rob had not seen Laura so angry before as she pulled her phone from a pocket and called in the digression from standard protocol. After giving Ranjeev a dressing down for not having escalated his situation when the local office could not respond, she invited him to brief them.

As expected, his report was uninspiring. There had been a slow but steady stream of people in and out of the travel agency. The frontage was faded but well maintained. As with Leicester, Ranjeev handed over a series of USB memory sticks and flash cards taken from his camera. Laura then stuffed them into a zipped pocket in her jacket. Ranjeev explained that he was certain there had to be a rear exit to the building because a few people, one in particular, had entered through the front door and had not reappeared by closing time. However, despite one sortie and umpteen searches on Google Maps, he had been unable to identify where that exit could be.

Laura scowled at him once again. He really should not be undertaking such enterprises by himself and certainly should not be holed up without maintaining a semblance of normal life, however one defined normal. Ranjeev merely gave an acknowledging 'but what should I do?'-type shrug as he pointed out the arrival of his prime suspect for delivering money to the hawala somewhere in the rear of the shop.

By mid-afternoon, with nothing else having happened, Laura suggested that it was time to leave and head back to London. As they left, Laura assured Ranjeev of how grateful they all were for his dedication and that she would kick up a stink to get him some support just as soon as possible.

Halfway to the car Laura changed the casual, chatty conversation, saying, "Don't look back, but we have company and have had since we left the flat. They're getting closer after each corner. We won't go to the car but will go to the hospital restaurant. I trust you remember the emergency number should we need it?"

"Of course, but I am sure we won't need it."

Two corners later, they came face-to-face with two young Asians and another two approached them from behind. "What you doing back there at that flat?" the shorter, but stockier of the two facing them spat as he squared up to them.

Rob felt his heart pounding and a trickle of sweat dribble down his back as he relaxed his arms and legs in the same way he did prior to any championship fight.

"Visiting a friend in his new home," Rob replied, taking the lead away from Laura.

"Don't believe you," the man shot back, pulling a knife out from behind his back, a signal that the others should as well. "Want to change your mind before white skin turn red?"

Rob didn't hesitate; he spun so fast, sending his right foot slamming into the speaker's nose, that the man had no chance to react. Rob's follow-through was like a whirlwind of action, focused on the accomplice, pummelling him with both fists, first to the face and then to the abdomen. Both men were floored almost instantaneously and left writhing in agony.

Rob approached them cautiously, reaching out to remove the knives from further use. As he reached for the second knife, the man lashed out, catching Rob with the tip, drawing blood across his hand. Rob lurched back, fell onto his behind and kicked hard, sending his right, hard leather heel into the man's jaw. As the man's head snapped back, Rob felt the crunching as his foot passed across the man's face. The man part gurgled from the blood in his mouth and part screamed in excruciating agony before passing out.

Laura, meanwhile, had swung round to face the other two men, who were stunned by Rob's sudden, unexpected, and highly effective counterattack.

One of the men lashed out at Laura with his knife. She ducked and took evasive action, letting out a muffled cry that brought Rob quickly around to her help. As Laura tackled her attacker, Rob approached the other, who immediately turned to flee. Rob gave chase and soon grabbed him from behind. He didn't know the protocol in situations such as this, but he instinctively knew he didn't want this guy escaping and talking to any others. The man twisted and slashed out with his knife, deftly fended off by Rob, with a parry to the forearm. The two circled each other briefly as Rob caught glimpses of faces in windows and heard the reassuring sound of sirens in the distance. Laura was likewise facing her assailant.

"Don't let him get away!" Rob called as his man attacked with a series of wild, vicious swipes and stabs that Rob had no difficultly evading. He soon established the man's rhythm and waited for the opportune moment before catching the man's wrist, twisting sharply and bringing his other hand down hard on the back of the man's elbow. The screech of pain muffled the crack of bone as the arm folded back on itself. Rob then kicked the man's knee from under him, flooring him to leave him writhing in agony on the pavement. That distraction was sufficient for Laura to take her man down with a couple of stinging blows to the head.

"You okay?" Rob gasped as he tried to catch his breath and control his adrenalin while looking around to make sure none of their assailants could slip away.

"Yes. We should wait for the police. I'll call Ranjeev, and you let Steven know."

While Laura was on the phone listening to seemingly endless ringing, she patted down their assailants, relieving them of wallets and various forms of identification, as well as a couple of knuckle-dusters, and scribbled down names and descriptions in her notebook.

Seconds later, three squad cars came tearing down the street from opposite directions. Laura jogged up to the first, even before it came to a halt, ID card held out in front of her. She yelled out Ranjeev's address and that they must immediately go there because an agent was not answering.

As those police tore off, Laura summoned the other police, handed over the items taken from the attackers, and said, "These four men must be detained under the Terrorism Act and not be permitted to see or speak to anyone until MI5 agrees. Get statements from anyone who was watching from the windows and is willing to speak." Fortunately, because she took the initiative, none of the police asked about Rob, despite frequent glances in his direction.

Laura hailed Rob with a wave, "We've got to get back to the office," and she headed off at a brisk walk.

Once they were out of earshot, Rob suggested, "What about Leicester?" Shouldn't they be warned?"

"Yes, good thinking," Laura replied, pulling her mobile from a pocket once more. "Abdul, hi. Is everything okay? Has there been anything out of the ordinary?" Then, after a moment's pause to listen to his response, Laura said, "Good. There's been a problem here in Bradford. Rob and I were just attacked, and Ranjeev is not answering his phone. Can I speak to Stu, please?

"Stu, hi. Bradford has been blown. We don't know how.

Please watch out for any unusual activity and beef up the security arrangements at your flat. Will keep you informed. Yes, that's right. Of course I will let you know about Ranjeev. Okay, bye for now."

Looking at Rob as they continued their march, she said, "This is not what Steven had in mind when he wanted progress. I really hope Ranjeev is okay and that the Leicester guys have not been blown. It will be interesting to see if the money laundering there increases. If so, that should be an answer. I'm confident we weren't tailed before we arrived, so there must have been some sort of counter-surveillance on Ranjeev's flat."

She then looked down at Rob's hand, having noticed that he had clenched his fist around a bundle of tissues. "You're hurt!" she exclaimed.

"Not too badly."

"Well, let me take a look at it once we're back at the car and then decide whether you have to go to hospital. At least we won't have far to go if you do!" Rob merely smiled weakly as the pulsing throb in his hand and the warmth of the blood distracted his thinking from the witty reply he wanted to respond with.

As they continued to walk, Laura said, "After the contretemps just now and the involvement of the police, I suspect that we need to get some sort of identification for you as well. It could become a little awkward otherwise." Then, holding her hand out to ward off the obvious riposte, she continued, "Yes, I know, you don't want to become part of the Service, and I acknowledge that. But some sort of compromise position has to be found. Otherwise you may just find yourself arrested unnecessarily!"

They had reached Laura's car, and she sat him down on the passenger seat as she took out a medical box and opened his hand to inspect the wound. Rob sucked in his breath sharply as Laura dabbed on some antiseptic and started to clean the wound. "You're fortunate; it's long but superficial. It'll be uncomfortable for a while because of where it is, but it shouldn't take too long to heal."

"Thanks. You'd make a great nurse."

"I'll take that as a compliment, but the profession holds no appeal. While I have to know how to do it, I could not face cleaning up wounds day in, day out. I have the greatest respect for both doctors and nurses; they are unsung heroes."

As Laura was about to drive off, the phone rang. "Yes? Oh, hello, officer, what's the status? ... Okay, many thanks, and yes, please place a guard on the door. We will require the space to be sealed off, ready for the forensics."

Rob waited patiently, knowing Laura would fill him in when she was done. Having hung up, Laura sat for a few moments in silence, head back on the headrest, staring at the roof. After a deep sigh, she started the engine and set off at pace back to London, calling Gurning on the hands free to brief him, enabling Rob to listen in and get up to speed.

Ranjeev had been found dead, beaten and viciously stabbed. The flat had been ransacked, and by all appearances, it had been a hasty job. The police had to break into the flat, indicating that Ranjeev had opened the door to his attacker or most likely, attackers. It was assumed that the assailants had left the same way because there was no sign of an open alternative exit. The tone of the conversation was very flat at the loss of a colleague in such circumstances. Gurning expressed extreme anger that Ranjeev had been by himself and consequently did not have a second pair of eyes and thinking to consider the validity and necessity of actions taken or not taken, such as Ranjeev's walk about to look for the rear exit to the travel agency.

After a brief pause for reflection, Gurning changed the subject to Leicester. At long last the members of the trio had been identified and warrants received to monitor their phone calls. Surprisingly, they did not appear to be discarding their phones on a regular basis, like many in the drug business. Since they didn't, it would make it much easier to eavesdrop.

They had also received warrants to enter both premises to conceal cameras and bugs so they could monitor what went on inside. That way, the camera in the flat could be removed, just in case someone had spotted that in Bradford to give the game away. Everything was pointing to the trio using the carwash as a hub for collections and distribution, presumably of both drugs and money. They wanted the cameras in place to find out if there was anything else as well.

With the conversation over, Laura disengaged the call and drove for a while in silence. Eventually, she sighed deeply. "We've got to catch whoever killed Ranjeev. And thank you. I doubt I'd have coped with those four by myself. Well, I know I wouldn't have been able to. I know you've seen the good side to Burak, and I'm pleased that there is one. The problem is the bad, legacy side now has way too much momentum, and sadly, I suspect that more people will lose their lives before this is over. How are you doing?"

"I'm not sure. At least the hand is not too bad. This is still all very surreal. I don't really know what to make if it all. The closeted, rarefied world at the bank did not expose me to such dreadful realities of life. Yes, it was dull, but it was safe. Being so close to so much death and being threatened myself—well, I don't know."

Rob paused, shaking his head, unable to complete the sentence. "I'm relieved I was there to help you. The thing that will keep me going is to try and keep those unwittingly caught up in Burak's enterprises safe. What sort of a man is he? Really deep down I mean. To knowingly and actively encourage activities that will result in other people's death and/or injury is something I just can't conceive."

"Well yes, I can fully empathise with you in that. It took quite a time for me to adjust to this job and even longer when a colleague was first killed during an op—someone I had known reasonably well. I suggest a good dinner and some stiff drinks when we get back to London. My place, that way we can talk openly."

"I'd appreciate that. Hearing of your past and experiences would be interesting and possibly helpful. And after all, you've already seen my place!" With both of them laughing at that last comment, the rest of the journey and evening took on a lighter mood, although the memory of Ranjeev's exuberant face was to remain for a long time to come.

13

The next ten days were a whirlwind of interviews and meetings for Rob to get his business put together. Laura joined him early on for the viewings of potential offices, and they quickly settled for one in Millbank Tower overlooking the River Thames. Not only was it reasonably close to home and very close to Thames House, but the view was also good, and it provided great accommodation. The previous occupier had been a firm of lobbyists funded by some large corporates with deep pockets. The firm had grown rapidly, relocating to larger premises after only sixteen months. They left the fit out, including much of the furniture, that Rob considered eminently suitable for his purposes, thereby accelerating the speed with which his new firm, Zouches, could start occupying the space. Security was also good, thanks to the presence of numerous politically affiliated organisations and at differing times, having formerly housed offices for both the Conservative and Labour parties thanks to its proximity to the Houses of Parliament.

Rob was delighted that everyone he approached to join his enterprise wanted to participate, and he was relieved that he immediately clicked with those put forward by Gurning and Jed. He also secured the services of two assistants to manage the administrative-type matters that come with any and every business. Both of the assistants were pleasant, chatty young women seconded from MI5 who were looking for a new challenge and came highly recommended.

As a typical grey, damp, and drizzly morning dawned, Rob set off for his early-morning run, a habit he had started years ago to fully wake up and think about his objectives for the forthcoming day. He was already deep in thought by the time he exited the maze of tunnels under Vauxhall Cross. Thankfully, his instinctive, lightning-fast reflexes enabled him to leap one of two other runners who collided just in front of him, sending one sprawling onto the dirty, damp ground directly in Rob's path. His leap saved him from ending up on the cold pavement alongside the man. The other runner, apparently off balance, grabbed for Rob, as though to regain balance, but Rob's pace carried him forward, beyond the man's reach. However, whatever was in the runner's hand just caught Rob's sleeve, pulling the threads of his shirt. "Hey! Watch out!" Rob yelled at them, annoyed. He glanced over his shoulder, and seeing both men back on their feet talking, and apparently okay, he continued out of the tunnels, passed a van parked illegally by the roadside and down onto the river path, passing two attractive young women who were also out for a run.

Such a pleasant frontal vision had to be checked out further, so he turned round to run backwards for the rear view—hopefully he would see them again another day! All those thoughts rapidly vanished as he glimpsed the two men with whom he had collided watching him before they ducked back behind a wall. Somewhat perturbed by this, and seeing St George Wharf rising high above their heads on the other side of the road, Rob decided to run a loop around the MI6 building, where he currently was, and circle back to pay Laura a visit, keeping a wary eye open for the two men.

Five minutes later, he was feeling fuzzy-headed as Laura buzzed him up to her apartment. By the time he walked through her door, he was wobbling and dazed, barely able to describe what had happened. Laura immediately had him lie down and phoned for an ambulance explaining all Rob had managed to stutter out and her presumption of a failed, full scrape of contact poison. Then she made a required call to Thames House both to alert the powers that be and also, more importantly, to place the medical services on notice to support, if necessary, the doctors who would attend to Rob at the hospital.

Laura was frantic by the time the paramedic arrived, daubing the now-unconscious Rob with cold water. An ambulance arrived a few minutes later to find the paramedic working hard to keep Rob's vital signs functioning. Rapid exchanges between the paramedic, the ambulance crew, and the Thames House medics on the phone were had as Rob's heartbeat and temperature rose. His eyes were dilated, and his tongue dry, even as sweat poured off his body.

"I've never seen anything like this," the paramedic uttered to the crew, looking bewildered and hoping for some inspiration from the ambulance crew.

The paramedic leaned close to Rob's left ear and spoke clearly. "Rob, I'm a paramedic. We spoke earlier. An ambulance has arrived, and we are going to lift you onto a stretcher to get you to hospital; we'll be as gentle as we can. Hang in there. We'll have you right as rain in no time."

Then, to everyone else, "Everyone ready? On the count of three." Following a series of nods, he continued, "One, two, three," and with that, they lifted Rob onto the stretcher as Laura watched on, very concerned.

Just as they were about to leave, she stopped them. "Hold up, we'll need his shirt for forensic examination. Can we remove it now and cover him with something else? That way it will get to analysis more quickly, and the faster we know what we're dealing with, the better."

"How about simply cutting the sleeve off?"

"That'll do fine. Just don't disturb where the material was cut."

Five minutes later, the ambulance raced to St Thomas' Hospital, and Rob was rushed into surgery.

While Rob was in surgery, Gurning and Laura waited impatiently for news. Gurning called the DG to let him know what had happened and agreed that Laura should be moved to a safe house; there was no way of knowing if Rob had been followed or why Rob had been targeted. This had been a professional hit, so it had to have something to do with the Service.

With that resolved, Laura arranged for one of her female colleagues to go to her apartment, with a couple of guards, to pack her necessities. She felt awkward standing there in front of Gurning giving directions to someone as to what personal items she would require and where to find them, but needs must. The question on everyone's mind was who had attacked Rob and why?

By the end of the day, Rob was conscious again and starting to show signs of a strong recovery. He was in bed in a single room at St Thomas' Hospital with two policemen standing guard outside. Meanwhile, the forensics teams were running numerous tests on some blood samples and on the material of Rob's shirt.

The next day, at the earliest opportunity, Gurning and Laura paid Rob a visit after many hours of anxious waiting. Following the inevitable pleasantries, Gurning took on a serious tone. "I'm pleased to hear that the doctors have given you a clean bill of health, Rob. We suspect that this was an attempted kidnapping and therefore need to keep you under close protection until we get to the bottom of this. You were lucky—very lucky. Once again, your training, instincts, and reactions saved you. If you'd hesitated or even paused to check on the two men, for that matter, the story could have been very different. We're reviewing all CCTV footage and have circulated the images of the two men. I'm sure we will identify them soon."

"Could it be related to Burak and this Emilio chap?" Rob enquired.

"Quite frankly, we don't know at this stage. Another possibility that has to be considered is related to the blown stakeout in Bradford and a cold case Laura worked on a year or so ago. The one saving grace of your visit to Bradford was that Ranjeev gave Laura all of his material. Interestingly, an alert dog walker handed-in Ranjeev's photographic collection of cars, also kept on camera flash disks. It was found discarded a few streets away. Ranjeev was an absolute car nut—not just sports cars but of all models, which could explain a camera looking down onto Leeds Road. We are hopeful that, as a consequence, the attackers have been comforted that the stakeout was not a stakeout at all but was totally innocuous from their perspective.

"This is important because, aside from those tagged by Ranjeev as being of potential interest, our team has identified another person of extreme interest coming and going from the travel agency: Sharif Al Rashid. He's a trusted number two for Mustafa Khartoum, who narrowly evaded capture eighteen months ago as we thwarted an attempted terror attack in London. Other parts of the Service are currently working on intel that Khartoum is planning another attack, so the Bradford connection is of extreme interest. We therefore arranged a re-lamp of all the streetlights in the vicinity and in the process fixed a number of wireless cameras onto the lights overlooking both the front and the back of the travel agency. The good news is that Al Rashid has returned twice, giving credence to our supposition that Ranjeev's cover was not blown."

"As an aside," commented Laura, "the thugs who attacked us are still locked up and not being allowed to talk to anyone."

Gurning then continued once more. "We think Khartoum somehow identified that Laura worked on the op that disrupted his last attempted terrorist attack. We also think he has had folks watching out for her, but not for that long. It is possible that they saw you with her, which is very troubling indeed. Every member of the team has had to up their own personal security as a result. The thing is, taking out an agent does not overly hinder an op focused on terrorist matters. Khartoum knows that. If it wasn't for the project with Burak, code named Network Break, by the way, it would be logical that Laura would work with the same team on the current op against Khartoum. So, if simply removing an agent won't get Khartoum anywhere, what about kidnapping a perceived boyfriend and attempting extortion for inside information? Everything about you suggests that you do not work for Her Majesty's Government, so, on that basis, we assume they pegged you as Laura's boyfriend or at least someone close."

Gurning paused to give Rob the opportunity to take everything in. While the bewilderment in his face was evident, the tension inside and the cold sweat running down his back were not. Rob also wondered whether Gurning had seen him taking the odd furtive glance towards Laura. She was attractive, but then many men took second looks when she passed, so why would Gurning think differently of him. *Grief, am I really up to all this?* he thought to himself for the thousandth time. Both Gurning and Laura were looking at him with a mixture of concern and possibly something else.

"We can come back later if you'd like," offered Laura. "I'm sure you're still tired and this is a lot to take in."

"No. No, I'm fine. Thanks for asking, anyhow. I'm curious—if they'd been following me, as you suggest, where was this surveillance team that you've got watching my back?"

"An excellent question and one I have asked as well. Let's put it this way, there are some folks who are feeling my wrath at the moment for having been way too lax!" Gurning answered. "Anyway, just to be on the safe side, I've decided that both of you are to be relocated to a safe house in west London, Ealing, as a matter of fact. That will provide accessibility for those from Thames House who will need to visit you, as well as for you to get out and meet Burak. Or, Rob, for you to meet your new employees. I bet that sounds strange, 'your employees,'" Gurning repeated with a grin.

Smiling in return, Rob said, "You bet it does. But what about our respective families?"

"That has all been considered, and protective surveillance has been installed for Laura's family. The team covering your family has not gone anywhere, although have been told in no uncertain terms to make sure there are no lapses. Everyone concerned has learned not to let their guard down."

"Thanks," Rob replied. He tried desperately to suppress a growing smirk, but failed dismally, so felt compelled to explain. "My parents are going to just love this. First Laura pays a visit and we go for a three-day trip around England together, and now I'm moving in with her! Mum will make my life a nightmare!"

All three burst out laughing, and after another ten minutes or so of chitchat, Gurning and Laura left and Rob drifted off to sleep.

14

Laura had explained that they were in a long-term safe house, hence the furnishings and general fixtures and fittings being of reasonable standard. Meetings with his own future team were arranged at pre-cleared restaurants in private function rooms. The future office in Millbank Tower was still a construction site and would be off-limits for a while to come, so even if folks weren't working out their notice periods, they wouldn't have been able to start.

On the second day, as they were working alongside each other in a room set up for them to do so, cups of coffee close at hand, Laura gasped, "Oh my word!"

"What's that?"

"It's those two men we heard about on the news—you know, the ones found floating in the Thames earlier this morning. I'm just reading an internal report seeking assistance with their identification. They were both beaten severely, brutally even. Take a look at these mug shots, would you? I'll spare you the photos of their bodies. Fortunately, their faces were spared, to a degree. Steven sent it across because they were both wearing running clothes. It's a hunch, but well, take a look."

"You mean you think they could be the guys who attacked me?" Rob said, shuffling his position to look over

Laura's shoulder. "Absolutely, that's them. But why kill them?"

"Khartoum's way. We know little about him, other than he has a brutal track record and does not tolerate failure. This will be meant as a message to others on his team: succeed or else."

"That's nuts! Surely it'll deplete his team?"

"Unlikely, they'd be non-core and replaceable."

"Is there any news from the stakeouts?"

"Good question. Pull up a chair, I've the reports open and am due on a series of conference calls shortly. You can listen in if you want."

Two and a half hours later, they sat back and looked at each other. "Conference calls like that are far harder than meeting in person," Laura commented. "That was exhausting!"

Laughing, Rob said, "That's life in the private sector, especially when covering multiple geographies."

"Well, I don't know about you, but I fancy lunch. There's a Carluccios just off the Broadway, so not far. How does that sound? The protective chaps will come as well, and I'm sure they'd appreciate a treat."

The reports and conference calls had provided an encouraging update. Matters were moving rapidly, and Laura and Rob would soon have to be springing into action for their respective roles. Rob would head to Leicester to, after the planned raids, provide an assurance to those who were working legitimately. Laura, on the other hand, would be in Bradford trying to piece together what Al Rashid intended. So far, there had been no sign of Khartoum. He had dropped off the radar entirely after the last thwarted attack, and Laura hoped Al Rashid would lead them to him. Everything pointed to an imminent attack, but still there was no clue as to what, let alone where, and nothing untoward had been detected at the London locations. Stress was running high.

The London surveillance had been relatively unexciting compared to Bradford and Leicester but no less revealing. The organised crime teams from Scotland Yard were delighted to have the additional help and a regular flow of information as more and more was uncovered through the days of generally tedious surveillance work.

Rob was shocked as he read through the daily briefings from both locations while holed up in Ealing with Laura. "Sadly, this reflects the daily life for far too many people in our home city," she said. "I couldn't cope with it."

"That's rich coming from someone who specialises in counter-terrorism and the associated atrocities that go with it!" Rob commented, glancing at her to make sure she appreciated he was teasing.

The Pimlico All Hours General Store and Money Exchange in Victoria had a booming trade, thankfully, mostly legitimate and therefore of little concern to Rob as a future viable going concern once the criminality had been expunged. Tails following some drug couriers from Leicester identified that following a few exchanges, a final mule often turned up at the Pimlico All Hours store to avail themselves of the hawala in the rear.

Likewise, the Fonthill Clothes store had not shown any sign of interesting activity to the teams supporting

Steven and Laura. All the same, the surveillance teams had uncovered some very unpleasant criminal activity. Fonthill Clothes occupied three ground-floor units turned into one at the lower end of Fonthill Road in Finsbury Park, close to the junction with Seven Sisters Road. A popular and busy store in the area, trade was brisk. The business manager had an informal arrangement with a hawala who operated out of a rear office, and both appeared to support the other in bringing business in. Land Registry records indicated that the manager had sub-leased the first floor out to two separate organisations. The name on the documentation—Roberto Borzi—was the same for both. Relations between the sub-landlord and sub-tenant appeared fraught at best, each trying their best to avoid the other.

Laura's favourite researcher, David Spalding, had proved his tenacity once again, delighting Laura and amazing Rob with his news when he paid a visit to the Ealing safe house. "It's great getting out of the office occasionally," he said as they settled around a table with cups of coffee. "I know I say that I like the relative safety of Thames House and the routine of my work, but the odd excursion is great."

"Glad you could come, David," Laura replied. "Coffee?"

"Oh, yes please."

"So what have you got for us?" Laura asked, pouring the coffee.

"Nothing much of interest for us. So far as I can tell, but plenty that'll be of interest to Scotland Yard. To think that I've been part of getting one up on them!" he said excitedly. "This Borzi chap runs both a modelling agency and a temp agency, specialising in Eastern European women. Essentially it appears to be a front for people smuggling, prostitution, pornography, and extortion. I can't believe there is any other organisation in Britain with a higher staff turnover rate. Young, mostly attractive women arrive, apparently legitimately and with valid work visas, and then disappear, only to be replaced. Borzi reports the disappearances as the women having simply not turned up for work and their whereabouts as unknown, having left the given contact address. Consequently, he has kept himself on the good books with the authorities.

"The women—I should probably say girls because some are so young—sometimes work for both of Borzi's companies, depending upon the woman's skills and beauty. His clients are not particularly reputable," he handed Laura and Rob a list of those he had identified, and a large majority had an asterisk next to them as an identifier of either a criminal record or as being under suspicion. I've passed details on to the vice team. A few of the girls have been tracked already to various, dubious establishments across the country. A wanted people trafficker has also been identified, and the team is tailing him, hopeful of tracing other locations and women."

Changing tack somewhat and taking a deep breath from having talked so much, David continued. "I suspect Fonthill Clothes can't cover the rent for the entire premises without the income from Borzi. Otherwise, I have no doubt the manager would kick him out at a moment's notice, assuming he's entitled to. Anyway, I've turned up some other information. Fonthill Clothes leased the entire building on the same day as the sub-leases were. The freehold is owned by Templar Real Estate Services, which is, as you know, one of your friend Demir's organisations. Interestingly, Templar

Real Estate Services also owns the Wilton Road premises occupied by Pimlico All Hours as well as the parade in Bradford, of which the travel agency is just one tenant. Additionally, Templar also owns the carwash in Leicester and the parade along Belgrave Street in which the money exchange is a tenant."

"You're joking!" exclaimed Laura. "Burak really does live up to his word that he set out to control as much of his operations as possible."

"What better way to launder the money you're earning in other dubious ways than to own the buildings that you rent to yourself and keep the money in the family, so to speak?" David added.

Rob sat there shaking his head. "How soon can we move in and close those operations down?"

"Steady on, Rob," Laura said. "While we have sufficient grounds to raid Borzi's premises, don't forget, we have a terrorist threat to deal with, and at least some of Burak's network is being used as a cover. The raids can occur after we've nailed Khartoum and Al Rashid. As yet, we have no idea of how extensive an act Khartoum is planning, and that has to take priority, however unpalatable it is to permit the status quo of other activities to continue for a while."

"Understood," Rob said simply, albeit with a great deal of personal difficulty in accepting such an approach.

As they were talking, the London team, led by Brian Jeffries, were debating the previous evening's football and some of the more questionable decisions by the referee. As always, the views were diametrically opposed.

"There was no way that was a penalty," Keith protested. "Your chap, Terry, dived. Clear as day!"

"Utter crap!" responded Andy. "You don't limp around as he did for five minutes if you dive. That was fair and square a penalty. Terry's game was badly weakened after that. "It was!"

"Oh shut up, you two," cut in Brian, "and come look at these guys paying a visit to Borzi. Seems intros are being made."

"How about a draw again to decide which we follow?" asked Keith. "And when are we going to get adequate resource? This is the fourth time we can't tail everyone."

"Keep your knickers on," Brian scolded in a friendly way, indicating he was equally frustrated. "You know the score and the money constraints. This time we take the guy on the left. I've a hunch. He appears to be calling the shots, even at times over Borzi, which is a first. Make sure we get good photos of these guys."

"So far we've only got partials of their backs."

"What!" exclaimed Brian in annoyance. "What about when they entered the place?"

"It wasn't through the front, that's for sure, and somehow or another they evaded the CCTV focused on the rear."

"Right, we get folks stationed to follow these guys, particularly the more senior, the moment they leave. And get photos!"

"Got you. Okay, I'll coordinate with the others. See you later, guv."

An hour later, a dejected team were back in the surveillance room, the two unknowns having slipped through their net without so much as a photograph, leaving Brian to try and re-motivate them. They always responded to energy and action, so he knew what to do. "Right lads, the priority is to get inside that building and understand how those guys gave us the slip. Keith, Andy, how do you fancy a bit of environmental protection work?" he said with a smirk.

They both knew he was up to something but could not fathom what, so they played along.

"Urrrgh!" they grimaced. "Sounds dreadful."

"Well my view is that you get your overalls on and some duplicate IDs sharpish, then with the help of a cover letter I will produce, you go in there to check all sinks, toilets, drains, etcetera, for risk of backing up. Haven't you heard of the problems reported by Thames Water further up the system? That requires the mandatory inspection of basement areas, the whole lot. Otherwise the force of law will come down on them. Got that?"

"Always the glamorous jobs," complained Andy with a grin of enthusiasm. "But aren't we sailing a bit close to the wind on this?"

"Very possibly, but so what! The system has let us down, and we need to know the layout of that place. I don't want any more folks giving us the slip again. You in or do we bottle?"

"We're in!"

15

Meanwhile, Al Rashid had been traced to an unassuming terraced house in Morley, just outside of Leeds, close to the station and the many junctions serving the north-south, the east-west motorway networks, and the Leeds ring-road. The surveillance teams were rotated regularly and constantly frustrated by Al Rashid's total lack of routine, preventing the easy placement of tails to take over one from another. Alerted by his vigilance in Bradford, the team remained away from the terraced house, and when Laura arrived, she based herself in the team's anonymous Bradford base, listening to the numerous communications as they kept their vigil for Al Rashid's next move.

Two days earlier Al Rashid had visited the travel agency and by all appearances had been frustrated with something. Somehow, at last, timing worked in their favour, and an agent was able to walk past the front door just as Al Rashid left, yelling, "In two days!" slamming the door behind him, leaving a concerned-looking assistant behind him.

Now, at 10:25 a.m., from the corner at the end of his street an agent reported that Al Rashid was on the move, getting into his car accompanied by an as-yet-unknown white male. As he turned out of his street, an old Peugeot 205 pulled out from another side street with a young couple inside, call sign Unit 1.

"Target Alpha in sight, two cars ahead, proceeding along Queen Street. Hold on that, Alpha pulling up. Having to pass. Alpha picking up another male, white, unknown. Alpha re-joining traffic behind us, turning left, left, left. No further visual." Shots from the on-board camera mounted in all of the surveillance vehicles were largely blocked by other cars, but everyone craned their necks to try for a glimpse of the new passenger, as though they were there and doing so would provide them with a different angle of the scene and an improved view.

"Unit 1, take next left. Roads will connect. Try to intercept. All foot units take position on street corners to look out," the controller called. "All others hold position." Laura felt quite giddy watching the streamed footage as Unit 1 raced through the side streets, trying to re-connect.

"Foot 3, Alpha has circled round and is passing along home street once more. Turning left, left, left on Queen Street again. Out of visual."

"Unit 4 nearly in position, will pick up." Then, following a few tense seconds of silence, not knowing if Al Rashid had slipped their net, they heard, "Unit 4, have contact approaching turning with Corporation Street. Left on Corporation Street."

Everyone in the control room expelled a collective sigh as the controller explained to Laura that this was one of Alpha's standard routes for starting his journey to Bradford.

"Unit 4, right on Fountain Street." The controller nodded to Laura again. There would be a few minutes as Alpha headed down Fountain Street to Bruntcliffe Road and the motorway.

"Unit 4, Alpha takes left, left, left on Baker Street going at speed. Unable to pursue without blowing cover."

"What the!" exclaimed the controller, studying the map and calmly relaying orders to all units directing cover for the possible exits Al Rashid had. Long, silent seconds ticked by as they waited for news.

"Unit 2, have Alpha emerging into Chartists Way. Will pick up."

Everyone watched the streamed video of Unit 2's progress as they followed Al Rashid, listening to the commentary for added flavour.

"This is not going well," muttered the controller to Laura. "This is the first time we're getting the run-around. Either we're blown or he's taking additional precautions because something's up. Do we stick with him?"

"Yes," replied Laura emphatically. "We must follow, if at all possible without making it overtly obvious, and hope he is simply taking precautionary measures because today is special. If it is, we really must not lose him."

"Unit 2, taking left into the High Street and the one-way system. Will follow."

"Unit 2, Alpha has circled the one-way system. Across roundabout, continuing on the High Street. Right, right, right into Harlington Road at speed. Unable to pursue."

"Damn, damn, damn," cursed the controller. "Potential exits again are limited, which is good for us, but I don't like this one bit. Units, take up positions on Fountain Street, Chartists Way, and motorway junctions. Unit 2, remain where you are and monitor Harlington Road. Report when in position."

To Laura, studying the map in front of her, Al Rashid had simply been going around in awkward circles, getting their units out of position and giving him maximum opportunity to either slip or spot a net if there was one. Why would he assume such tactics unless he either knew of the surveillance or wanted absolute certainty of not being followed?

A silent five minutes ticked to ten and then to thirty. Eventually the controller turned to Laura with a sigh. "We've lost him. He either slipped out of the net or has gone to ground within this area." He circled the Fountain Street, Chartists Way, High Street, and Britannia Road quadrant. "What do you want us to do?"

"Stand down for now, keep roving teams in the area on the off chance. Alert the teams around the travel agency, although I suspect he will be a no-show," she replied dejectedly. "Good effort, though, thank you. He gave us a real run-around and hopefully still doesn't know we've been tracking him." With that, Laura stood and walked off to a quiet meeting room, grabbing a coffee on her way—she had to think.

Should she order a raid on Al Rashid's house? She could see who else was there, if anyone, and find whatever information might be available to point them in the right direction. The thought was very tempting. There was, however, one potentially massive flaw that nagged at her instinct. If, as she suspected, Al Rashid's evasive actions indicated Khartoum was on the verge of a terror attack, then the house had no further purposes and had been abandoned. As an experienced operative, he would not leave anything incriminating behind, other than traps. Therefore, nothing of use would turn up, and Al Rashid would be tipped off and would take additional precautions, which they really did not want. The opposite would be preferable. No raid, then—at least not for now.

A few hours later, a technician monitoring the surveillance cameras popped his head round the door. "Thought you may like these," he said, placing a range of unappetising-looking sandwiches on her desk. "You'll need the sustenance. Also, Khalif, one of the travel agents, hasn't returned from lunch. He usually takes just thirty minutes, but it's been ninety. What would you like us to do?"

Laura didn't bother to smother her groan. She leaned back in her chair and rubbed both sides of her head. After a few moments of contemplation, she responded, "Have someone call in and ask for him to talk about some genuine-sounding travel plan that has supposedly been discussed with Khalif previously. I'd like to speak to whoever makes that call as soon as he or she has finished."

Laura sighed as she watched the retreating back of the young man who had come to break the news. The tension throughout the small office was palpable, and this latest twist did nothing to alleviate it.

Less than ten minutes later, the same young man knocked politely on her door and waited to be invited in. "Come on in. What's up?"

"Well, I made the call you asked for—thought I would since we'd had the conversation."

Laura smiled. She was warming to this unknown member of the team. "I like your initiative. I'm sorry, I don't know your name."

"Talal Fara, and thank you. Not encouraging news, however. Mr Singh sounded frustrated, although he tried to hide it. All he'd say was that Khalif has taken some holiday and will be back after Thursday, whatever that means."

"Oh great. Our leads are disappearing like flies in front of a waving hand, and we're nowhere nearer knowing what they're up to. And it appears that we have three days until whatever happens! I'll speak to London. Thank you, and please let the team know how much I appreciate all your efforts."

Laura called Gurning and patched in Stu and Rob at the Leicester base to update them all on the morning's happenings. "In conclusion, Steven, my hunch is that whatever is intended will take place on Thursday."

"I agree. I'll have Jill dig around to find out what, if anything, official may be happening over the coming few days. Stu, any update from your side?"

"Well, our trio appear to have been busier than usual, but nothing that would raise any alarms. The only matter of real interest has been that they've been visited by the same Range Rover five times now over the past week and a half. Other than that, there have been a couple of guys bringing different cars in on separate occasions. All went for the Extensive, so the cars were out of sight in the one area where we weren't able to gain access to place a concealed camera. If you remember, we mentioned that area of the building is too well secured, and we didn't want to risk leaving signs of an encroachment and tip them off."

"Yes, I remember," Gurning sighed, "and I still agree that your decision was the right one, even though I'd love to know what goes on inside that area. Anything else?"

"Yes, a couple of things. First, as we review footage of the cars going in for the 'Extensive', they generally leave either a lot lighter or a lot heavier laden. That's not drugs or cash. And before you ask, getting a tail on them has failed.

We tried, but they disappeared down circuitous side streets far too rapidly. Second, we have more evidence of the trio making exchanges in the toilets and then visiting the hawala over the road. When they don't visit him, our presumption remains drugs, and we've been able to follow a couple of the couriers to drop-offs with known dealers throughout the Midlands. Unfortunately, we have not been able to follow those bringing the primary supply in, and that's a frustration. Hold on a tick, Abdul's waving."

A few moments later, Stu was back on line. "Two of the trio are on the phone. We can expect to be busy in the next few hours."

"I would love to know what goes on behind those closed doors. Steven, I think we are at the stage of having to act and find out," Laura opined. "We need to either discount aspects from a possible terrorist link or disrupt it, potentially forcing Khartoum's hand in the hope he will make a mistake and we will gain a lead."

"Agreed. Stu, make the arrangements. If we learn nothing by close of the day, you are to go in, making sure you take the trio. Clear?"

"Crystal. Not a problem."

"Good. Ah, here comes Jill with what appears to be news." Everyone waited patiently while Gurning read whatever she had produced. "As always, there's a raft of high-level engagements and activities going on. Jill has already sent a copy to you all by email. They could be focused on any number of places. Laura, please establish what facilities could be a target within a hundred-mile and a fifty-mile radius of Leeds, where Al Rashid appears to have made his base. I'll get the team here to assess what could be going on in or around London in case they're using the Midlands simply for grouping purposes."

"Steven, if I may?"

"Of course, Rob. You're part of the team."

"Well I've scanned the list Jill sent through..."

"Yeah, and oh boy does Rob go fast. I gave up trying to keep pace!" interjected Stu.

"It's just that towards the bottom of the list for Thursday, there's a pharmaceutical conference in the Peak District with both a flag and a tentative against it. What does that mean?" Rob asked.

"Interesting. Hang on, I'll get Jill to pull up the details."

Everyone could visualise Gurning waving to Jill, as was his way, pointing to the entry on the list and waiting patiently as she tapped away at his computer for some more detail.

"I agree with you, Rob. This is potentially interesting," Gurning said a few moments later. "The tentative indicates that there is currently nothing requiring our attention, so it is of note only. The flag contradicts that because—and this is where we should have been informed and what could well be of interest—our Minister for Business and Enterprise, along with many of her European counterparts, could be attending a conference. This is crazy! Two days to go and it's not even confirmed what senior members of various governments are or are not doing! Jill! I want this prioritised!" Gurning called, ignoring, or forgetting those on the phone, nearly deafening them in the process.

"It appears that the CEOs, their COOs and heads of distribution from Europe's top pharmaceutical companies are meeting to discuss the increasing disruptions to the supplies of critical medicines across Europe. Incidences of serious illnesses and deaths have increased over recent months due to the apparent sabotage of the distribution channels, and rightly, this is being taken very seriously. No wonder the various ministers may want to be present. Jill, I want to know why this conference was not explicitly flagged. It certainly meets all the criteria!"

Everyone on the phone pictured the scene as Gurning became more enraged. "And I want to speak to the Minister immediately this call ends. We require her intention to attend or not. She needs to be aware of the security implications of the Service being informed, for her sake and that of her counterparts. This is a travesty! Then I want the DG to speak to Sir Gus MacDonald, as Head of the Civil Service. Right, Laura, pending the Minister's response, I still want you to focus on other possible targets, as discussed. Stu, you are to raid both of the Leicester premises regardless. God help us if we are to secure a conference venue in just a couple of days!"

"Can it be postponed?" enquired Rob.

"Probably not, considering the topic. Blasted politicians—you'd have thought they'd learn, or at least have someone appointed to babysit them properly! Ah, this is the Minister on the other line now. Chop to it, folks, and good luck. We'll speak later." With that, Gurning cut the line.

Abdul and Rob returned to their surveillance, while Stu made arrangements for the raid. Laura, meanwhile, set to trying to identify other potential targets. By the time Gurning had everyone on the phone again a little over thirty minutes later, Laura had identified two. The first was a military research establishment in the Peak District and the other a research and development centre north of

Birmingham and west of Nottingham, supporting GCHQ in Cheltenham. Both facilities should be totally anonymous and highly secure, as well as presenting attractive targets for terrorists.

"Interesting research on possible targets, Laura," Gurning started. "Either could be a target. You'll need to assess both. Jill will arrange for you to visit both. You'll have to figure how you will manage everything. Sorry, it's going to be a pressurised few days. Unfortunately, to add to the burden, we have a very sheepish Minister. Both she and her European counterparts will be at the pharmaceutical conference. She has no idea why it was presented as being tentative because her attendance has been scheduled as confirmed for weeks. To me this is either unacceptable incompetence or something more sinister—something deliberate. Whichever, it will have to wait. I'm arranging for a team to secure the hotel as a matter of urgency. The details are being sent to you all as well. You'll all have to find, as well as follow, all leads necessary to narrow the field to a single target."

"Steven, I appreciate that a witch hunt within the Ministry would distract and take time, but if it was deliberate that we didn't hear about the conference, wouldn't that be a strong indicator of where our attention should be focused?"

"A fair comment, Stu, but there is deliberate and deliberate. There's deliberate to avoid fuss and aggravation on top of a heavy workload, which sadly happens all too frequently. Then there's deliberate to place a person or persons at risk. If that's the case in this instance, it would adversely affect the European health system. Otherwise, why target this conference?! I don't want to discount options too early, just in case this is an instance of lazy deliberate. If it is a sinister deliberate, then any investigation would take more time than we've got. Anyway, how are things looking at your end?"

"All quiet at present. The team is on standby to raid at a moment's notice. I do want to wait to see if either of the calls received by the trio requires the 'Extensive', before pressing the button."

"Okay. That seems sensible. I'll leave you guys to it. Laura, if you leave now, you should be able to assess the military establishment today. Rob, welcome to the deep end of our work. Exciting, but the ramifications are immense. They also cannot be discussed with anyone other than those already in the know. We're all reminded of this regularly, so don't worry, the reminder is not a reflection on you. Keep in touch one and all. Good luck and safe endeavours."

Despite Gurning's assurances, Rob did wonder if he could read minds. Had Michael mentioned that Rob suggested they get together for a drink a couple of weeks back? Oh man, what a life! But time to contemplate that life was cut very short; Stu was tapping him on the shoulder.

When Rob looked out across the street, he saw that the trio were looking agitated and no wonder. A standard delivery or pickup car had just arrived and was parked outside for a more basic wash. Meanwhile, a Ford people carrier had pulled in and positioned itself in front of the roller-shutter door reserved for the Extensive, and Stu was barking orders into his radio to mobilise everyone and initiate the raid. Rob would accompany Stu, who did not want anyone left alone.

16

Upon Stu's orders, two matte black armoured vans with POLICE emblazoned across the sides and front travelled rapidly and silently up Belgrave Road from their holding position and came to a halt, one each at the entrance and exit to the carwash. Police cars followed, and came from all other directions to cordon off the vicinity, blocking the side roads and running tape across pavements to keep innocent bystanders away from the activities at the carwash and money exchange. More police officers from accompanying standard police vans entered the shops in the cordoned-off area, requesting people to remain inside and apologising for the inconvenience.

The rear doors of the armoured vans swung open as soon as the vans were stationary, and armed police, in their dark-blue padded uniforms, flak jackets, and helmets, stormed out. Four approached the money exchange. Two remained at the front door waiting for the signal that the other two were ready at the back door. The others focused on the carwash forecourt and building, some charging around both sides to cover the rear.

A small group of the armed officers quickly entered the waiting area inside the building and, following a confirmatory check of each person there, guided those there outside to a waiting van in the side street. A further group of officers stormed the toilet area to apprehend the one member of the trio who had headed in that direction behind the suspected drugs or money courier. As they burst in, the courier, with head bowed, was in the process of checking the contents of the plastic shopping bags handed to him for stuffing into his own large brown holdall. Immediately the trio member shoved the courier hard in his chest, sending him sprawling into the oncoming police officers, a flurry of bank notes flying into the air as a result.

The trio member raced in the opposite direction, flinging yet another bag at the officers, covering them in a heroin powder, making the officers grateful for their masks, which protected them from inhaling the stuff. Having lost ground, all but one of the officers set off in pursuit, seeking the exit taken by their quarry. One remained behind to drag the courier outside in handcuffs.

Meanwhile, Stu, Abdul, and Rob had entered the waiting room and looked around the spacious area. While not designed for comfort, it was certainly pleasant enough, with a reasonable-sized confectionary, car parts and accessories shop off to one side. Two televisions, one with the BBC News Channel and the other with a cartoon network, were placed high on the wall in opposite corners. As they looked about themselves, a burst of gunfire sent them scurrying into the shop area for cover.

The rest of the armed officers had tackled the enclosed valet area. Two stood guard outside the vehicular entrance, having earlier decided that access that way would be futile. Instead, they forced their way through the heavy, well-secured internal side door. The inevitable noise alerted the other two members of the trio, giving them sufficient time to arm themselves and dive behind various crates at the rear of the oversized garage.

The driver of the Ford people carrier, on the other hand, jumped into the driver's seat and started the engine, the boot still wide open with a couple of long cases sticking out of the rear. Moments later, he rammed the car into the closed doors, reversed, slammed into some mobile equipment racks and sent them spinning in all directions, spilling the contents over the floor. Accelerating forwards once more, the car crashed through the doors, debris from the frame and surrounding brickwork flying in the wake of his attempted escape.

A few rapid and well-placed shots into the tyres from the two police officers outside, coupled with the blocked exits, put paid to the driver's escape. Moments later, staring up the barrel of a sub-machine gun, the driver was hauled roughly from the car and shoved onto the ground before being cuffed and led away.

The gun battle inside the garage had settled down to a periodic exchange of fire as the officers repeatedly called out the standard warning of, "Armed police, you are surrounded. Lay down your weapons, come out with your hands above your heads, and lie down on the floor."

Each time, in response, the two members of the trio squeezed off a few more rounds from behind the steel crates where they had based themselves. Following a radio exchange with Stu laying out the scene and situation, the officers were advised to secure the area and position themselves safely to establish a siege, minimising gunfire to avoid unwanted injury. The objective was to take these two alive. They were too important and could hopefully provide useful information to understand what Khartoum was planning, when, and where.

The team following the other member of the trio pursued him through a doorway, along a narrow corridor, and up some open-sided timber stairs, leading up to a mezzanine floor. As he ran, the man produced a handgun from his clothing and sent a couple of wild shots slamming into the concrete block walls. The police followed cautiously, crouching low as they emerged on the mezzanine floor, just in time to see the man, now accompanied by two others, each gripping larger firearms taken from lockers lined up along one side of the otherwise open but cluttered space, exiting through a hatch in a side wall. Disappearing through the gap, they fired wildly over their shoulders—sending the other few occupants scrambling for cover behind benches and chairs, screaming in alarm at the gunshots.

As the officers shouted at these folks to stay down, they made their way across the floor to the hatch. Suddenly three shots rang out. Two of the four officers fell to the floor, one unmoving. The other, groaning loudly in pain, rolled away, seeking cover. The remaining officers flung themselves aside, rolling to end up in a crouched position from where they both fired well-placed rounds to the head and chest of a new gunman, killing him instantly.

While covering the other people to avoid further ambush and keeping a wary eye on the hatch, one of the two officers radioed Stu. "Urgent assistance required on the mezzanine! Two officers down, one in need of medical attention. Guarding five unknowns, presumed standard employees, with a further assailant dead. Trio target plus two others at large, escaped towards rear of building in the roof area."

During the radioed report, the other unwounded officer shuffled in a crouched position over to his fallen colleagues, keeping his gun levelled and pointed towards the five workers. After confirming that the first colleague was dead, he continued over to the other to rest a hand on his arm.

"Hang in there, mate. Help's on the way. We downed the bugger that got you."

"Heard," responded Stu. Then to the others in the garage he said, "Need the team split. Half maintain position and secure the siege status to keep the trio two in place. Expect them to test resolve as they see forces leave. All others are to assist officers upstairs. Go!"

A group of four broke away from the garage and headed cautiously to the mezzanine. Stu and Abdul readied their own weapons and hailed the two officers from outside to support them now that the Ford driver was in custody.

Minutes ticked by as near silence fell across the building and the group of four worked their way to support their colleagues, checking that the end of the corridor was secure before climbing the stairs.

Across the road at the money exchange, the four officers entered the building, two from the rear, two from the front. As expected, the business manager and hawala were both present, chatting to each other from across the room. Their eyes opened wide at the sight of the armed police. A rapid glance around the shop, which also acted as a card store and stationers to attract a greater flow of business, confirmed the pre-raid reports that no one else was present, at least at ground level. Giving no resistance, the two elderly men accompanied one of the officers outside for a quick search before joining the others who had been safely evacuated from the carwash.

The remaining three officers rapidly went from room to room, first covering the remainder of the ground floor and then slowly went upstairs. They eased the first of the closed doors off the landing open, senses on high alert following the initial burst of gunfire they heard moments earlier from across the street. Gradually, thoroughly, they worked through the upstairs flat, not letting their guard down one iota as regular reminders of the unexpected dangers of raids were heard from across the road as sporadic gunfire continued to rattle out. Finally, they eased the hatch open that led to the roof space, wary from the signs of regular use. Using a ladder propped up against the wall, the first of the officers mounted the steps. The flashlight atop his weapon illuminated the space, the beam of light slicing through the darkness, seeking out any potential threat. His relief was evident as he announced, "All clear. The space is empty, but there's an opening between buildings that leads all the way along the terrace."

A few minutes later, he and his colleagues emerged at the far end of the terrace, back at street level, having followed and cleared all of the roof spaces and the presumed route taken by those who had not been observed re-emerging from the shop. Having completed their task, the four officers jogged briskly back towards the carwash to support their under-fire colleagues, who were facing far greater challenges.

The team of four reinforcements emerged on the mezzanine to take over from their colleagues. Three stayed behind while one accompanied his colleagues back out of the building, covering them as they carried the wounded officer to a waiting ambulance.

Having helped their wounded colleague, they combined forces with the four coming back up the street—their objective to go through the hatch and flush out the missing member of the trio and his two unidentified companions. Opening the hatch, they went in, surprised by the amount of light pouring in through the roof lights. In pairs they worked their way along a series of narrow metal walkways covering the remainder of the roof void. Try as they might, they couldn't stop the loose metal sheets from clanking with every step, preventing any chance of stealth. As they peered around the corner of the wall to locker and break room, a single shot twanged off a steel roof truss beside one officer's head. The other officers all dived onto their stomachs, craning their necks to try and spy their quarry and identify where the threat came from.

Suddenly there was a deafening boom, the noise reverberating throughout the building. Clouds of billowing grey-white smoke rapidly filled the space as dust and other debris from the roof filled the air, disorienting the officers. The explosion's lingering ringing in the officers' ears partially covered the cracking and crunching sound of masonry, wood, and plasterboard. The rapid-fire radio conversation that ensued confirmed that no one could determine the direction from which the sound came. With such poor visibility, it was going to be slow work worming their way along the narrow walkways on which they found themselves.

Stu, Abdul, Rob, and the two armed officers with them looked around in horror at the sound of an explosion above their heads, instinctively ducking as ceiling tiles and debris poured down upon them. Caught by surprise, they found that, with the debris, the one trio member and his two new colleagues had dropped through the ceiling, landing nimbly on their feet, spraying bullets all around. Abdul and the two armed officers fell, wounded, taking a number of bullets in their arms and legs. Rob and Stu rolled for cover, Stu opening fire. One of the injured officers, who had been chatting to Rob, shoved his weapon over to Rob, grunting in pain with the effort as he sought cover.

A second explosion, coming from the garage, rocked the building as the three men dropped in from the ceiling. This second blast blew a hole through the outer wall of the building enabling the previously trapped trio two to send a hail of bullets throughout the garage as they fled the space. Escaping through the hole, they ran down the side street, away from Belgrave Road. As they raced passed the rear of the building, the second man was hit firmly in the belly with the butt of a police officer's firearm who had been guarding the rear for just such an eventuality. The man doubled over in agony, breathless and unable to move. The leading member of the trio swung round, spraying bullets as he did so, but another officer dropped him with two well-placed bullets to the chest. The writhing trio member on the ground was rapidly disarmed, searched, and cuffed by the officers.

❖❖❖

Stu and Rob found themselves separated at opposite ends of the car accessories shop, heads down, peering around themselves. Stu waved to Rob that the three hostiles were in front of them and two aisles away. A spanner clattered across the floor as Stu and the remaining trio member exchanged fire.

Rob ran, crouching, to the next aisle and came face to face with the other two hostiles, who had quietly closed the distance to Stu and Rob. Taken by surprise, they swung their weapons up to fire at Rob, who first flung the firearm he was holding at their faces and then dropped backwards onto his hands and kicked up at their faces. Startled by this unexpected tactic the two men staggered backwards to avoid being hit. One dropped his gun as he stumbled on some screwdrivers and other tools spread across the floor. The other tried to squeeze off some shots at Rob, but was left frustrated as his weapon jammed. Both grabbed some stainless steel exhaust tubing from a nearby rack as new weapons, more suited for close-up combat. Flipping himself upright as though a gymnast, Rob found himself between them, ducking to avoid the first few manic onslaughts of swinging pipe, which clanged loudly on the metal shelving as each narrowly missed Rob's head.

A further exchange of gunfire rang out as Rob heard messages in his earpiece informing everyone that, of the trio members from the garage, one was dead and the other apprehended. At the same time, Stu was desperately calling for assistance, horribly aware that three of his men were down leaving Rob and himself to fend of three assailants!

Tense moments followed as the two on either side of Rob squared up for the next assault, waving their pipes in the air menacingly. Reading the moves correctly, Rob ducked the attack, grabbed a piece of cloth from a shelf and held it up to dampen the next incoming swing from one of the pipes. Wrapping the cloth around the pipe, Rob twisted sharply, sending the pipe flying from the attacker's hand and clattering onto the concrete floor a few metres away, out of harm's way. Totally surprised, the man stumbled forwards and off-balance from Rob's move. He immediately received a well-placed kick to the solar plexus, sending him crashing into some shelving before slumping to the floor, loose items from the shelves raining down on top of him.

Yet another exchange of gunfire followed, and Stu's voice rang out loud above their heavy breathing. "Assailant down!" Having winged the man, sending him spinning, Stu had quickly followed up with two shots to the man's chest that flung him backwards into the shelves.

While not used to fighting people with steel piping, Rob was in his element, so not to be left out, he in turn yelled, "One down, one soon to follow!" He grinned at his opponent and took up his standard fighting position before launching a series of wicked and rapid kicks. The man quickly saw sense and dropped the pipe, held his hands up in submission and knelt on the floor, just as Stu came around the corner, gun up and levelled, ready for action.

Stu quickly assessed the situation, cuffed the kneeling man, and then cuffed the other, who was still curled up in agony from Rob's kick.

As Stu pulled them up, ready to be led from the building, he turned to Rob with a broad grin. "Laura said you were useful in a scrap. I wish I had seen the action for real. I've watched a few of your championship bouts on *YouTube* and they were impressive, but I suspect the real thing is something to behold. Well done!" He clapped Rob on the back. "I think we're done."

Then, picking up his radio, Stu repeated his call for urgent assistance for Abdul and the other two officers, one of whom, despite the pain, commented, "I did see the action, and boy, it gave me some real pleasure!"

As they walked out into the sunlight, Stu turned to Rob. "Great work, Rob. A real pleasure working with you. This was a tough one. I want to follow Abdul and the chaps to hospital to check up on them. However, you still have some work to do. Let me introduce you to the local Community Police Officers as they'll take you to the holding area for all those who've been working here and as far as we can tell are legitimate. These people know the CPOs, whereas we need to retain anonymity. The CPOs will introduce you so you can explain whatever it is you need to about what's been going on, the transfer of ownership, and hopefully obtain their allegiance. Good luck."

"Thanks, Stu. I've learned lots." With that, they shook hands and Stu made the introductions and left.

An hour and a half later, Rob felt exhausted. The adrenalin from the operation had worn off, and for the past sixty minutes he had been chatting with the impacted people in a rapidly commandeered hall nearby. The change of pace from a raid situation to one where he had to depend upon his wits, his best influencing skills, and blending a carefully balanced combination of charm, reasonableness, and firmness had been challenging.

Initially he had addressed everyone, saying that the previous owner of the buildings was also part owner of their businesses. This, he explained, had been achieved through a network of offshore companies so that it was not clear the same person was involved. That person was now in police custody for criminality, and all assets, including the buildings and the part ownership of their businesses, had been transferred to Rob's company, Zouches. This was because that same individual was a much-wanted international criminal who had abused his position as part business owner to funnel criminal activities through their businesses.

This represented a new approach by the government, as proposed by Rob, to support those impacted by crime through no fault of their own. The objective was to keep the businesses running and people employed. It would be Rob's job, together with his team, to support their businesses going forward, to help re-build where necessary, and to assist developing new business to replace any that was lost as a result of closing down the criminal elements.

He emphasised that he was totally independent of the government, and therefore, so were they. That was why there were no government representatives at these meetings and why the Community Police Officers had left after making the introductions. Their presence at the start was simply to provide an assurance that Rob was legitimate.

Following that, Rob met separately with the two business owners and the hawala to reiterate his support for legitimate enterprise and that they were not currently under suspicion. He explained that there would have to be the inevitable checks to confirm this presumption, and he hoped they would understand. Only then could the police, other agencies, plus Rob and his team support them and vouch for their integrity, helping to rebuild reputations that very possibly would have been tarnished as a result of today. After that, they would not see any interference from the police or the government. These institutions respected that communities throughout the country did not want interference. His firm, likewise, would not interfere. They would merely take an active interest in how their business was progressing and assist when appropriate. They, the people in front of him now, were responsible for running their businesses.

During that second part of the discussions, as confidence in Rob grew, all three mentioned their unease at the involvement of the trio and the other three men who had not previously been identified by the surveillance. Their attitudes had been threatening, but the owner's representative had introduced these men and required their employment within the carwash business. He had also insisted upon cooperation by the money exchange and hawala as part of the deal to provide the initial start-up investment and accommodate their respective businesses. This representative, they explained, held a lot of influence over them because he had a Power of Attorney to sign documents, collect a share of the profits, and provide additional investment or not, as well as introduce new business, or not.

Rob referred to the arrangements each had with respect to the profit sharing and cooperation drawn up as part of that initial investment. As far as Rob was concerned, the type of cooperation that had been required previously was history. The only cooperation he expected was in terms of sharing relevant information on the health and progress of the businesses and agreeing a business plan for them to work towards in the future. Update meetings and board meetings could be held either at the premises or at a hotel in central Leicester. The choice was theirs.

All Rob wanted from them at this stage was two things. First, he wanted them to agree when they would meet again to discuss taking the businesses forward. Second, he wanted a copy of the Power of Attorney they had mentioned. Both were promised.

Later that evening, and at last in the comfort of a decent hotel after a healthy dinner and a glass of wine, Rob updated Gurning and Laura. As he finished, he assured Gurning that as soon as he had copies of the Power of Attorney, he would send them through for further investigation.

17

As the raid on the Leicester premises had unfolded, Laura was in her car heading south to the first of her destinations: the military research establishment in the Peak District. She had listened anxiously to the escalating events in Leicester, desperately wanting to be where the action was, providing whatever support she could to those engaged in the operation. She felt partially responsible, so not being there was odd. She was also acutely aware that she was too far away, had a vital task to perform, and quite possibly would simply get in the way.

Likewise, she also knew she should not try to make contact with any of her direct colleagues—Stu and Abdul, or even Rob—to check on their safety, however desperately she wanted to. They would be far too busy to take a call, particularly if the reports of gunfire were correct.

Late in the afternoon, having at last relaxed sufficiently to enjoy the drive through some beautiful parts of the Peak District, Laura slowed down as she meandered along a narrow, twisty, one-way lane. The directions, which she had been required to commit to memory, had provided that after the seventh corner there would be a very narrow, obscure turn to the right. The appearance was one of a passing point, which for a one-way lane was not required. She was to pull in at that point and then reverse a car length to the hedge behind, at which point a further opening would become obvious. She was to then drive slowly along that new track, ready to stop at any time if challenged. She should expect up to five checkpoints before reaching the security gate and fence. At the gatehouse she was to ask for General Marshall-Jones, who was expecting her but did not know the reason for the visit.

Following the directions explicitly, she found the way—just. Laura marvelled at the cunning simplicity of the disguised track as she drove along slowly and was challenged just once, although she did see the other checkpoints because they made their presence known. If it hadn't been for that, there was no way she would have spotted them—she was clearly expected.

Whatever it is that goes on here, not only is it well guarded, but by association, it must be an attractive target, assuming it has been identified in the first place, she thought as she arrived at the gatehouse. But for her trained eye, it appeared to be an averagely maintained cottage in the middle of nowhere; however, she identified some serious firepower at various concealed places in the walls. Ten minutes later, she arrived at the main house, accompanied by an armed escort wearing civilian clothes, driving a Range Rover. The mansion was breath-taking, a perfect hideaway for the wealthy with its immaculately manicured lawns.

Another armed escort, again in casual clothes, materialised at the front door as the Range Rover returned from whence it came. "Ma'am, please follow me. The general is expecting you."

As Laura obediently followed, she tried not to gawk at the magnificence of the place, feeling completely underdressed for such stunning surroundings, with a grand staircase leading from the large, stone-floored entrance hall with portraits of various people hanging throughout on the wood-panelled walls. As she looked about her, she did spot some CCTV and movement sensors and was sure there were more she had not seen. Laura was shown into a library and waved to a set of chairs and sofas. "Please take a seat. The general will be with you shortly. Would you like a tea or coffee?"

"Just some water, thank you."

The escort produced some bottled water from a sideboard with a small fridge inside, placed the tray in front of Laura, and left.

"Miss Grahams, I presume?" came a commanding voice from behind her. She turned to find that a powerfully built man in his late fifties had materialised silently through the wall. *Presumably there is a secret door somewhere in the wood panelling,* Laura decided.

"And no doubt a cover name for a lady in your line of work," he said, smiling. "I'm General Marshall-Jones. Pleased to meet you—on the basis that I have to. Please, do sit. I can't say I'm at all happy to meet you. I'm surprised your organisation even knows about the place."

The general was smartly dressed, with a dark blue roll-neck shirt, trousers, and blazer. His comportment and presence were such that one's attention was immediately grabbed. Laura had met many powerful and commanding people in her time, but this was different. The general was the real thing.

"We didn't, not even the DG. It required some digging," Laura said, refocusing herself so as not to be overawed.

"Ah, then you'd better explain just why you were digging, my dear, and how your digging identified this facility," the general asked in a kind yet demanding manner. "As you may imagine, I am not best pleased that outsiders are able to find out about our existence, let alone our location."

"Well we're extremely confident there's going to be some sort of terrorist incident within the next few days, quite possibly Thursday, somewhere in this region. However, we have no pointers yet on what the target may be. One of the key suspects was able to give us the slip earlier today, and we have raided a facility in Leicester this afternoon. You'll hear about it on the news, if not already, because there was gunfire and some explosions."

"Hmm, yes. It's been flashing across all the newswires imaginable. Caused quite a stir by all accounts."

"No surprise there, then. Well, to answer your question, at least in part, our systems are designed to perform deep searches under specific circumstances. However confidential the matter, it will be registered in the system but only accessible under certain circumstances and provided that appropriate authorities are obtained. Your facility was identified following one such search and was flagged as one of the three possible targets. My purpose today is simply to meet with you and firstly assess your security and secondly the likelihood of your facility being the target. May I ask what happens here? That was not recorded on our system."

"Delighted to hear that no one can simply dial us up, and sorry, no, I'm hardly going to enlighten you with any detail, merely a smidgen to whet the appetite, so to speak. I'm sure you'll get the same from other sources. What we do here is not done in the house; my ancestors would turn in their graves. Yes, this is my ancestral home. Nor would our business be visible from the sky. From that I'm sure you can figure something out, what!" The general guffawed at his little witticism.

"For all intents and purposes, I'm some oddball former military buffoon living out my years in my ancestral home. It was previously left to decay somewhat, but I came into the money and did it up. There is the formal driveway that I use, but I have left it unmaintained to actively discourage curious visitors. Clearly, to maintain some sense of life, I do have the occasional visitor and I even open the house and gardens for the village fête. I also take a periodic trip into the village at the end of the drive to show myself and spend a little money, but that's about it.

"When I had to take on a desk job, I pressed for one of my specialties to be taken more seriously. Got nowhere initially, what! But by gum, it wasn't for the sake of trying! However, after some of our more recent international engagements kicked off, the armed forces asked me to research my ideas. That was because it became clear I had indeed hit upon something. We needed somewhere secret to develop the idea. I suggested this place. The rest is history, as the saying goes. There are no relatives for me to leave the place to, so I'll form some sort of trust to maintain the balance of stay away, you're not welcome unless invited, with being semi-amenable to the locals, while ensuring the highest level of security to continue with the on-site activities.

"If you'll allow me," the general said, standing up suddenly. Laura got a sinking feeling that she was about to be dismissed and would have to kick up a stink. "If you follow me, I'll show you my security audit room. I developed it for military audit purposes, so the arrangements can be checked without giving anything away about the place. We don't want some bureaucratic auditor spilling the beans now, do we? That should hopefully give you a sense of comfort."

I already have it, thought Laura.

"That said, I will raise the alert status until the weekend. It'll be a good exercise for the chaps, what! But I would appreciate a call when the threat has passed."

"Not a problem. Of course I will."

"Oh, and Miss Grahams, I presume you will require somewhere to spend the night. You're very welcome to use one of the guest rooms and save the Services some money. You'll bump into all manner of other folk here over dinner and breakfast, but please respect the code of this place. Conversations are actively discouraged."

"A room would be wonderful, thank you. I haven't even had the chance to think about sleep, let alone food. Presumably I can make calls from my room?"

"Absolutely. You'll find it far better equipped than most hotels. All recorded, of course, so make sure you don't say anything you don't want overheard."

An hour later, following a very engaging explanation and question-and-answer session on the facility's security, Laura found herself in a luxurious suite with fabulous views over the grounds. She put in a quick call to Gurning to update him, giving him her instinctive assessment.

"In conclusion, Steven, this facility would be an excellent target, disrupting our research into our next-generation attack and defence capabilities, all of which are of a technological nature that many parties, including terrorists, would love to get their hands on, if they knew about it.

"Apparently, in the hands of any other organisation, Britain would be at great risk. That aside, a successful attack on this place would also be a tremendous coup, as well as providing a huge propaganda opportunity. However, unless there has been a leak and serious breach of security, this place is unlikely to have been identified. Also, if it is the target, they'll be more than able to look after themselves. Therefore, my recommendation is to consider this a target, but focus our efforts elsewhere until such a time, if it comes to it, that all other options are discounted.

"I also somehow suspect that the general would not be at all enthused by the idea of having an additional layer of security foisted upon him for three simple reasons. First, the security here is the best I've ever come across. Second, the number of people becoming familiar with the place would in itself be a weakening of security in his eyes. Third, a greater presence would undoubtedly draw more attention to the place, detracting from the anonymity that is currently enjoyed."

"For now I'm happy to go along with your logic and recommendation, but I will want to reconsider the position after your assessment of the next possible target tomorrow," Gurning replied with a sigh. "Have a good night's rest; you'll need all your energy over the forthcoming few days."

18

First thing the next day, Rob joined Stu at the carwash with some more members of Stu's team.

"Okay, folks, listen up," Stu called over the chitchat, seeking silence and attention. "Clearly we are going to focus on the garage after the guns that were found in the Ford people carrier and the explosives those guys used to blow their way out through the wall. However," he emphasised, "I repeat, however, we need to go through the whole place with a fine-tooth comb. Remember, weapons were taken from the lockers upstairs, and there could well be other locations used to store or even split up their merchandise. We must not lose sight of the initial brief indicating that there is a concealed room in the roof for drugs. Any questions?"

After a moment of silence, Stu finished up with, "You've got your pre-assigned teams, so let's do it."

The teams of men dispersed for their assignments, leaving Stu and Rob to wander around checking on progress. The long crates from the Ford had been taken away the evening before for security reasons after they had revealed two sniper rifles, complete with a substantial amount of munitions, not only for the two rifles. That find had created an air of expectation for the teams.

Rob watched on from the side-lines as two teams in the garage started unpacking many more boxes of munitions of various sizes and types and then started carrying the contents to armoured vans outside, ready to whisk the items away for further examination. Seeing Rob's interest, Stu walked over to explain.

"We will take the finds to a secure facility ready for tests prior to subsequent disposal. We really hope something will indicate the source of this stuff. Often the manufacturing process will leave little hints for us to follow, provide a trace to an initially legitimate-sounding purchase that ultimately was a cover. Alternatively, we may find that it was siphoned off from a larger consignment. Knowing this detail could help trace the financiers, the locations, and even those involved."

"Stu, over here," a man called, waving. "We've got explosives here, with components for timers and some grenades."

Rob wandered off, not entirely comfortable with his proximity to so much destructive power. Walking across the otherwise-deserted mezzanine floor, he received an enormous fright, jumping back in surprise and shock as the scattered, overturned chairs and small tables also bounced on the slightly bouncy vinyl-covered wooden floor. As he had been walking past the row of lockers, one section just in front of him toppled over with a huge crash, sending a cloud of dust into the air. A couple of heads then materialised from a concealed opening where the lockers had stood. Half-laughing at Rob's expression and half looking rather sheepish, two officers emerged to apologise at the shock created.

"Sorry about that, although your expression was priceless, well worth the racket! Well at least we now know where they split and diluted the drug consignments. A veritable factory in there," he continued while signalling behind him with his thumb. "This was a massive operation.

Moments later Stu was at Rob's shoulder, breathing deeply from his sprint to find out what the noise had been all about. "No more of that please!" he barked. "We're not sure yet that all of the explosives downstairs are stable!"

"Come on, guv," one of the men replied, "the whole place would have gone up ages ago if anything was unstable."

"Yeah, yeah, okay," Stu conceded. "Just be careful, okay. So what's up?"

"Come have a look. If we find any CCTV, I want a copy of Rob's expression and reaction. Guv, you should 'ave seen him."

"Okay, okay, now budge over and let's have a look."

They all squeezed through the narrow opening into what appeared to be a dead-end corridor the entire length of the mezzanine floor. It was fitted out with a full-length smooth vinyl worktop, a number of chairs, scales, and other drug paraphernalia. Everything was rudimentary but perfectly functional. There was a stockpile of various drugs at one end, and at the halfway point, there were various powders all neatly labelled and ready to mix with and dilute the stocks of far higher purity drugs that the trio had accumulated. Incongruously, and wholly unexpected, at the far end were a number of piles of gold in a variety of forms. There were rings, ear studs, and a surprisingly large pile of shavings. Next to the gold were some more scales and various items for melting the gold, ready to pour into the moulds all neatly lined up against the wall.

Stu whistled a few expletives before ordering, "Right lads, let's have loads of photos, and then bag and label all this up. Then keep on searching. Oh, and guys, good job."

By lunchtime the search was over, so the forensics folks could have the place to themselves. Rob surveyed the haul of weapons, explosives, drugs, gold and an odd assortment of other items found in the packing crates at the rear of the garage, amongst which were garden forks and spades, a large number of golf balls, and colourful back sacks. The team milled around, joking about the assortment of items as Stu checked the inventory before clearing everything to be removed.

At the same time as the Leicester team started their searches, the London team were drinking coffee and drawing lots on which regular Borzi customers would turn up that day and who they should follow. After the first few tails, to break the monotony of an otherwise straightforward surveillance op, the team soon realised that many of the regular visitors had something to hide and were building quite an extensive dossier for further examination by other agencies. However, they could not follow everyone at the same time.

"Ah, the young, smart, nervous chap is back," said Keith, not taking his eye from the camera. "Take a look. He appears more apprehensive than usual today."

"Agreed," came Alan's reply not long afterwards. "As the saying goes, 'First come, first served.' Let's follow him. Not quite 08:00 hours. It'd be interesting to see where he works and if any of Borzi's ladies are there, or at least find out the connection. This chap's been here, what, six times now?"

"Five," Keith corrected, looking at his list. "Surely this guy is too young for anything significant, and while presentable, the cloth is certainly not of the quality worn by many of the others and this chap doesn't have the same swagger either. Why not wait for another?"

"That's what makes him interesting. I've a hunch. Contact reference will be Delta."

Ten minutes later the young man re-emerged and walked directly to Finsbury Park underground station, with Wes easily keeping up with his long-legged, casual strides. Taking the first southbound Victoria line train towards central London, along with many hundreds of other commuters, Wes had to join Delta in the same compartment just to keep him in sight. *Far from ideal*, Wes thought to himself as Delta looked around at his fellow travellers, eventually letting his attention settle on an attractive young woman sitting not far from him. He got out at Green Park. Delta then headed north into Berkley Square and up the west side of the square. Shortly afterwards Wes called in for support.

"Control, I need support with this tail. Delta has walked right around Berkley Square and is now heading back south out of the square. This is not going to be easy. He eyeballed everyone in his carriage, so he could well spot me."

"Onto it," responded the team's controller.

"Thanks. Now cutting through an alleyway beside the Holiday Inn towards Dover Street. I'm exposed, too few other people around." A few minutes later, Wes called again. "Back on Piccadilly heading west. Went east on Stafford Street and south on Old Bond Street. Now heading into Green Park."

"Okay, Wes, stand down, but hold position to monitor progress from a distance, just to make sure Delta does not cut back again. Others will pick him up at the other exits to the park."

"Control, I've got a visual. He's approaching the Mall," a woman radioed a few minutes later.

"Okay, Marjorie, Delta is yours."

"Thanks. Delta has sat down on a bench and is making a poor show of reading a paper while looking around at all the people. Good job Wes held back. I'll need to pass on to Paul. This guy is clearly agitated and concerned about possible tails, or is looking out for a meet."

Five minutes later, Paul reported in. "Delta is on the move, heading into St James Park."

"I'm on Birdcage Walk and will pick-up."

"Thanks, Marjorie," responded the controller.

"Have visual again. Delta's looking around. Heading east and has cut through to Old Queen Street heading towards Storey's Gate. Damn it, he's turned into Matthew Parker Street. I'll be blown soon."

"Okay, drop back or go into a building. Paul, pick him up on Tothill Street please."

A few tense minutes of not knowing ticked past before Paul's radio burst into life once more. "I have a visual on Delta, heading towards Victoria Street. He's slowed down ... Blast it, he's legging it and has crossed Victoria Street on amber. Lots of horn blowing—the idiot could have got run over!"

"Suggests he made you," commented the controller unhelpfully. "I'll flood the surrounding streets with cars to try and locate him before he goes to ground."

"He's heading down Great Smith Street, crossing as though towards the DTI or the Department for Business or whatever blasted name the politicians have given it nowadays, and has gone round to the rear but can't see if he's entering or passing it by."

"Okay, keep walking the streets. You may come up lucky. Stranger things have been known."

The London controller called Laura, informing her that they had lost a target, code named Delta, in the Westminster and Victoria area and that they would keep people in the vicinity throughout the day and evening rush hour, and stake out surrounding underground stations as well.

"Do you have any idea what Borzi and this guy were talking about?" she asked.

"None at all at this stage. The warrants have not come through yet to bug the place."

"Blast! Get a message to Steven and ask for his help to expedite matters. Sounds as if we really need to know. People don't do a runner unless something is up." Then, with a sigh, she said, "Okay, well keep me informed how it goes today, but sadly I suspect you won't get very far. Speak to you later." With that, Laura disconnected and refocused on the road ahead.

19

Laura had reluctantly left the grand surroundings of General Marshall-Jones's home. Her room had been exquisite. The bed had enveloped her in silken, soft luxury, giving her the best night's sleep for ages. She had ambled about the room in the extra-long T-shirt that she wore at night, feeling that her attire was totally out of place for her unexpected surroundings, while trying to soak up every aspect of the place. For once, she had not rushed to check e-mails, whether personal or work, and neither did she check for any text messages on her phone.

Instead, she spent quite some time sitting at the dressing table preparing for the day and looked out across the open countryside through the windows. The day that dawned was a perfect British autumnal one, although it was still only late summer. She enjoyed the clear blue skies, the early dew twinkling on the lawn in front of the house from the snap cold spell, and the last of the morning mist rising through the trees, dissipating over the fields as the temperature gradually rose.

There was no sign of the general when she left, merely the note that was handed to her at breakfast thanking her for the visit and asking to be kept informed. The note also reminded her of the checkpoints that she might encounter as she drove down the track, and that he really did not want anyone to hear about his home.

With that, Laura climbed into her car and set off on the journey south towards the GCHQ research and development facility. The tranquillity she felt remained as she drove through the Peak District, but soon evaporated as she passed through the more urban environments of Sheffield's suburbs. By the time the London controller's call came through, she felt as though all the benefit gained at the general's house had well and truly gone, but she would still be able to picture the place in her mind's eye and dream.

The next facility was not hard to find. It was a little to the south of the Peak District, north of Birmingham and almost directly off one of the many main roads that cluttered the otherwise beautiful countryside. It was conveniently sign posted as 'The Peaks Business Park'. As she approached the handful of low-rise buildings, she could have been anywhere in the country. The establishment gave the impression of a typical small business park that had sprung up between the late 1980s and early 2000s. The main distinguishing feature was the security, which impressed her for how discreet it was.

Laura pulled up at the gatehouse and the lowered barrier. An elderly uniformed guard emerged as she wound down the window.

"Good morning, young lady. How may I help you?"

"I'm here to meet Simon Jones. He's expecting me. My name is Lisa Grahams."

"Certainly. I'll let him know that you are here. I'll be right back."

Laura followed his progress. His expression had not given anything away at all, which was good. She could also see a number of other shadows in the gatehouse, and instinct suggested they would not lack the agility that the guard who had greeted her clearly was deficient of.

"That is all okay, Ms Grahams. Presumably you have a form of identification?"

Laura presented the ID card for her alias and gave him time to inspect it. "Thank you. Please proceed straight ahead; Mr Jones is in the second building on the right. He will meet you in reception. You'll find a visitor's parking space at the front of the building."

"Thank you," replied Laura brightly, and then as the barrier was lifted, she drove forward slowly to give her time to scan and review the complex. As she did, she noted a slight change of sound as the tyres ran over a marginally different texture of roadway. Laura glanced down and saw a couple of rectangular outlines in the road surface that she presumed were concealed tank traps. "Neat," she muttered.

As she continued her slow drive, she kept her eyes open for other forms of security but saw no clear evidence of anything very much. Although that did not mean additional measures were not present, it was not encouraging. All she did see were a couple of CCTV cameras on the corner of some of the buildings, but not all of the buildings by any means. Those she did see appeared new. *Interesting*, she thought. *I'll have to ask about that.* There were none overlooking the fence—well, at least, not as far as she could tell.

Simon Jones came out to meet her as Laura pulled into the parking space and got out. "Ms Grahams, pleased to meet you. Simon Jones."

Laura gave him an appraising look. He was reasonably good looking, slim, fit, approaching middle age, and had what had surely been a happy, pleasant face, but the dark bags around the eyes and early greying hair told a story of their own. His pale blue, open-necked shirt complemented his eyes, and dark blue trousers completed the picture of a man generally comfortable and confident in himself. It was just that the tired eyes and streaks of grey hair suggested otherwise.

"Please, Lisa," said Laura, shaking hands. "It's good to meet you and kind of you to do so at such short notice and minimal explanation."

"My curiosity has certainly been piqued, although I suspect that I have a good idea. I've been expecting a visit from someone," he replied, turning towards the building. "Anyway, please come in. Coffee is brewing, and it will be more comfortable to discuss whatever you wish in my office."

Laura frowned, puzzled at his comment.

"You chose a fine day for an outing. I trust that you had a pleasant journey?"

"Very pleasant indeed, yes. I spent the night in the Peak District since I was coming down from a job further north, and it was just delightful. It's just a shame not to be able to spend more time in surroundings like that."

"Oh, I agree entirely. It's one of the benefits of living around here. In weather like this the Peak District is stupendous. If the weekend has similar weather, I'll be over there for some wonderful walking. Anyway, this is the admin block and restaurant," he said, holding the door open for Laura to pass through into the large, light lobby that ran the full width of the building with floor-to-ceiling glazing along three sides. Two lifts faced them, with stairs off to one side, the steel handrail gleaming under the lights. To the other side of the lifts was a set of wide double doors with a lot of chairs and a variety of small café-type and long bench tables beyond. *That's the restaurant then*, she thought as the lift doors opened.

As they settled down at a small meeting table in Simon's office, Laura decided to take the initiative. "So, why don't you tell me why you've been expecting a visit?"

"Ah, now that would be telling, wouldn't it, particularly if I'm wrong. So it's probably better that you start. I hope you don't mind. I don't want to be rude."

Okay, thought Laura. *Polite, genteel, and comes across as unassuming, but sharp and cautious with it. That's fair enough.*

"No offence taken. That's a perfectly reasonable stance to take." Laura was keen not to antagonise the man so early on because, hopefully, he would become more forthcoming with a gentle approach. "I'm here to discuss your security arrangements because we have reason to believe you're being targeted."

Simon sighed. "As I suspected."

"Really? Why's that?"

"We've had a few security breaches recently. Strangely, they've only been through the perimeter and not into the buildings. As far as we can tell, nothing has been taken. All very curious, but alarming all the same."

Laura sat up, even more alert than initially. "I'm sure. How do you know there's been a breach in that case? And when was this?"

"It's been periodic over the past few weeks. The perimeter patrol has found the fence damaged on four occasions now. Of course, as site manager I've taken a good look because I'm responsible for getting the damage fixed. And therein lies the curiosity; only once did it appear that someone could have got through."

"I suppose that it's always possible whoever was trying to force entry was disturbed," Laura suggested.

"True, but our patrols have never reported seeing anyone. We're certain that it's not an animal—I've seen animal incursions many times during previous jobs, and this damage is most definitely man made. I've asked for additional security, even though it's not my responsibility, so we have some troops stationed here now in the gatehouse until arrangements are finalised. I hope they will become permanent. There are plans to install a lot more CCTV with twenty-four-hour on-site monitoring, even though that will start to destroy the low-key nature of the place."

"Why would anyone want to break in? I know you're a research and development section for GCHQ, but from the external appearance, you may as well be a standard office park."

"That's precisely the intention. Create our security through anonymity by being boringly normal in appearance and by being in everyone's face. You know the expression, no one pays attention to what's in front of their noses. But therein also possibly lies the problem." At Laura's raised eyebrow and quizzical look, he continued. "Simple really. Standard offices in these parts rarely have good security and therefore offer easy, rich pickings for opportunistic thieves: computers, other pieces of technology and stationary, lots of stuff that we workers take for granted, and even grounds maintenance equipment. All has a ready resale value and is easy to pass on."

"Yes, I can see that. Are you sure it's as simple as that?"

"What, you think it could be more serious?"

"Not necessarily. Your explanation is perfectly plausible, but surely, simply because of what this place is, there should be consideration of more serious intentions? And that is precisely why I'm here."

On hearing that, Simon looked increasingly alarmed. *Simon wouldn't be a good poker player*, Laura thought. *At least that helps my cause because I'll know if he tries to hide something.*

"I have been troubled by these breaches for the reasons I've given," he continued, cautiously. "Local police, who have no idea what we do here, have warned all office parks and commercial users in the area about a spate of office burglaries. I don't want someone discovering what we do here as a result of petty crime, particularly at the moment because there are a few important initiatives in testing phase and close to formal release. That's why I escalated my concerns to GCHQ. Don't ask me what these folks are doing. I'm not cleared to know what the clever souls here do; all I do know is that the work is vital for our nation. Now you've got me really worried."

Laura proceeded to give the worried man the same information as she had shared with General Marshall-Jones, bringing a distinctly grey, ashen expression to his face as his shoulders slumped further and further. "Oh gawd," was all he could say as she finished. "Presumably the powers that be in Cheltenham know?"

"Absolutely, they do know now. That's why I'm here. Another quick question, if I may. It's one that I expect you cannot answer, but you may have heard something."

"I will try, fire away."

"Have there been any leaks about the work undertaken here, or has someone been acting strangely, or as though under extreme pressure, or even, has anyone disappeared totally?"

"If there have been any leaks, I've not heard. In terms of people's behaviour, well yes, many people are under pressure, and it is showing. All I know is that each of the different work streams are highly sensitive and are to be delivered as soon as possible. From what I've heard, they are on schedule but only just. The entire contingency was eaten away a long time back. No one has disappeared as far as I am aware."

"Okay, thanks, that's helpful. I was hoping you'd be able to show me around and give me the details of the security arrangements here in order to assess the potential risk profile and likelihood that this facility is the target. I would have cut to the chase far earlier had you not said what you did at the outset. I wanted to give you the opportunity to expand in your own way, which you did and that was helpful, so thank you. Maybe you'd be so good as to show me around, if that's possible?"

"Certainly, that's not a problem. A walk will do me the world of good, particularly in such fine weather. We won't have access into any of the other buildings while people are working. Those are the rules. If something breaks and requires attention during the day, a blocked toilet or replacement light bulb, for example, then everyone has to clear their work away before the swipe access is downgraded to a level for me or members of my team to go in. It's a right old palaver. We can certainly walk around the perimeter, and I will show you where the damage occurred. It will cost a fortune to place tremblers and covert cameras to cover the entire complex. I suspect that the chiefs of Cheltenham, as I call them, know it is necessary but are trying to delay the expenditure until the next financial year. As I understand it, they've already over-committed their capital spend for this year."

"Well that's their problem, not ours," replied Laura comfortingly and smiling at his reference to the chiefs of Cheltenham. "The long and short of it is that they need to, and after today, they are likely to also get hit with the cost of additional guarding and very possibly a severe kicking from my boss!"

With that they stood and had a pleasant stroll around the perimeter, chatting amicably as they went. Simon pointed out places of interest and concern and where the fence had been damaged. Following that, Simon suggested that they have lunch before she left, an idea that Laura readily accepted. She was hungry and ready for something far more substantial than she would buy for herself on the road. Simon was also an easy man to talk with, and as they ate, he happily chatted away about his wife and family, why he had applied for this job, and how enjoyable it had been until these security breaches had occurred. As Laura prepared to leave, Simon handed her a number of sheets of paper.

"Forgive me—these are copies of the e-mails I've sent about the paucity of the security, even before the breaches. As you'll see, I recommended changes. I've also included my e-mails and reports covering those incidents. Yes, I suppose it's been a bit of an arse-covering exercise, but the primary purpose is because I believe you will be able to make something happen, and ideally before anything more serious occurs."

"Thank you, Simon, this is most helpful. Well, very good to meet you, and I am sure you'll be hearing from folks shortly. I hope it doesn't become too much of a headache for you."

They shook hands, and Laura departed, eager to find a deserted lay-by or other place to pull over, read Simon's materials and then call Gurning.

Laura found herself talking with Gurning from the car park of a roadside café, where she had parked as far from any other vehicle as possible.

"I can't believe how amateurish and idealistic the place is, Steven. I've read the e-mails that Simon Jones has given me, and they go back a good few years with him warning people that security should be a lot tighter. While I fully acknowledge the plausibility of Simon's comments that these recent breaches could well be the typical criminal that targets office buildings, I would not discount this as a possible target. That said, professionals should have been able to gain access easily the first time."

"Unless the lack of apparent security perversely put the infiltrators on edge, thinking there might be something a lot more sophisticated. They could have been testing the security. Anyhow, I agree that this facility has to be on the list as a potential target. I have spoken to the head of station at GCHQ, who told me what they're doing there. Essentially, it's a breakthrough that will place us years ahead of everyone else in electronic eavesdropping, for both voice and electronic communications. They have also had a breakthrough for encryption and decryption techniques. We are known as a powerhouse nation of technical expertise in this arena, so it would not surprise me if others, whether at a national or terrorist level, would seek to snaffle our ideas and capabilities."

"And to think that such advancements have such poor security. It's inexcusable!"

"Exactly."

"But Steven, because the security there is so poor, we don't know for sure that the breach was only of the perimeter. There is no evidence that a search was undertaken to ensure that no listening or other recording devices were installed. Regardless of being the target or not, the entire facility requires a huge amount of attention."

"Agreed. You need to come back to London and work on coordinating efforts against Khartoum and on this. Sorting Burak's wider mess will have to wait a few days. We're going to be stretched horribly thinly, even leaving your general to protect his own."

"My general, indeed," she replied, cheering up slightly at Gurning's leg pulling. "See you in a few hours, but you know I can't help but think we're missing something."

"I agree. That's why last night I asked David Spalding to work on this with you as well. I know the two of you work well together."

"Great! Thanks, Steven."

20

As Laura disconnected speaking with Gurning, her smartphone started beeping like a thing possessed. When she glanced down at the display, a flood of emails and texts came through. One of the texts indicated she had a number of voice messages. *Great! There's either been a network outage, or no signal, or the blasted contraption is playing up because it's so old!*

There were two notes from the London team. The first informed her that Delta had not been seen again. The second reported that the two men seen with Borzi two days earlier had given them the slip through a basement tunnel leading to a nearby garage hitherto unknown as being connected with the premises and therefore had not been watched. Some photos of the backs of the men's heads were attached, but the small size of the display prevented Laura from getting a reasonable perspective of them. She was pleased to note that David Spalding had been copied on both emails.

David had also sent a text message, as well as a crisp voice message asking her to call him as soon as possible. So, with a sigh, she called him back.

"Gracious, Laura, where have you been? I've tried calling you dozens of times!"

"No dratted signal."

"You sure Rob's not with you?" David teased.

"Humph! So what's got you so excited? Surely not ill-informed and idle gossip!" Laura was smiling widely by now and was sure David would be as well. The two of them enjoyed verbal sparring and had engendered an excellent, trusting work relationship.

"Not at all. It's the notes from the London surveillance teams. I want your approval to circulate Delta's photograph across the HR departments for all Ministries, particularly the Ministry for Business, since Delta was close at the time of his disappearance. It's just a hunch. The London team are not aware of the European Ministerial Critical Medicines Conference tomorrow so would not have put two and two together. It could be coincidence, but …"

Laura cut across him, having heard more than enough. "Do it. I will e-mail my approval now. I don't believe in such close coincidences. I always like working with you—you catch things the rest of us don't."

"And just to let you know, I'm working on trying to get identifications of those guys in the photographs with Borzi. The one they said was domineering is a complete unknown, but the other—well, it wouldn't stand up in court, but the posture and ears are very like your old adversary, Khartoum, just with a very different hairstyle."

"Work on Delta until I get back. I want to see the comparatives you are referring to before setting any hares running. It sounds intriguing. I'll be a few hours. See you soon."

When Laura walked through the entrance security at Thames House reception, she could sense that tension filled the air.

She was also staggered to find that Gurning was sitting with David Spalding at her desk. She gave one her famous raised quizzical eyebrow glances at Gurning as she hung her jacket on the stand, left her overnight bag at its base as well, and dropped her handbag behind her desk.

"What's up?" she asked as she unpacked her work items, including locking her handgun in the secured desk drawer.

"Delta is up," replied Gurning. "It required some pushing to get the Ministry for Business HR department to engage with us, because they were dealing with an irate Minister, frustrated at the no show of the member of her admin team who is dealing with the arrangements for the conference. With that knowledge and a bit of prompting, we got them to look at the photograph from Fonthill Clothes, which was immediately recognised as one Nazim Omar, the no-show admin.

"We're therefore now focusing on the conference. I've alerted the team up there, and sorry, you're on your way out again. I've asked Brian to release one of his lads to join you and for him to do the driving. You've done enough today. Study these photos on your way, and give me your opinion. It's a good enough resemblance for me if you're onside as well. I will have to pull a few favours to get authorisation to raid the Finsbury premises, but with the growing links between Leicester, Bradford, and now Fonthill Clothes, I will push for it."

Laura was aghast at how rapidly matters had moved in a few short hours. She was also mightily relieved that she would have a chauffeur for the journey back up north. She started to pack her things again while saying with a grin,

"You intentionally waited for me to finish unpacking, didn't you?"

"Absolutely! Unfortunately, we have to assume that Khartoum and company are aware by now that we are onto them, or at least sniffing around. They will know they are neither as well manned, nor equipped as planned. However, from his past record, I can't see him aborting whatever is planned, so I want you there to take charge.

"Just think, we would have been completely blindsided by this thing if it hadn't been for looking into Burak's operations! I'm heading off to confront him with this now, during the proverbial quiet before the storm of what will be tomorrow. Hopefully, with this clear link to terrorism, he will become more amenable to sharing information more openly and quickly. I'm probably flying a kite, but it's worth a try."

"By the way, the conference starts at ten o'clock tomorrow morning," David added. "The news from the venue is that the entire place has been searched and there's nothing to report. With the local police we are flooding the place and the surrounding area, but as we know, the countryside can be like a sieve for anyone sufficiently determined."

"Well, there you have it. Let's jump to it." Gurning stood to leave.

"Right you are," replied Laura enthusiastically, caught up in the moment of high tension and imminent action. "However, I still think the GCHQ facility requires immediate attention as well. I accept that everything now points towards the conference, but that doesn't mean that, like the conference, we haven't stumbled upon something there."

Gurning hesitated at the door, thinking through the logic of Laura's comments and the implications on resource. "I'll speak to the DG," he said eventually, in a thoughtful, cautious way, despite his apparent agreement. "As always, your logic is faultless."

A few minutes later, Rob walked into the office area and wandered over to her desk. "Hi! How're things?" Seeing Laura with her gun in hand, he hesitated. "I trust you are not intending to use that thing!" he joked. "I saw you walking through reception, so thought I'd come and find out how things are going, but I can come back again later if you want."

"No, it's all right, Rob. I'm just packing again to head up north again. Steven was here with David, and they've just briefed me. I'll fill you in while I pack. I also want to hear from you about Leicester."

"I can also update you on the office for Zouches. It looks fabulous and is nearly ready for occupation. The teams here and their contractors have really pulled all the stops out. When you're back, you'll have to come round."

"I'd love to," Laura replied. She then summarised the current situation, leaving out the details relating to the two secret facilities, merely commenting that the conference was their focus because there were too many coincidences.

Laura arrived at the conference hotel late that evening and ate a tuna sandwich and salad with the ever-present stack of fries on the side as Nat McCall briefed her on the hotel, the grounds, the surrounding land, and the couple of hills overlooking the hotel. He outlined the steps taken to secure the area as far as possible, including regular patrols of the hills. He also discussed, in detail, the agenda for the following day.

Nat looked tired, as well he might, not having slept for forty-eight hours. His eyes gleamed, however, and his energy level was so remarkable that Laura was tempted to ask how he did it, but she was not entirely convinced that she would like the answer.

Nat was apparently in his late-thirties but looked a lot younger. His reputation was legend. Muscles rippled beneath his white, open-necked shirt, with the rolled-up sleeves exposing a string of tattoos on his forearms, all gained during his years in the special forces. Whether a long-term member of his team, or a new recruit, everyone said the same thing: they didn't want to work for anyone else. Now that Laura had met the man, who had been drafted in at short notice for this conference, she could understand why.

"How are the transfers being covered?" Laura asked.

"A separate team, thankfully," replied Nat. "As each minister arrives at Manchester airport, we'll be informed. A security detail has been allocated to meet, greet and then accompany the minister here. Our own minister is travelling up by car. The arrangements and route were changed hastily once that admin chap went AWOL and the connection established by you guys. I don't suppose you know who they are targeting, if anyone specific, or is the thinking that it's the conference as a whole?"

"We really don't know. It doesn't appear logical to target an individual when a conference offers greater potential, but I agree we can't rule that out. From your short time here, have you even an inkling for the most likely tactic for any attack?"

"That's the six million–dollar question and really depends on the objective or target. If it's an individual, I'd vote for a sniper from the overlooking hills as whoever arrives or departs. But why wait for a conference to take a shot at someone? It doesn't make sense. It's generally far easier to penetrate the security detail of daily life—at some point either the target or a member of the protection squad will slip up, whereas security at an event like this is always scrutinised. Anyhow, just in case, the current patrols over those hills and among the trees will become a permanent presence tomorrow, from early until after departure."

"Don't forget that a couple of high-powered sniper rifles were found during the Leicester raid. Whether that disrupts or changes anything, only time will tell."

"That aside, assuming that this is the target, I'm expecting a broader attack, but I really cannot conceive how it will be executed. Everywhere and everything has been swept for explosives. Divers have checked out the lake, and we've even been through the sand in the bunkers over at the pitch and putt. Manchester airport have an extra body on duty solely to monitor all aircraft and report anything potentially suspicious from miles out, at which point the RAF will be scrambled. An air strike seems improbable, however. That would leave a rocket attack, which is plausible but unreliable."

"What about the staff here?"

"That is one area of concern that has not yet been fully closed off. Whether a suicide attack, poisoning, or some other type of individual level of atrocity. There simply has not been the time to complete the vetting for all employees. I've frustrated the hotel's manager and those of the caterer by insisting that no temporary person or contractor be used, and only permanent staff of three plus years' standing be engaged."

"I guess that didn't go down well, but good call," commented Laura thoughtfully. "But if the attack were to come from someone on site, how would they get the necessary weapons in? I'm sure you're frustrating everyone with searches."

"Sure am," Nat said with feeling. "Their cars as well, all of which I'm requiring to be parked well away from the building and behind trees. I have also insisted that all deliveries are made prior to the arrival of any delegate and that all vehicles have departed by that time as well. I suspect that the manager here has changed his view of governmental conferences being easy and 'money for old rope'! This certainly started out that way, but he's had a rude awakening," Nat chuckled, giving Laura a wicked grin. "Well, there's not much more we can do now, so best you get some sleep. I'll just go do my final rounds. Hopefully you've been shown where you're staying?"

"I have, yes, thank you. Good night. See you around six?"

"I'll be there."

21

Nat, carrying a plate piled high with scrambled eggs, bacon, sausages, mushrooms, tomatoes, and toast, joined Laura at the breakfast table where she was seated, studying the day's agenda again.

"I'm pleasantly surprised to see that they have to work for their pay at this one," she said wryly as Nat sat down. "No element of a jolly at all. It appears to be all business."

"That's the positive influence of senior business folks being present, coupled with the severity of the matter at hand," commented Nat. "A brief and to-the-point conference. I understand that this was the only day they could all accommodate. That said, apparently the pitch and putt, as well as the driving range, attracted some attention from the delegates, many of whom are keen golfers. Hence the choice of this venue, as that will provide a short respite over lunch. Well, at least that's what the manager said."

As they finished their breakfast, Nat asked, "Care to join me on my rounds? I'll focus on the golfing area on the basis that presents one of the two external opportunities for attack."

"And the other?" encouraged Laura.

"Oh, the inevitable conference photo, which will be taken on the steps at the rear. Both elements are overlooked by the hills, so they provide a good opportunity for a sniper or rocket attack." Shortly afterwards they headed off around the grounds, stopping to chat with the patrols as they passed.

Rob had also risen early, as was his way, and went for a run around Walpole Park in Ealing, followed by an out-of-breath protection squad. After a hearty breakfast of muesli and a plate of cheese, mushroom and tomato omelette, washed down with a strong coffee, Rob headed off to his new office. In between his engagements and activities in Leicester, he had maintained contact with his newly recruited team, all of whom had enthusiastically accepted the terms offered to join the newly founded firm, Zouches. As matters came to a head and approached a conclusion in Leicester, Rob had contacted them once again, proposing a meeting at the nearly completed new office.

At 8:30 a.m. they congregated in the bright and tastefully colourful reception, clearly the inspiration of a high-end interior designer seeking to create a modern, young, and professional working environment, while also somehow appealing to traditionalists. Rob marvelled at how so much could be accomplished with such simplicity. The builders and decorators had disappeared, leaving the technology folks to their work. As the team looked on, drinking coffee, the workmen were setting up the comms room, the desktop computers, and the all-important multimedia gadgets. There was video conferencing and collaborative projection whiteboards with associated computers and printers. There were also various other toys that the technology folks of MI5 had conjured up for the team's pleasure. There were the inevitable large flat-screen TVs hanging on the walls of the reception to display a variety of news channels and market data information. Each desk had at least two computer screens, and some had four.

Rob dinged a teaspoon against his cup for silence, feeling incredibly self-conscious and ill-suited for the role that he was now embarking on. However, he was determined to portray the confidence and assurance he was known for.

"Welcome, everyone, to our new head office. I've arranged that we can have access to the board room essentially from now, and afterwards we can wander around the office as we want, although please be considerate of those folks still working through the office setup. Expectations are that we will have a live environment within two weeks, although for many of you, because of existing commitments, it won't be possible to join until after that date. Well, shall we go through?"

Rob guided everyone through some impressive light-coloured wooden double doors into an expansive and well-equipped boardroom. At the far end was a large-scale plan of the office, showing a number of smaller meeting rooms, also directly off reception, and a large open-plan office area behind accommodating twenty stand-alone desks and two pods of four linked desks for the administrative and support teams. These were placed near the windows, as they would be permanently in the office, with all of the other desks arranged in an arc around them making the admin team a focal point within the workspace. Against the inner wall were a series of small meeting or quiet rooms. The reception and waiting area, boardroom, and most of the other formal meeting rooms had excellent views over the River Thames, which was running at near high tide, with gusts of wind whipping the dark water into sporadic bursts of small, white-topped waves.

"Welcome again all," Rob said as they settled down in their seats. "The agenda for today is short and simple: Explain some more about this setup—about Zouches, including its ownership. Explain the need for confidentiality and why both a firm confidentiality agreement and the signing of the 'Official Secrets Act' have been necessary and the consequential obvious link between Zouches and the government. Then I will cover the objectives for Zouches. Finally, there will be time for everyone to mingle and start to get to know each other some more. I'll keep the chat as short as possible to provide the most time for Q and A, and time to mingle.

"So first, Zouches. You were, I am sure, enticed to join by the words 'a start-up private equity firm' and that Sir William is involved." At that Rob gestured to Sir William Shields, who was sitting among the group and due to take an active chairmanship role and as a special adviser. "So why am I standing here instead of Sir William? Simply because I own Zouches and am the primary beneficiary of the revenue generated. Well, that's after paying off some fairly hefty debts, that is!"

Upon that announcement, there were startled expressions from all those who had known Rob previously. He smiled before continuing. "And no, I have not always had the wealth to establish such an enterprise. How I came to effectively inherit the wealth that justifies a private equity firm leads on to explain why it's been necessary to sign two sets of confidentiality agreements and the seriousness with which you need to treat the knowledge that you will gain."

Rob looked around the room to ensure he had everyone's attention. "Essentially, I saved the life of a billionaire master criminal, who has to remain nameless. As part of saving his life, it was agreed that he would both hand over his entire empire to me and also accept coming to Britain to face justice. However, before facing justice publicly, he will assist the efforts to bring his criminal network to its knees. This is the essence of the need for confidentiality. The man's network spans many countries. Until such a time as the network has been dismantled, he will continue to be at the forefront of all communication with those elements that have not been transferred into Zouches. This may take quite some time.

"There are both legitimate and criminal businesses. You can split the legitimate businesses in two. First, there are those businesses that have absolutely no connection to any criminality. Unfortunately, there aren't very many of those. These businesses will transfer immediately to Zouches for you to start to manage, support and grow. Then there are other legitimate businesses through which criminal activities are channelled without the operating manager's knowledge. In some instances, this crime lord has planted people into those businesses to run the criminal aspects. In other instances, the criminal activity is simply pushed through as though legitimate, daily customer interactions. These businesses will only transfer as and when the criminal elements and activities have been expunged. This is where the combined expertise of this group will come into its own and leads to our objectives.

"Put very simply, we will help those business managers rebuild and expand what has been disrupted, potentially severely, and we will maintain and create employment. If it weren't for this arrangement, once the criminal elements are shut down, many hundreds of innocent people's livelihoods could be destroyed. We must remember, these businesses will not only have been disrupted, there will be damaged reputations, both to the business and most likely also to those caught up in the mess. They will be in shock, having been completely hoodwinked and let down by the primary owner. In some instances, the local manager has a shareholding. In all cases, this crime lord has remained anonymous and worked either by phone or more frequently, through a Power of Attorney given to one of his henchmen, or other delegate from an off-shore company. It is highly likely that those affected, once they realise, will lose confidence, and almost certainly their willingness to trust anyone will have evaporated.

"I'm sure you read in the papers or watched the TV coverage about a raid two days ago in Leicester that disrupted a major drug-smuggling operation. Well, I was there because those two premises are examples of legitimate businesses being abused for this man's criminal activities. However, in this case, and there are very possibly many more like it, this man's sidekicks have expanded their operations and embraced the support of terrorism. There were not only drugs found at those premises, there were also weapons and explosives, giving a real example for the need of extreme confidentiality. Nothing gleaned within these four walls or during the course of your work is to go anywhere. Absolutely nothing!" With that, Rob paused briefly for effect. Whether the silence was from respect to let him finish speaking or because they were too stunned, Rob had no idea, but he had noticed a few of them wriggling in their chairs. *I hope no one is getting cold feet,* Rob thought to himself.

"I spoke to the managers of the Leicester businesses afterwards, and they were thoroughly dejected, were in shock, and really are unsure who they can trust. We need to gain their trust, and those like them, and keep otherwise successful businesses successful."

"Rob, sorry for interrupting, but isn't this therefore potentially dangerous for us as well?" asked Huw Thomas, who was joining Zouches as their corporate lawyer.

"Fair question, Huw, and thank you for jumping in; I was getting concerned that everyone had lost their tongues!" Fortunately, everyone laughed, lightening the atmosphere.

"Anyway, to answer your question, no, I don't believe so, provided we respect the confidentiality, mind our part of the equation, and not involve ourselves until businesses are transferred to us. At that point, the businesses should be post-criminal and should hold no interest for those groups. I must emphasise the confidentiality once again because we will sometimes have access to information prior to the authorities acting. That won't be frequent, for obvious reasons; the fewer people who know, the better. But sometimes it may be necessary. Much of the time I will know and help the authorities with the judgement call on whether to share or not."

"Ever the one for seeking the excitement of danger, eh, Rob!" Julian Smith, Zouches' COO, called out, raising some more laughter throughout the room.

"Rob," jumped in Yves Aussourd, one of the asset managers.

"Yes, Yves."

"So there are all these businesses out there and the boss has disappeared because he is in custody. So how does that work? Surely they'll go native or someone else will move in?"

"Ah, that's the interesting aspect of the planned arrangements, while also being difficult to stomach. As briefly intimated, this man will continue to manage them until the authorities are able to close down the criminal element. Personally, I find it tough to swallow that criminality is being permitted to continue, but having followed the preparation for the Leicester operation, seen the outcome and now knowing that links to other terrorist activity have been established, I can understand why it's necessary. Those links would not have been identified if the authorities had gone straight in and closed the operations down, thereby leaving other activities unidentified and able to continue unabated somewhere else. So in essence, I am working hand-in-glove with the security services. Our combined intervention is absolutely essential. The extent of the links to terrorism is unknown but is thought to be considerable. A pack listing the legitimate businesses ready for immediate transfer will be circulated shortly. The managers are still unaware of the change, and one of our first tasks will be to determine a strategy for on-boarding them and bringing some structure, cohesion, and good, but not burdensome, reporting and governance.

"Before taking any more questions—I can see a few itching hands—there is one final objective that I have for Zouches." At that point Rob could see Sir William raise his eyebrows. Sir William was appointed by Jed to both support from a business perspective, as well as to keep a wary eye on proceedings. Thus far Rob had not shared his final objective with anyone.

"The extent of wealth to be managed by us far exceeds the requirements of any single individual, even should I marry a lady with expensive tastes and have a large, demanding family!" Rob paused as his friends of old had a good laugh at his witticism. "Therefore, I also intend to establish a philanthropic trust through Zouches to make the best social use of much of that wealth. I am still drafting my intended focus for that trust, but much of it will focus around children, young adults and a reasonable proportion for the elderly. Right, any further questions?"

As he had spoken about the trust, Rob could see Sir William's relief and apparent support by way of a gentle nodding of his head.

"Rob, can you give us an idea of the types of business coming our way?" Timothy Havering, the CEO-to-be, asked.

"Absolutely. It's a mixed bag. In Leicester, for example, there is a carwash and a money-exchange business. There are also real estate and construction companies, farms, florists, travel agencies, technology companies and logistics businesses, including couriers and transportation businesses, the latter comprising cars, planes, helicopters, and boats. Those are the ones I can mention. I haven't totalled up the number of countries covered yet, but it's quite a lot."

There was a moment's silence as the extent and magnitude of what had been discussed was absorbed before Julian Smith aptly commented, "We'll have our work cut out then!" raising a good few chuckles.

"Rob, a question for curiosity purposes as much as anything," said Karen Ayles, who was to be the CFO. "Why have you chosen Zouches as the name for your firm?"

"I was wondering if anyone would ask," Rob chuckled. "I came across the word as the name of a farm during my research for a university project. I liked the sound and thought it would make a great and unusual name for a business and have harboured that thought ever since. The word apparently originates from a similar-sounding old French word meaning 'tree stump' and may also derive from the French place name, La Souche. The name Zouche without the S is also an old aristocratic English name with a long lineage. As I say, I just liked the sound of it!"

The meeting then broke up, and folks milled around, initially gravitating to Rob, probing him with questions about how he came to save Burak and cut the deal with the government, during which he explained that a lot of the cost of the many forthcoming operations would have to be covered by Zouches.

22

Sarah Puddleford was understandably nervous as she sat in her ministerial car heading towards a conference she knew was important. Ordinarily, as the host, she would have felt the tingling nerves of expectation ahead of her required speeches. Now, however, the nervousness was for her life and that of all the other conference delegates. The presence of the unmarked police Range Rover escort did little to comfort her. If anything, its proximity simply served to exacerbate her nervousness.

She had been badly let down by Nazim Omar and was disappointed beyond words. She had offered Nazim a job just over a year earlier having visited his college on results day and had been impressed by his alertness, questions, and above all, determination to excel. He had apparently turned his back on working at his parents' back-street café in the east end of London so he could pursue his studies, much to his parents' disappointment and familial pressure. She had wanted to encourage both him and the many others who knew his story.

Mrs Puddleford felt she had also been let down by the personnel vetting procedures. As Nazim had progressed and subsequently joined her administrative team, his proximity to her and his access to confidential information had necessitated additional background checks, all of which had been clear. That had been only five months ago. Somehow, whatever it was he was mixed up in had escaped the vetting team's attention. He apparently had no political, ideological, or religious allegiances of note. Some serious questions about this failure were being asked even now as she made her way up north to face goodness knows what.

As she sat in her chauffeured car, she thought of her family back at her constituency and family home. Mrs Puddleford pulled out a notepad from her case, wrote two letters, and folded them away into separate envelopes. Turning to the bodyguard assigned to her for the day, she asked, in as confident a voice as she could muster, "Dylan, if anything terrible happens, please make sure my family receive this and my parents receive this."

"Certainly, ma'am. I will look forward to giving them back later today on the journey home."

"Thank you." Mrs Puddleford settled back into her seat again, thinking about Dylan's lifestyle and his complete lack of surprise at her request. *Do many of his charges make similar requests,* she wondered, but did not dare ask. She wanted to put on a show of strength from now on.

The first of Mrs Puddleford's European counterparts' aircraft touched down at Manchester International Airport and taxied to the private terminal, where a series of smart limousines and escort vehicles awaited their arrival. The officials and other ground crew had been gossiping all morning about the suddenly imposed heavy security for the arrivals. Flights from France, Germany, Italy, the

Netherlands, Spain and Switzerland were expected, with businessmen accompanying the relevant country's minister where appropriate.

The plan was that there would be a precise fifteen minutes between each transfer, and regular communication between the respective convoys would ensure that gap be maintained. Nat's intention was that there would be no grouping of the participants, other than at the conference venue. Assuming that any terrorist attack was intended to target multiple people for maximum damage and effect, he wanted to limit the potential locations to make maximum use of the resources available to him.

As the airplanes were landing and their respective convoys set off, it became busy at the hotel entrance as the staff and deliveries started to arrive. Every delivery was logged and compared against the list of what was expected. Nat was due to review the log shortly before the arrival of the first delegates.

Each vehicle and individual was searched while each member of the staff was quizzed, and the required original form of identification was carefully scrutinised. Many of the staff were nervous and uncomfortable at such close attention, and a few had failed to turn up. Their names and addresses were noted, ready to be passed on to Immigration for their residency status, to the Inland Revenue to ensure they were paying the correct taxes, and finally to Social Security to ensure there was no benefit fraud going on, as well as to the police for criminal checks.

Together with one of the roving patrols, Nat and Laura reviewed the grounds. At the pitch and putt course and driving range, they stood and surveyed the surrounding landscape and hills with their powerful binoculars. Nat pointed out where he would position himself as a member of the Special Forces on a covert op to take out an enemy position. Radio in hand, he gave directions to the patrols on the wooded hillsides to make sure those spots were thoroughly checked out.

Next up was the rear of the hotel, where the obligatory conference photo would be taken. As they were walking, Nat called each of the police checkpoints scattered throughout the surrounding area for a status update. They were positioned on the roads leading to the surrounding hills, the roads leading directly to the hotel, and the quiet back roads within striking distance of the hotel grounds. The reports came in satisfactorily, confirming there were no unaccounted for vehicles and no suspicious traffic.

Finally, they meandered through the woodland at the edge of the hotel grounds, Nat and the accompanying patrol using their training to seek any traces of recent human passage. It was a tough task, and as they finished, they could not be absolutely certain but were reasonably confident no one had been in the woods since the previous day. That said, Nat appointed a team of six to split into pairs and constantly patrol the woods just in case.

Nat's radio burst into life. "Ten minutes, sir, and the Minister for Business will arrive."

"On our way."

Immediately, they turned and headed back to the hotel. Nat wanted to be present when the delegates arrived, particularly Mrs Puddleford. He expected she would want both an update and an assurance. Her bodyguard had sent a text a little earlier stating her evident and understandable nervousness.

By the time the Minister's car glided to a halt in front of the hotel's elegant façade, the small welcoming committee was lined up. The hotel manager welcomed her first and then introduced her to the in-house event coordinator, who would be at her beck and call for the day. If she wanted anything at all, she just had to press the call button on the small gadget he presented her with. Hesitantly she took hold of it, the tension in her face clear for all to see. Politely, as required, she thanked him whilst giving her bodyguard a look saying, "Is this safe?" Dylan glanced at Nat, who nodded. It had been pre-cleared—Nat had held on to it after it had been checked over, only handing the gadget back to the manager just as the Minister arrived. The manager had also been searched just prior to arrival so there was no chance of a swap.

As Laura looked on, she wondered how any productive work could be accomplished while the possibility of a terrorist attack hung over the place like a dark storm cloud, echoing the weather above. When she had woken up that morning, Laura had been convinced it was going to rain. Even now distant rumbles of thunder threatened to prove the weather forecasters wrong again. It was supposed to be overcast but dry for the entire day. Could it last?

The manager had by now introduced Nat, who quickly briefed Mrs Puddleford on the current status and arrangements for the day before turning and introducing Laura. The Minister then uncharacteristically hurried into the relative safety of the hotel's interior. She had decided that future welcoming committees would be indoors, using the weather as an excuse.

The Dutch would be the next to arrive. The Italians would be last. Those businessmen not accompanying a

Minister would arrive whenever in their own chauffeur-driven cars. They were not considered suitable individual targets.

In between arrivals, Laura called Simon Jones at the GCHQ research and development facility for an update. He sounded stressed as he described the influx of security personnel and the fact that there had been another breach the previous night. This time there were evident marks of an attempted break-in on the front doors to three of the campus buildings. One door had been left hanging open, but the intruders had been disturbed by a patrol. However, the perpetrators had given them the slip.

The news made Laura anxious. Had they focused on the wrong place? Should she relocate? Both locations were equally vulnerable and equally attractive for terrorists. She didn't like knee-jerk reactions and tried to think rationally. Gurning would have the same information as she did and would call immediately should he require a change of emphasis. Simon handed his phone to the day's head of security, who updated her on their arrangements, giving her some, but little comfort.

Amid her troubled thoughts, Nat had studied the log of deliveries and was now muttering curses that barely registered about the golf pro from the nearby golf course bringing an unannounced stack of new boxed golf balls and collections of the latest clubs, bags, and other goods. He planned to give out some of the goodies and hoped to sell other items. Otherwise, everything else was in order.

Laura mumbled her response, caught slightly by surprise. "Typical that someone would try to buck the system. Presumably everything checked out?"

"Yes. The manager assured me that he's well known and the search and sniffer dogs came up with nothing, so he got away simply with a good ear-full! I can't blame the guy for trying to be entrepreneurial, but everyone was told very clearly not to bring anything that has not been pre-cleared!"

François Maranville was bored. "Why do the British have to be overdramatic with everything? First the conference and now the security arrangements. It is almost like being the president!" he said to Nadia Trivette, his attractive assistant who was, as always and as he preferred, showing rather a lot of her shapely, slim legs, which were stretched out in the long wheel-base limo.

She had been looking out of the window when he spoke, which had enabled him to yet again admire her feminine curves. She turned as he spoke, flicking her long blonde hair as she did so, releasing an invisible plume of her alluring perfume into the air. François breathed in deeply as she did. He longed for those moments of her scent.

They were on the M67 motorway near Hyde. The silence in the car was tedious and the quiet thrum of the speeding tyres barely audible.

"It is, isn't it?" Nadia replied sweetly, flashing a beaming smile of perfect, gleaming white teeth. "It's a shame we can't stay over. The write-up for the hotel is very good, and I hear that the Peak District is beautiful, despite the gloomy English weather."

François was just starting to imagine an overnight stay with Nadia when their car swerved sharply, the driver cussing loudly as he slammed on the brakes. As he did so, there was a second, more jarring jolt, accompanied by the sound of squealing tyres and grinding metal as a car slammed into their rear—it was not one of their convoy. Nadia screamed and François instinctively reached out to protect her. As he did, he saw that another car had come in between them and their escort in front.

Horrified, he looked on as two men jumped out carrying guns. Shots rang out and the rear windshield disintegrated upon the impact of the bullets. The police response was rapid and incredibly efficient in its ruthlessness. Even before their vehicles were stationary, the armed men in the rear of each escort car, one in front, one behind, were out and rolling on the tarmac, raising their handguns and firing rapidly at the attackers with great accuracy.

Moments later the attackers from the rear car were lying dead on the road, as was one of those from the other car, which, facing overwhelming and superior firepower, sped off, tyres squealing, adding the smell of burning rubber to the cordite from the guns. It was all over in such a short space of time that François wondered if the attack had really happened.

The police allowed the perpetrators to flee, their near-suicidal behaviour a cause for concern. If they were pursued, the French Minister would be left with less protection and therefore more vulnerable to a second attack, should one be planned, which was very possible.

François quickly consulted the driver, who gave his consent for a brief sortie to inspect the scene prior to continuing their journey to the conference. The standard motorway police quickly closed the motorway to perform the necessary search of the area for evidence and to clear away the bodies. Other patrols gave chase to the fleeing gunmen, but it proved fruitless.

Nat quickly arranged that the other arrivals each take a different route to the venue and liaised with Mrs Puddleford as to her intentions. Should the conference be cancelled or would they continue? Her response surprised him. While clearly tense, she replied that the decision should be left to François Maranville when he arrived.

"Wow, she has more guts than I gave her credit for," he confessed to Laura as soon as they were alone.

"It also says a lot about the importance of this conference. But why did they have to target the French Minister in Britain? Why couldn't they just do it in France?"

"Good question, but unanswerable at the moment. For now, we have to concentrate on the safety of our charges. I'd like to think that attack settles it—that the threat is over and we can relax a bit—but it's still early. I agree with you, why the French Minister and why here as opposed to anywhere else? That said, multiple terrorist attacks in the same area are incredibly rare, so we may be lucky."

"Okay, but even if he wants the conference to continue, we also need to consider the implications of this to his mental capacity. Should we allow the conference to proceed?"

"Let's play it by ear when we're able to speak to him. We need to keep our options and minds open."

Tense minutes passed as they waited for the battered limo to arrive at the hotel and an ashen-faced François Maranville to emerge, supporting his more-troubled assistant. Some hotel staff took her off to a quiet area, ready for some counselling and a medical assessment that had been arranged for them both. Maranville was escorted to a second room, where Laura and Nat sat him down and first tried to determine his frame of mind, intentions and whether he had any ideas to why he had been attacked.

Laura took the lead. "Monsieur Maranville, we are from the security services. We can assure you that the hotel is safe. You are safe now. Are you happy to talk for a few minutes? Any information we can get at this stage could be very helpful."

"Absolutely, mademoiselle. I am, of course, happy to talk and help you in any way I can." His thick French accent had been made deeper, thicker through his habit of smoking fifteen Gauloises cigarettes a day.

"Thank you, Monsieur. First, how do you feel about the conference continuing?"

"It must, of course, continue. We don't come a long way to resolve a crisis of profound magnitude and cancel because of personal scares. We must look to history and learn from past heroes to know how we, too, must respond."

As he finished, François Maranville fumbled inside his jacket pocket and fished out a packet of cigarettes. He extracted one and lit it. Neither Laura nor Nat was going to challenge him on the legality of smoking inside a public building, but both noted that his hands were as steady as a rock. Nat simply hoped that any smoke alarm in the room would not be sufficiently sensitive to send the hotel into evacuation mode and send everyone's stress levels off the Richter scale!

At a loss as to how to respond to such courageous words, Laura replied "Thank you, monsieur. As you'd expect, we've received a good account of what happened from our colleagues. What we would like to know is if you know of any reason why you would be specifically targeted, whether at home in France or here in Britain? We wish to determine whether this is more likely to have been a random one-off attack or if there is an imminent risk that further attacks on your person could occur."

"Ah, mademoiselle, a good, a deep, and searching, yet difficult question. My profession will inherently place people in one of three camps for how other people regard me: They don't care who I am or what I do. They approve of, maybe adore me and my philosophies, or they loathe and possibly hate me." At this he gave a very French and resigned shrug of not knowing. "Would anyone want to kill me in such a fashion? I should think not. Why? I am a minor minister. *Pas importante!*" he finished off with flair.

"We understand. That's very helpful." As Laura spoke again, both she and Nat exchanged their agreed signal of twisting their pens to signify their perception that he was not only willing but also capable of continuing with the conference. "Please, just a couple more questions. I understand that you asked to exit the safety of your vehicle and review the scene before continuing the journey. Why was that?"

"That is simple, mademoiselle. I wished to look into the eyes of those who wished me harm and who wish to disrupt the work I hold most dear. To see the persons who would try this. That is all."

"And what did you see? Did you recognise anyone?"

"Oof! *Non, mademoiselle.* I did not recognise anyone. What I saw was young men with no hope and probably brainwashed by those without the courage to stand up in public and discuss their points of view because they know their perspectives hold no substance!"

"Monsieur, that has been very helpful. Thank you. We will let you join the conference now and can assure you that your safety and that of all the delegates here is of paramount importance to us and will be protected with our lives if necessary."

"You are both very gracious, but let us pray it does not come to that, *n'est pas?*" he replied as he stood, straight backed, and shook hands with them, his double-breasted dark blue suit still looking immaculate, off-setting the crisp white shirt and pale blue tie.

As the door closed behind him, Nat whistled air between his lips to show his appreciation of what he had just heard. "There goes one cool customer and a tough cookie!"

"Now look who's talking," Laura said, smiling. "That said, my sentiments entirely. But I don't think this is over yet."

"Yes, I tend to agree. I'll take a swing around the guys shortly to emphasise that we remain on alert, at a higher level of threat than before, if that's possible. But I can't make heads or tails of this. If that was a diversionary attack or one to tempt us to drop our guard, it was first, a suicide mission for those who went and second, a pretty lousy attempt. It just doesn't make sense."

"I'm with you on that. Anyway, you need to rally your guys while I make some phone calls. The media will be braying for information, and the French authorities will want assurances."

23

The conference got off to a late, hesitant, and tense start, but eventually the doors were closed and the proceedings got underway. Every delegate was very aware that the reason or reasons for the interruption to the distribution of critical medicines throughout Europe had to be determined and a solution for fixing the problems found. They had also openly discussed over pre-conference coffee whether the disruption and the morning's presumed terrorist attack on François Maranville's car were connected.

Were there previously unrecognised built-in failures at their organisations, or with their processes? If so, what fixes were required, and who was best placed to action those remedies? Alternatively, was something more sinister at play? To date, this had not really been contemplated, although it was not taken off the agenda. Now it was to be taken far more seriously.

By the mid-morning coffee break, it was clear to everyone that the focus had not been lost, despite the morning's dramatic distractions. The delegates were talking with great fervour as they moved into the rooms set up ready for drinks and biscuits. Mrs Puddleford's expression had changed from one of bordering upon a startled hare caught in a car's headlights to one of her usual professional gravity and seriousness as she contemplated what lay before them to resolve the crisis. She even managed to smile as Nat approached her to very quickly provide her with the assurance she wanted—everything was quiet in the vicinity, and others were taking care of the enquiries from the world's press about the morning's events. All in all, she had nothing to worry about.

Mrs Puddleford even curtailed the length of the break to get everyone back around the table, so great was her desire not to lose the momentum gained from the previous session and to make up on lost time. She even sent the kitchen staff into a complete spin as lunch approached by agreeing with everyone that it should be a working lunch instead of the planned more formal affair in the dining room. The intended waiter- and waitress-served meal had to be rapidly rearranged to become a serve-yourself buffet in the conference room.

"Well, hopefully such zeal will put pay to the golf," Nat commented to Laura when the hotel manager informed them of the planned change to the lunch arrangements. "That should make matters easier for us, at least."

The additional stress caused by the request was tangible throughout the hotel as people scurried around and exchanged conversations kept as quiet as possible, although the language used became more colourful.

However, at 2:30 p.m., Nat's hopes were dashed. Everyone required a break and fresh air. Mrs Puddleford announced that they would first have the obligatory conference photo call. Then those who wished to could hit a few golf balls for fifteen minutes, while the others could either simply relax or wander the gardens, which, she announced, had been designed by some famous gardener of ages past. She proceeded to speak eloquently about some chap Nat had never heard of and that there were some rare plants.

Now it was Nat's turn to stress—no one had said anything about garden walks! How could Mrs Puddleford's love of gardens not have been noted and associated with one of the venue's key attractions?

He and Laura had walked through the garden and he recalled thinking, *Not bad. Nice if you have the space and money,* but he had not been overwhelmed. Now he had to split and thin down a couple of patrols to cover this activity as well! He was fuming, but refused to let it show as he rallied his teams.

"Base to all, delegates are emerging for their photo, followed by fifteen, I repeat fifteen minutes of recreation. Both golf and walking the gardens. I need someone to cover the gardens pronto. Hill patrols one and two, report in."

"All very quiet, Nat. Pass through traffic only. Hill One out."

"Same for Hill Two, Nat."

The responses were the same for the perimeter patrols and those spread throughout the grounds.

Both Nat and Laura stood behind the photographer, their backs to the delegates as they scanned the surrounding area.

"Grounds patrol four!" barked Nat suddenly, sharply, but quietly. "Movement in the woods, at least two people! Move!"

Nat continued his search in greater earnest through his powerful binoculars but could not locate the movement he had seen. The photographer was happily snapping away, and the conversation between shots among the delegates was light-hearted, so Nat really did not want to alarm people by bundling them all back inside if it wasn't necessary.

A few tense minutes later, they received a reply. "Just a couple of kids out for a bit of loving stuff, sir. All okay." Nat and Laura just looked at each other. There was no need for words; their faces articulated the relief that they felt.

"Good, but make sure we know how they got so far in without being traced. That's an unacceptable lapse!"

"Sir!"

Then, turning to Laura, he added, "Someone's going to feel the toe of my boot on their behind for that one!"

By this time, the delegates were starting to disperse, some heading off to the gardens and others to the golf, carrying their clubs as well as the freebies of golf balls, tees, and cleaning clothes that had been left for them in the coffee room.

Laura and Nat trailed those delegates who fancied the golf in the direction of the driving range and pitch and putt. As they let the delegates walk on ahead, they listened to the banter and challenges being levelled to see who could drive the furthest with the new balls they had just picked up and how they should all hit the balls simultaneously. Not particularly interested, Laura and Nat turned off towards the gardens via the pro's shop.

"Well, at least it appears that the conference is going well and that the earlier fracas has been put behind us," Laura commented.

Nat merely nodded and made an affirmative noise as he continued to scan the horizon.

As Laura strolled about the shop, fingering the clothes and other items for sale, Nat chatted to the pro, taking an interest in the new balls he was giving away. "So why give all these balls away? What's wrong with them?" he asked in a half-teasing tone.

"Oh, they're the latest and the best, or so I'm told. But as with all new things to enter a traditional game, it is difficult to get take-up. So what better way to get something established than to have a promotional giveaway, particularly to influential people who will hopefully like them and tell others?"

"Yeah, I guess that makes sense," Nat replied, unconvinced, his mind trying to fathom how another attack could be perpetrated, if at all.

"Would you like some, sir?" the pro was asking.

"Huh, oh, yes, thanks." Nat was looking out of the windows towards the distance, searching for anything at all that could be out of place. The pro handed him three boxes, each containing three balls. Without really looking, Nat flipped a packet open and rolled a ball into his palm, toying with it as he watched the delegates approach the range.

"Hmm, an odd feeling to them. Different somehow."

"Exactly, sir. It's as you'd expect from something revolutionary."

"I suppose. Hey, Laura, you play golf?"

"A little, why?"

"Take a look at these new balls." With that he tossed one over to her. "They feel real different." Then, turning back to the pro, he said, "So, tell me the sales talk on why these are supposed to be so good."

Laura caught the ball adeptly and fingered it thoughtfully for no more than two seconds before exclaiming, "Shit!" She carefully placed the ball on top of the golf sweaters beside where she was standing and charged out of the shop, shouting to Nat to put everything down. Then, as she approached the delegates, she yelled, "Stop! Stop! No one do anything! Stand still!"

"What the…!" exclaimed Nat, taken aback by her language and action. He partly moved to follow, but hesitated and reviewed the ball in his hand and the one Laura had laid on the sweaters. He then stared intently at the pro, examining his face properly for the first time, noticing that it was covered in sweat and he had large sweat marks beneath his arms. "What—" he started, but the pro placed a finger to his own lips.

"Maybe, sir, you need to follow your colleague," he uttered whilst holding up a piece of paper upon which was scribbled, "I can't talk," and he pointed to his lapel.

"You're right. I'll be right back for the balls—anything to help my game," Nat then opened and closed the door to the pro's shop, but did not leave. He quietly walked back over to the pro, who was scribbling on a piece of paper, muttering, "Crazy people. A dozen balls and two sweaters—a good start. That's been worth my time." However, he had written, "*They have my family. I had to bring the balls but don't know why.*"

Nat nodded and wrote on another sheet, "*OK. Stay here. We can help. What's the address?*"

Armed with the address, he quietly left the shop, breaking into a sprint to follow hot on Laura's heels the moment the door was closed.

When he arrived, Laura was nearly bent double, trying to catch her breath while continuing to say, "Don't touch anything, don't do anything," to a lot of bemused and very concerned people.

"Okay, Laura," started Nat. "Take it slow and explain what it is about these balls. Presumably it is the balls, right?"

Laura nodded, breathless after her sprint and barely able to talk. Then between deep breaths she replied, "I don't know what it is about the balls, but they're new and you say they feel different. That's what some of the guys reported about the hundreds of golf balls found and confiscated during the Leicester raid the other day. Too much of a coincidence."

Nat had no hesitation in agreeing. "Okay, everyone, sorry about this, but no golf today. All balls received today, whether free or bought, are to be left where they are, or handed to me immediately please."

Addressing everyone in a very authoritarian voice, François Maranville declared, "I think, messieurs, mesdames, that if the good lady and gentleman here consider that golfing holds potential danger, we should adjourn back to the hotel. More excitement will unduly detract from our intended purposes here today, and it does appear that the challenges ahead of us are of another's purposeful and menacing makings."

The murmurs of assent were unanimous. There was just one voice expressing a level of curiosity. "So just what could be the danger posed by a golf ball? The security services say that they have had sniffer dogs out and thorough searches throughout the hotel and grounds, so I'm curious."

"A fair question, sir, because we also checked these balls," replied Nat, looking directly at the speaker, whose name he did not know. He recognised him as being one of the business leaders attending the conference. "Quite frankly, I don't know what risk could be posed by these things, but they feel different from a normal golf ball and only arrived today with the golf pro, who says he has been obliged to bring the balls here today by way of a direct threat against his family. Clearly, I trust that what I've just said goes no further because I have a team racing to his home address as we speak, and we don't want more trouble than we already have.

"That said, I too am curious, so since we have a couple of minutes, may I ask you all to head back to the hotel and I will then try to find out. You will be able to watch from the steps."

Once Nat was confident everyone had both handed in all of the golf balls and was well away, he picked one ball from the pile and walked towards the fifty-metre marker, a reasonable-sized concrete pillar in the ground. Taking aim from a good distance, he hurled the ball at the pillar, confident he would be able to hit the target, which he did with ease. The explosion, while not huge, obliterated the pillar and would have comfortably killed anyone within the close vicinity. However, a second, far larger explosion occurred almost instantaneously behind him as the pile of balls erupted, sending shreds of balls in all directions.

Laura, watching Nat closely through her binoculars, saw him spin around, mouthing expletives as he saw what had happened. Somehow the explosion of one had caused the detonation of the others within a certain distance. Fortunately, the pro's shop was beyond that critical distance as it remained standing, although she did see both the pro and the two security men watching over him emerge from the shop in a great hurry, mouths open in speechless shock.

François Maranville broke the silence of the onlookers. "This is too much, Mademoiselle," he continued, addressing

Laura. "There are many questions and so far, no answers. I am sure you will inform everyone present of the conclusions you reach when you do. I am grateful to you for preventing our deaths. But I do suspect that your services will be required at the end of today to assist in unravelling what we think may be happening to critical European medicines."

"You have my word, Monsieur, that everyone will be kept informed. This is most disturbing. We are fortunate that no one has died here today, and let's hope the golf pro's family can be released safely as well. If there are links to what you have been discussing here today, then, most certainly, we will be ready to assist in whatever way necessary."

As everyone trooped back into the main conference room, Laura held back, waiting for Nat. "Now I wasn't expecting that!" he announced as he drew near. "Bloody impressive though, I must say. Each ball individually is a phenomenal weapon, but being linked to all others within a certain distance is sheer, evil genius! How they got past the sniffer dogs is beyond me. At least, assuming the pro is telling the truth about being bugged, those listening in at the other end will assume the dirty deed has been done and was a success. Hopefully, therefore, his family may be safe."

"Ah, so that was your game. I was very surprised by your actions, I must say, but that does explain things."

Nat smiled. "Always sense in my madness!"

"Glad to hear it. My concern now is the stockpile in Leicester. We need to find out where they came from and if they are being distributed elsewhere. Imagine this going off at clubs around the country!"

"Just don't go there! I don't want to contemplate the potential, but of course you are right."

❖❖❖

Half an hour later, Laura and Nat were in a meeting room busy making and taking phone calls and briefing people about the golf ball situation when Nat's temper blew.

"Shit! The bastards!" he exclaimed viciously as he slammed the phone down. Looking over at Laura, he elaborated, "Sorry for the language, but the team have just entered the pro's home and found his wife and two children dead—tied up and shot through the heads at close range. The neighbours heard and saw nothing. We need to find these guys and just let me know where and when. Then me and my teams will want to participate and give them some of their own medicine! Now I have to go and tell that poor man. Shit!" With that, he stormed off.

Laura sat there shell-shocked. She knew Nat would be the consummate professional by the time he arrived at the pro's shop. She also knew she felt exactly the same.

Both were relieved when the conference finished and all the delegates had departed. Laura agreed to keep Nat updated on seeking the distributors of the golf balls and left, pleased that she had a driver, and she was soon asleep in the passenger seat as they headed back south to London.

24

As soon as the full details of the events at the conference and the pro's family were relayed to them, Gurning and Rob paid an urgent visit to Burak at his place of incarceration, a farmhouse that was a heavily secured safe house.

Gurning wasted no time in briefing Burak and getting to the point. "Do you have any idea where these golf balls could be made and/or be distributed from? Saturday is nearly upon us and will be a typically huge day for people to play golf!"

Burak merely sat there, silent, a look of profound horror on his face.

"Burak!" Rob chimed in. "Innocent people have died today. It had nothing to do with the nature of the businesses you built up, but was because of terrorism. They were needless deaths, which I know you abhor. You have to help us. Think of Evelyne and what she meant to you and your change of heart for the sake of both her and for Anja. Think of how the golf pro feels right now, if not more so because his entire family has just been wiped out!"

Burak looked at Rob through sad, defeated eyes. He had become a shadow of his former self in recent weeks.

"Burak, this is not like you! Where has your spirit gone? Is this how you want Anja to next see you and remember you? Come on. You have a great role to play here. I know Emilio's use of your network and links with terrorism has been hard on you, but let's *take him and them down*! *Let's take them down!*"

Aware that a relationship and level of respect had grown between the two men, one he could not hope to emulate, Gurning left Rob to it. He was certain Rob's words would have a far greater effect than his own entreaties.

Burak regarded Rob thoughtfully. "Of course you're right, Rob. It's just having lost Evelyne and effectively lost Anja as well as my freedom, coupled with the realisation that what I created—however dreadful it was—has been hijacked for terrorism is worse than hard."

"Burak, you know you don't deserve freedom! What you have is far more than most in your position. You have access to far more than others and are not incarcerated in prison. Look at you! You're living in relative luxury to enable you to see Anja from time to time, purely and simply on the basis that you agreed to help me and the authorities. This arrangement also provides you with your life which, I am sure you are all too aware, would not be long if Emilio and others were aware of your current arrangements!"

"Okay, okay, I get it. I need to stop moping, snap to it, and regain my zeal. I would love to see Emilio and that lot suffer. To answer your question, the most likely place is Kiln Farm in Milton Keynes and a pair of adjoining warehouses. One is a legitimate distribution business that belongs to Tracy Bond. She's a tough lady who takes no nonsense. Emilio persuaded me to let him use the other unit since it was sitting empty. Said he wanted it for the preparation of materials. The only time I went there, without Emilio's knowledge, the place was decked out big time. At least a quarter of the warehouse space was set aside as a clean room, with a lot of scientific-type equipment in there. I didn't hang around for long; I didn't have the time. Nor did I have the inclination to ask any questions.

"I do know that Emilio, through someone in his network, has struck a lucrative deal with Tracy to distribute his wares all over the place. She, of course, only sees a legitimate business and a profitable contract."

"Sounds worthy of a try," Rob suggested to Gurning.

"I agree, but we don't have time for potshots. That's my concern," Gurning replied.

Turning back to Burak, Rob asked, "What's your business relationship with this Tracy Bond? Since you are still pulling the levers, would you be able to ask her what orders she has and what shipments she has made in recent days?"

"I guess I could, yes."

Without hesitation, Gurning handed Burak a secure phone, one that could not be reverse traced. Burak gave him a hard stare but took the phone and walked over to the corner of the room, where he made the call, speaking in soft tones, disguising his voice in a way that neither Rob, nor Gurning had heard before. They could not hear the conversation clearly, but it was evident that the early minutes were exchanging courtesies and pleasantries. After a while, however, the tone took on a serious, business-like note. Finally, the tone changed again to the typical concluding pleasantries.

Burak leant back against the wall with a deep sigh and stared out of the window. The silence weighed heavily on the three men, none wanting to break those precious moments of private thought. The room was quite small, but the light colours of both the walls and the furniture made it feel more spacious. There were five lounge-type fabric chairs with a small coffee table beside each. A bookcase stood either side of the only door, each one stuffed with dog-eared paperbacks.

Eventually Burak broke the silence, aware of the two pairs of eyes fixed firmly on him. "Yes, she confirmed that her firm has delivered large numbers of golf balls across the country in recent weeks for a launch on Saturday. She also has an order to pick up many more boxes tomorrow from the neighbouring unit for further same-day deliveries. She's got a pile herself and intends to share them with her friends. I didn't have the courage to tell her not to use them. I will trust you to do that and save the goodness only knows how many souls who will otherwise be killed, maimed, or injured. Tracy's a good girl. Go softly on her."

With that Burak walked out without saying anything further to his visitors; he merely muttered, "What have I done?" over and over to himself. As he left, he dropped a piece of paper with the exact address and Tracy Bond's contact details onto Gurning's lap, together with the mobile phone. He had done his bit for now. Much more would be demanded of him in time.

"Come on Rob, let's go. We've got work to do."

They walked out of the farmhouse to the car, ready for the return journey to London. Gurning's mobile phone was already firmly held against his ear, and he was talking earnestly by the time they settled back into the leather seats and the driver set off.

"Rob, I will leave the communication with Tracy Bond to you," Gurning said. "We will go in tomorrow morning, as soon as Emilio's building appears to be full of people. Your empire is growing, and from what I hear, you're doing pretty well as both owner and ambassador to soothe the transition."

"No problem, will do. It was a shame that Burak left as he did. I was hoping to ask after Anja and how she is doing."

There was a momentary hesitation from Gurning before he said, "I'm glad you didn't. It would have been a little awkward."

To answer Rob's questioning glance, Gurning continued, "Katherine and I have adopted Anja. Burak would have expected you to know, but I decided to keep this as low key as possible. She needs a home and ideally one that can understand the complexities of her situation and provide the required security. She also needs to go to school. Katherine is a linguist; that's how we met. She also has a degree in psychology, so she should be able to appreciate what Anja is going through. Apologies—I should have let you know. It was clear that you'd grown fond of her, and she of you. However, for her sake, opinion is that it's best that connections with the Services are minimised. Unfortunately, that includes you. I hope you understand."

"Yes, I guess I do, and I probably would not be the most reliable contact for her, which likewise would not help in her progression."

Laura knocked on Rob's bedroom door at the Ealing safe house and popped her head round at 5:00 a.m. the next morning. Rob was still in bed. "Wakey, wakey," she said brightly.

"Urgh! How can you? Surely you're not ready yet?"

Laughing, she entered, still wearing her nightwear of extra-long T-shirt. "No chance. Just wanted to make sure you'll be ready to leave in forty-five. Coffee's brewing downstairs. See you soon."

"Laura."

"Yes?"

"I heard yesterday was rather hairy. I'm glad you're okay."

"Thanks. I'll fill you in on the way to Milton Keynes. We need to get through today as well." With that she withdrew and left Rob to get ready.

Two and a bit hours later they were sipping the day's second cup of coffee at a command centre set up on the forecourt of a vacant warehouse two kilometres away from the target premises. They had driven up in a services-issue saloon and laughed frequently as Laura activated the wipers, making them swish and judder over a dry windscreen, instead of operating the indicator lights.

Rob was in a light grey suit with open-neck blue shirt. "So, are you ready for your meeting with Tracy Bond?" the day's commander asked. "She's expecting you any time after eight o'clock, aware that you may be caught in traffic. She said her diary is clear, and she has not arrived yet. I will let you know when to go. We want you there shortly after she arrives so that she does not take any calls or in-person meetings from the golf ball folks, so you must keep her talking. I suspect that will be easy enough considering your message and the implications for her business.

"It will only be when the other unit appears to be fully operational that we will strike, but no later than nine-thirty. You are not to tell her about the strike until it happens. At that point, a liaison team will come in to evacuate all employees from the side fire escape. A coach will be there to whisk them away to a safe distance. I sincerely hope the explosives won't be used, but we can't be sure. Everything clear?"

"Yes, but I think it's the wrong approach. An hour and a half is too long for me to keep her talking without coming clean about the raid. In her place, she may well ask me to leave after the first five minutes so she can, at the very least, seek confirmation of what I'm saying and very possibly seek legal advice. My arrival with an unannounced message of this nature will be like a bombshell. This is not the usual way of communicating the corporate change of ownership!"

"Okay then, we will have to play everything by ear and let you go in say fifteen minutes before we strike. That means you will have to wait until the target premises are fully operational. We are monitoring all phones into Bond Distribution, so if she receives a call from next door, if it's at all concerning, we will have to cut the line, in which case we strike immediately and you will follow afterwards, as you did in Leicester. How does that sound?"

"I still think it's the wrong approach, but I am happy to run with it, if that's how you want it played."

"Excuse me, sir," a policewoman said as she turned around from her monitoring position. "Prime Zulu has turned up with two others, one of which is Delta from the London op. Delta was held by the third person and appeared both unwilling and possibly beaten."

"Just so I'm clear and that code names have not changed," interrupted Laura immediately, "Prime Zulu is Khartoum?"

"That's correct," confirmed the commander.

"In that case, there is no way that Rob goes in ahead of us. We think Prime Zulu is aware of who he is, possibly even has seen photographs. If he saw Rob going in next door, this operation would be blown, as would the potential for many others! Let me see the third person. If Prime Zulu is here, I'm willing to bet the other is Sharif Al Rashid."

Laura leant over the woman's console to review a replay. "Yes, that's Rashid all right. If both Khartoum and Rashid are here, we should go in now and not risk them leaving."

The policewoman interrupted, adding, "There are still cars arriving at the site, though, and there's quite a lot of traffic on the estate roads."

"Okay," said Laura, turning to the commander. "If you agree, this is how we play it. Prime Zulu must be apprehended, as well as the golf ball operation being taken down. I know we are trying for low key, but if he's here, we must act. If someone mentions they've seen a police command centre in the vicinity, then he's gone, no hesitation. We should block the surrounding roads for incoming traffic—now—and allow existing estate traffic to dissipate, get to where they are going and then strike. Agreed?"

"Okay, agreed."

Rob could see that the commander was uncomfortable at being given such explicit orders, but he sensibly recognised he had no choice and put everyone on standby. Then he set about making arrangements for the road blocks. A covert surveillance team moved in to cover all possible exits to ensure Khartoum did not get away.

A painfully slow twenty-three minutes slipped by before the commander gave the green light to the strike force. Laura accompanied Rob and the liaison team to Bond Distribution, walking through the front door moments after the strike force went into the adjoining unit.

The strike force went in through the three visible people entrances: the front door and side and rear emergency exits. The vehicular roller shutter door was left closed but guarded. Their instructions were clear: no flashbang or any other sort of explosive device was to be used. They just did not know enough about how the golf balls worked to risk using anything of their own.

The strike team smashed the doors in using their handheld battering rams, with teams of eight charging in immediately once the doors were down. Half the team entering the front door headed for the stairs to cover the small first-floor office space.

The remainder all found their way into the warehouse space, guns pointed directly in front of them and shouting instructions to stop what they were doing and lie face down on the floor, creating pandemonium among all who were there. The space was mostly open but, as Burak had described, a quarter of the space was partitioned off, creating the equivalent of a single-storey large box room. There was a heavy door and viewing panel in one wall, complete with an electronic keypad to control access. Otherwise the walls were solid and blank.

Apart from that, the space provided adequate room for a large van to reverse in and allow the roller-shutter door to close while the remainder of the space was fitted out with work benches, some of which appeared to be used for packing and others with mounted vertical drills and polishing equipment for some sort of assembly. Boxes of golf balls were stacked up close to the loading area, and hundreds more balls were in large wire-mesh baskets with empty cardboard boxes waiting to be filled piled high on the work tops. There was no mistaking that they were in the right place.

Most people immediately obliged and fell flat to the floor, only a few hesitated momentarily. Four went for their own weapons, either on their belts or lying beside them on a worktop. The armed police wasted no time in killing them, the bursts of gunfire echoing around the large space. Seeing their colleagues fall to the floor, their heads and chests caving in from the impact of the bullets, was the only incentive required for those who hesitated before taking a prone position on the floor.

The police then cautiously worked their way through the area, handcuffing those already lying on the floor and ensuring that no one was hiding in some unseen place. In time, they came to the secured box room. The lead man raised a mirror to see through the visibility panel without having to expose himself.

"Activity seen. Unknown number of occupants," he reported before trying the door handle, which did not budge.

However, as he spoke, a burst of gunfire pepper-potted the door and the police rapidly retreated behind some nearby workbenches. Gunfire continued sending bullets in wavy lines all around and through the walls.

"Okay, we treat this as a hostage situation and consolidate our positions until we know everyone else is safe and all explosive material and golf balls are removed," the team leader ordered over his radio.

Meanwhile, part of the team worked their way rapidly up the stairs, crouched and ready for action. The fire door at the top was helpfully, but illegally, propped open with a fire extinguisher, giving them a clear view of much of the open-plan office floor, with a meeting room and office at the far end. As they rounded the half landing on the stairs, shots rang out from the far end of the office, sending bullets slamming into the wall above the oncoming police, splattering them with dislodged plaster and dust. The police immediately returned fire to provide cover as they scampered up the remaining few stairs to gain access to the office space and shelter behind a row of filing cabinets.

A few more shots rang out before a small explosion occurred that sent smoke, dust, and debris flying into the office space.

"Brace!" called the team leader as they all expected the rest of the building to blow because of the golf balls downstairs in the warehouse. Precious seconds ticked by. "Must be clear. Hold! Someone's heading our way!"

From out of the billowing smoke, a figure started to emerge carrying a machine gun. The police called for the person to drop the weapon, put his hands on his head, and lie on the floor. Instead, the still-shadowy figure raised his arms rapidly, gun still firmly held and swinging forward.

Four shots rang out from the police, hurling the person backwards and onto the floor. The team of four worked their way forward cautiously but without experiencing any further resistance.

When they reached the downed hostile, the lead officer checked him for life signs before confirming he was dead and cursing. "Damn it, he was a decoy! There's no magazine in the gun, which is taped to his hand! We were forced to shoot a potentially unwilling accomplice! Looks like Delta."

They continued to work their way forward until they reached the office and meeting room. Darting his head forward and back around the doorframe, the lead officer looked into the office. "Office and meeting room are connected. Someone's in a chair sitting in the doorway between the two rooms. Appears to be alive. You two, take the meeting room doorway. Joe and me will take this one," the team leader announced, pointing to two of the officers.

When they were in place, those at the meeting room door reported in, "Ready, guv. We can see a hole has also been blown through the wall into the neighbouring unit."

"Understood. Assumption, therefore, is that this person is another decoy, but be careful. You two watch that hole and cover us. We'll take the chair." They moved in, sweeping their machine guns around to cover the area, and crept around the desk to check for potential unpleasant surprises there. Having secured the room, they approached the chair.

The lead officer gingerly approached the seated figure. A man turned slowly on the swivel chair to face him. In the dim light, the officer was confronted with a pale and utterly expressionless face with blank, lifeless eyes, as though looking straight through him. There was not a flicker from the eyes nor a twitch from the mouth as the figure slowly moved his arms to open his jacket.

"Shit! Explosive belt!"

That was the last the command centre heard from those four officers as a large explosion ripped through the front of the building, blowing out the walls, both internal and external, the roof, and the floor. A cloud of smoke and dust rose into the air and covered the officers in the warehouse area below with debris. But still the golf ball explosives did not blow.

The explosion provided the required distraction for some officers to storm the box room, shooting the lock off and rolling into the confined space, avoiding the reactive burst of fire from the two occupants. Bullets smashed and scattered jars, boxes, and other items that had been on the worktops. One of the officers, prone on the ground, sprayed a long burst of bullets at just above ground level, catching both hostiles in the shins and sending them crashing to the floor, screaming in pain. Rapidly, the officers ran forward, kicking the hostiles' weapons out of reach before rolling them over roughly onto their bellies to handcuff them.

Radioing in, the lead officer reported, "Rear box room hostiles wounded and secured. Assistance required. All other areas secured."

As they entered Bond Distribution, Laura showed the receptionist her identity badge and asked where Tracy Bond could be found before telling her to leave her position immediately and follow the instructions provided by the uniformed police who had entered with Rob and herself. The receptionist was required to guide the police around the building's ground floor to evacuate all occupants. Laura and Rob would cover the first floor as they made their way to find Tracy Bond.

Laura announced her arrival on the floor with style. "Police! Please evacuate the building immediately by the nearest emergency exit. You will find officers on the ground floor and outside ready to support you. Go!"

Tracy Bond emerged from her office at the far end, clearly frustrated at the interruption. Her loose-fitting trouser suit was elegant and flattered her large build. She had a commanding presence, with a kind, open, and friendly face. As she emerged, the staff who had stood up and started to leave faltered, looking back at her for guidance.

"Folks, that's an order. Leave! Now!" yelled Laura, having seen the sudden hesitancy. By now she and Rob were two-thirds of the way across the floor to meet the boss lady. "Ms Bond? I'm Lisa Grahams, Security Services. This is Robert Krane, with whom you had an appointment. Unfortunately events have overtaken us, and we need to evacuate the building. Now! We will explain once we are safe."

There was no need to say more as the muffled sound of gunfire was heard from the neighbouring unit, sending the now-panicked staff scuttling towards the stairs.

Tracy Bond fixed Laura and Rob with an initially firm stare and then said pleasantly, "I'll be with you in a moment. I'll just gather my things."

She turned and ignored Laura's protestations not to return to her office. A long minute dragged by before Laura popped her head in the door to insist that they get moving.

Laura and Rob became impatient as they walked slowly through the office, Tracy Bond pushing chairs under the desks as they passed. "Ms Bond, this really is unnecessary. We need to speed up and get you to safety. There are explosives next door!"

Tracy Bond looked at them blankly and as if they were stupid. "I know," she replied calmly, leaving them stunned, momentarily speechless, and totally off guard. With that, Tracy Bond produced a handgun from her oversized handbag and pointed it at them both. "Now, shall we start this conversation again?"

Rob judged the distance between them and sadly realised he was too far away to take any action. "Let's return to my office, where we can discuss my safe passage. I would like my friends from next door to join me, assuming you haven't killed them yet. If you haven't, then all hostilities next door are to halt immediately. While we wait, you can also enlighten me as to how exactly you traced the golf balls here. That idiot of a golf pro didn't know anything, and he was the only outsider I can think of. If you fail to answer satisfactorily and in a timely manner, I will have to use non-lethal parts of your bodies as target practice!"

Laura was quick to respond, aware that Rob was trying to get close. She hoped her response would divert Tracy Bond's attention towards herself and potentially help him. "I'm not sure what you mean about golf balls or of your involvement in anything, but it certainly sounds like something we should know about. We were merely following some known criminals and tracked them to next door. You could have walked free without our knowing, had it not been for this." Laura waved a hand casually at the handgun.

It was now Tracy Bond's turn to look slightly surprised. "Uh-uh," she said quickly to both Laura's hand and Rob's proximity.

She then squeezed off two shots at a uniformed and unarmed police officer who had appeared at the top of the stairs, sending him toppling backwards down the stairs with an agonising scream. "Now that'll be a useful message to say that I mean business! Now come on, let's go to my office."

She moved to face them, placing herself equidistant between them, the gun steadily alternating between them. "Turn round and move!" she ordered again as Laura and Rob, who had their backs towards the office, realised that their opportunity to distract Tracy and act against her was gone.

Just then an ear-splitting explosion tore through the space from the office, sending fragments of concrete block, stud partition, and glass flying and smacking into them like blunt shrapnel pounding their bodies. Instinctively all three bowed their heads, and Tracy Bond shielded her eyes with her free arm. Rob took the opportunity to close the distance and kick out to disarm Ms Bond, sending her gun flying off beneath a nearby desk. Laura pulled her own handgun from her bag, but a chilling voice cut her short.

"Drop that pathetic piece of metal, Ms Grahams. I thought I saw you and your boyfriend here as your colleagues broke the peace and quiet."

She turned to see Khartoum standing in the billowing dust with a machine gun pointed at all three. "Ah, Tracy, so pleased you weren't next to the wall when I pressed the button. The mess would have been so much worse. Since you're still alive and didn't leave with everyone else, perhaps you'd be so good as to help keep these two under control—Ms Grahams has proven to be a frustrating nuisance in the past. And now that I get a good look at the boyfriend, I would like to know whether it was him who caused Emilio so many problems in Slovenia. His appearance is very similar to the description I heard. I thought it could be, but wasn't sure. Emilio will be *so* pleased. It's a shame I didn't let him know my suspicions as he'd have given me greater resource. He is one seriously annoyed man at the moment."

Laura and Rob looked at each other in a combined mix of horror that Rob had been identified and of relief that Emilio did not yet know.

Tracy looked around unsuccessfully for her gun. "Take Ms Grahams' gun, you stupid woman!"

"Mustafa!" Tracy said, sounding hurt. "Don't be like that, I thought…"

"Exactly your problem! Thinking too much while flouncing around as some successful businesswoman, instead of obeying me, or staying at home where you belong!" Khartoum spat his criticism of her out. "Now let's see if you can be useful, and I will consider taking you with me." Then, turning to Laura, he said, "I presume you have a radio. Give it to me."

With the barrel of his gun thrust into her face, there was little choice but to comply. Laura reached with her left hand into her jacket pocket. "Careful!" exclaimed Khartoum, thrusting the gun at her once again. Laura extracted her radio, carefully pressing the emergency alert and system wipe buttons as she did. *At least the command centre will now know for sure that we're in trouble*, she thought, *even though it should be self-evident.*

"Good," said Khartoum. "Now, to the meeting room over there. We will wait there."

As they started to pick their way through the rubble another explosion blew more debris over them. Rob immediately fell over, stretching his hands out as he landed and hit the floor. Tracy kicked him in the ribs. "Get up! And keep your hands open and where I can see them."

"Ah, that will be my comrade. Hopefully he killed many others with him!" Khartoum stated flatly, his attention also on Rob, although his gun never moved from Laura. Rob shuffled his hands beneath him to get into a good position and slowly pushed himself up, opening his hands and moving them wide as he did so.

A few minutes later, Rob and Laura were bunched together, sitting on the floor, in a corner of the meeting room while Khartoum and Tracy sat in a couple of dusty chairs. Khartoum was banging the radio, trying to get it to work when a voice called from outside using a loud hailer. "Mustafa Khartoum! This is Commander Peeves. Let me speak to your hostages."

Khartoum slammed the radio down onto the table and wriggled through the debris, out of the meeting room, always beneath the eye line of the windowsill, the blind swaying gently in the breeze. "You are in no position to give me orders!" he yelled. "I want an Audi RS4, fully fuelled, outside in thirty minutes and clear passage to wherever I choose to drive. Otherwise I'll start throwing pieces of your woman out this window! ... And I'll take pleasure in doing so!" he added as an afterthought.

With that he worked his way back to the meeting room. As he did, Tracy turned her head momentarily to say, "That was fabulous, Mustafa," even before he got to the room.

As soon as she turned her head away, Rob leaned in closer to Laura and slipped Tracy's gun beneath Laura's now-ruffled and untucked blouse and into her waistband, whispering as he did, "Picked this up when I fell." Then he resumed his initial position again. Laura didn't flinch.

When Khartoum reached the meeting room once more and stood up, he kicked a chair across the room. He didn't like being cornered and trapped. Turning to Laura and Rob once more, he flicked the dirt and debris off the meeting table at their faces, making them flinch and duck.

"You!" he yelled at Laura, thrusting his machine gun at her once again. "Move over to the other side. I don't like you being together." Laura stumbled up, hunched and flinching, apparently in pain, cradling her right arm to keep the gun hidden. "Enjoy your pain whilst you can feel it!" Khartoum jeered, letting his gun dip towards the floor.

Laura spun suddenly, the dirt scrunching under her feet. She stretched her arm out straight and squeezed two shots off from Tracy Bond's handgun into Khartoum's chest. He stumbled back, gurgling with a look of startled shock on his face. His involuntary reactions squeezed off a burst from his machine gun into the floor as Laura then shot him through the head before he could wreak further havoc and injure or kill someone.

At the same time, Tracy Bond swung around, turning her gun on Laura. While she was still rotating, she fired once, too quickly, just missing Laura's head. Seeing his opportunity, Rob kicked out hard and shoved the meeting table into Tracy Bond, toppling her over a chair with a screech. Both leaped up and raced at each other. Tracy, screaming with rage, raised the handgun, wanting to shoot Rob at near point-blank range.

Having despatched Khartoum, Laura turned her attention upon the raging Tracy, and registering the danger, yelled "Rob!"

The call distracted Tracy Bond, making her both hesitate and lose focus. She was off balance sending her shots wide, missing Rob by a wide margin. Laura then had the precious few moments required and shot Tracy Bond.

Laura and Rob sagged into each other's arms with immense relief, aware that each had saved the other.

"Strange place to be romantic!" a familiar voice commented, announcing they had company and an armed policeman appeared. Lifting his protective headgear, Nat's face materialised, smiling at them. "Come on, you two. Let's get you out of here for a well-deserved drink and a brush-up."

"Nat! What are you doing here?" Laura exclaimed.

"I couldn't let you handle all these golf balls alone, now could I? Not after all my experience!"

As Nat led them back outside, members of the medical team wrapped blankets around them and guided them to one of the nearby ambulances to cleanse their wounds. "Numerous but all superficial," they were informed as the dirt was washed from their faces. "You've been lucky. Your clothing protected you from the worst of it."

Once they had been released from the medical crew they moved away to make room for more needy folk. Nat then wandered over to the nearby perimeter wall on which they were perched.

"No sign of Al Rashid. We'll review the footage from our team's head cameras shortly, but we assume it was Al Rashid wearing the explosive belt. Whether willingly or not,

I doubt we'll ever know. We lost a lot of good men today. I'm glad you guys are okay. Rob, it's a privilege to meet you. I've heard quite a bit about you from this young lady and have also followed your competitive career. I'm too old, so I wouldn't stand a chance against you," he said with a wink and a smile. "Catch you both later."

Emergency services people were milling around, tending to the minor abrasions or other ailments suffered by others from the strike team, while police led the arrested folks away.

As Laura and Rob continued to survey the scene, the forensics teams arrived to sift through the debris and collect all of the computers and paper files. The expression on their faces said everything. They were under extreme time pressure to identify where all the golf ball shipments had been dispatched to. Gone was any hope that Tracy Bond would help them with that task! Only after they had found out where the shipments had gone would they start to piece together whatever other information could be gleaned from the two premises. They would start questioning the other employees as soon as possible as well, in case they could shed light on the locations of their recent deliveries.

Meanwhile, the commander was briefing the media at a hastily arranged live news conference. "Ladies and gentlemen, as you can see, there has been great devastation here today. Sadly, a number of heroes from our security forces have lost their lives. They died in the line of duty and in the process of saving many lives around the country. Our thoughts are with their families and friends at this time.

"I now implore all golfers and all golf clubs and shops throughout the UK to call a special crisis hotline immediately if you have received new style golf balls in recent weeks ready for promotional activities starting tomorrow. The hotline number will appear on your screens now alongside a picture of these golf balls.

"It is not possible to over-emphasise the dangers posed by these golf balls. If these balls are used, people will die. It is as simple as that. We do know that shipments were dispatched throughout the country, and we are currently trying to identify where they were sent to, but that will take time and we require your help. Call the hotline or your local police immediately. Do nothing with any shipment you have received. You will receive instructions from those on the phone. That is all for now. There will be a more detailed briefing in two hours. Thank you."

"Excuse me, Ms Harding, Mr Krane?" They looked up to see a smartly dressed young man standing in front of them and in the process of producing his MI5 identification. "Mr Gurning asked me to come and drive you home. He added that with the demise of the hostiles, there is no requirement to return to the safe house, other than to collect your belongings."

"Perfect," they said in unison, staggering to their feet to follow the Service driver.

25

Three weeks later, Rob was sitting in the office at Zouches, his injuries sustained in Milton Keynes now barely visible. He had become comfortable in the new surroundings during the weeks since the office had been formally handed over and the contractors had left, despite the somewhat eerie feeling of being alone in the vast space. Rob was pleased with the result. It was light and very pleasant. There was colour and the space felt modern, but would not be off-putting to traditionalists. Importantly, it felt professional, it had style, and he loved the views and the wide-open vistas across the River Thames and London—something that was lacking where he lived, although he did not really spend sufficient time at home to worry about that! In any case, he loved his apartment for its quirkiness.

The administration team had joined him two weeks earlier to familiarise themselves with the systems that had been installed and set up the filing. They also discussed and then established office processes and systems and the contracts for the smooth daily running of the place and generally organised themselves to be ready for this day.

The excitement was tangible between them all when Rob had taken the eight-person team—five women and three men—out for lunch. The chatter was all about the arrival that afternoon of everyone else and the formal opening of Zouches. Shortly after lunch Gurning, Spreachley, Jed, and Laura would arrive to meet with Rob and discuss how and when the next phase of dismantling Burak's network would commence, including a discussion about how much should be divulged to everyone else. They would then stay on to join Zouches' opening and Rob's briefing before the early evening fun started with an opening party. Unfortunately, because of their business, there could be no guests, but between the twenty of them, the administration team were determined to create a good time.

Rob was waiting in the boardroom, enjoying the view over the Thames, when Gurning, Spreachley, Jed, and Laura arrived. He was lost in thoughts of distant lands and pleasant weather thanks to a couple of sightseeing boats gently gliding by and a small pleasure cruiser that bobbed about on the resultant bow waves. Snapping out of his reverie, he welcomed his visitors and gave Laura a polite kiss on the cheek.

Once everybody was settled, Gurning got straight to the point, in typical fashion. "The last series of ops were an overall success and will certainly have disrupted matters for this Emilio chap. Unfortunately, we haven't worked out yet why they targeted that conference. Most satisfactory was the taking out of Khartoum and his UK terrorist cell, even though at a high price. We've also been able to pick up a number of others from the information found in Khartoum's car, which is great news. Ideally, in future we will be able to plan ahead, but I know that's not always possible. I also want to bring in some additional expertise to help out. With your agreement, therefore, I will invite Nat McCall to join this team."

"I'll be delighted to work with him," Laura replied, with Rob providing an assenting nod.

"Good. And Rob, you and I will pay Burak another visit. He is still sufficiently horrified at what we uncovered through Leicester, Bradford, London, and Milton Keynes that with your persuasive skills, we may just be able to get him to open up."

"I'll brief you and your team on the structure of the businesses transferring at a later date," commented Jed. "There's still a lot of work to do, and I'm hoping your team can help."

"What all this tells me," continued Gurning, "is that while Burak shifted focus to his legitimate businesses, Emilio and possibly others solidified their grasp on their portions of the network. Emilio, at least, subtly changed emphasis without Burak's realisation, hence his being blindsided with respect to the links to terrorism. We need to find out if there are any others like him.

"Therefore, the intel that Burak is able to provide remains invaluable, but we have to accept there are distinct limitations—Tracy Bond's involvement with Khartoum being a prime example. Frustratingly, Burak still remains reticent to share everything he has and knows. Why he thinks playing such games benefits him is unclear. That said, he's told me one of the hubs of activity revolves around the Black Sea, so we'll need to start looking in that direction as well. Not forgetting, of course, that I expect all of us to keep our ears open for this W person, whoever Doc is, Emilio, of course, and the other leaders of the network. Laura, because of the international flavour of this, I have agreed an unusual pact with Graeme and his management in that your responsibilities cut across both Services. This will ensure that any links, any commonality, however small, will not be missed.

"Rob, I suspect you will enjoy the next element because Burak has informed me that he has a yacht under construction in Istanbul and it should be ready for handover quite soon. Depending upon suitability, you could use it to cruise the Black Sea and follow any links through into the Mediterranean. Burak has shared that there are locations in many of the ports throughout both seas, as well as throughout the Aegean and Ionian Seas.

"Here's a list of locations I want you to focus on with Laura. There are rather a lot, and you will need to settle on a strategy and order in which to approach this."

Jed re-entered the discussion. "From what I hear, there will be no problem about covering the many ports you'll have to visit from the yacht Steven refers to. It sounds really rather impressive, so I'd like some photos please! And an invite on board, should you ever head this way."

"If it's that grand, we can have a firm's party on board!" Rob suggested, smiling.

"Right, let's have a review of some of the detail within this document," Gurning said, lifting his copy of the previously handed out file.

As they pored over the information in the file and began to discuss the details, the chink and clunk of glasses, plates, and cutlery could be heard in the reception area. Shortly afterwards the delectable aromas of quality party food wafted into the boardroom. An hour after they had started their meeting, the receptionist knocked on the door to announce that the others had started to arrive.

"Any other business before we close?" asked Steven.

Fifteen minutes later, they had joined the entire Zouches team, and Rob raised his glass.

"Welcome, and I am delighted to announce that Zouches is now open for business."

Everyone cheered and clapped. "My final comment before we party is let's toast our collaboration with the authorities to smash international crime and terrorism!"

A chorus of hurrahs and cheers rang out across the office as everyone started to sip their champagne and enjoy the canapés, while admiring the blistering red-orange sunset shimmering on the River Thames.

About the author

James Hanford has been writing, primarily as a hobby, since 2012 alongside his day job in corporate property. James recognises and appreciates the benefits that his career has granted, meeting a great many wonderful and interesting people. Through work and personal travel, as well as daily life, James has experienced many situations that have helped his writing as he relives the emotions of potentially (or mostly imagined) dangerous situations. He was born and still lives in London, England, with his wife and two sons.

    www.jameshanford.com
    www.facebook.com/James.Hanford.Author

The story continues in....

Intervention: Eavesdroppers

The second book of the Intervention series that finds Rob Krane jetting between Bulgaria and Britain trying to untangle a web of apparently unconnected criminal activities. Soon, security operations are being launched across Europe as global financial melt-down could be triggered.

Intervention: Murky Depths

Burak Demir displays his true colours in the third book of the Intervention series while Rob Krane chases leads across Europe that link counterfeit money and weapons smuggling to forthcoming anti-capitalism demonstrations. But time is about to run out with thousands of peoples' lives at stake.